MAYDAY
FROM MÁLAGA

MAYDAY
FROM MÁLAGA

MICHAEL KIRK

PUBLISHED FOR THE CRIME CLUB BY
DOUBLEDAY & COMPANY, INC.
GARDEN CITY, NEW YORK
1983

All of the characters in this book
are fictitious, and any resemblance to actual persons,
living or dead,
is purely coincidental.

Library of Congress Cataloging in Publication Data

Kirk, Michael, 1928–
    Mayday from Málaga.

    I. Title.
PR6061.N6M3   1983   823'.914
ISBN 0-385-18969-9

First Edition in the United States of America

Library of Congress Catalog Card Number 83–7328

For Eve and John

The said Company doth further promise and agree that the insurance aforesaid shall commence upon the said Ship, at and from as above, and shall continue until she hath moored at anchor in good safety at her place of Destination and for such period afterwards not exceeding twenty-four hours from such mooring, and upon the Freight and Goods or Merchandise on board thereof from the loading of the said Goods or Merchandise on board the said Ship or Vessel, at as above, and until the said Goods or Merchandise be discharged and safely landed at as above AND that it shall be lawful for the said Ship or Vessel to proceed and sail to, and touch and stay at, any Ports or Places whatsoever in the course of her said voyage for all necessary purposes without prejudice to this Insurance.

EXTRACT FROM A STANDARD PRESENT-DAY
INTERNATIONAL MARINE INSURANCE POLICY.

MAYDAY
FROM MÁLAGA

CHAPTER 1

The two-thousand-five-hundred-ton *Sea Robin* was twenty years old, flew the Panamanian flag, and had spent most of her working life on a general cargo run between the Mediterranean and northern Europe. She flew the Panamanian flag for the same reason that the nearest thing she knew to a home port was Piraeus in Greece —both kept down costs. Currently she was managed by a London agent and owned by an obscure but profitable shipping company headed by a one-time Romanian refugee based in Switzerland.

All of which was about normal for her kind of veteran.

It was the month of May. Her voyage began at Marseilles, where her cargo manifest showed she loaded a cargo of timber, agricultural machinery, fertilizer, and several container tanks of bulk *vin rouge*. From Marseilles, she ambled across to Barcelona, where more cargo was waiting. When she sailed again, her course was a south-west curve that would take her towards the Straits of Gibraltar and from there to the Atlantic.

Two days after leaving Barcelona, the *Sea Robin* was still plodding along the Spanish coast. It was dusk, Gibraltar was a distant, bulking haze on the horizon ahead, still several hours away. Much nearer, to starboard, a bright ribbon of light was beginning to appear along the shoreline. Several crewmen eyed the light enviously—it marked the start of the high-rise hotel and apartment-block resorts of the Costa del Sol, Spain's luxury holiday playground. Behind that, like a dramatic backcloth, a long, brooding mass of mountains formed a stark silhouette against the evening sky.

Dusk gave way to darkness. The lights ashore began to thin as hotel developments gave way to fishing villages and isolated farms.

Most of the *Sea Robin*'s crew were at their evening meal when her time-worn engine gave one despairing, warning, clank. It was a clank felt in every nook and cranny of her rusting hull. Then came a grinding scream of metal followed by a long shriek of hastily released steam.

When that stopped, there was a silence broken only by the rhythmic slapping of the sea against her hull.

Helpless, wallowing in a moderate swell, the cargo ship began to drift. Fevered attempts at repairs got under way in her engine-room.

Two hours later, the lights ashore much nearer, her engine remained silent. The *Sea Robin*'s radio, powered by stand-by batteries because the emergency generator wouldn't start, wheezed out an SOS request for tugs.

She was still drifting in towards the shore, completely at the mercy of tide and currents. On the bridge, her captain and mate argued about what to do. Her captain was Dutch, her mate Greek, and they loathed each other at the best of times.

But they were equally worried. Neither knew much about this stretch of the Málaga coastline, and the *Sea Robin*'s meagre collection of greasy, tattered charts was about as little use as a school atlas.

Maybe they should try to anchor.

They were still arguing when a fang-toothed ridge of undersea rock ripped a long, fatal gash in the *Sea Robin*'s bottom. Lurching, shuddering, she stubbornly drifted clear. Then, with a final, matronly dignity, she began to sink.

Now, there was only one order that could be given. Scenting the inevitable, the *Sea Robin*'s crew had taken time off to pack their suitcases. Her boats were lowered and hardly a man got his feet wet as they abandoned ship.

Her captain was the last to leave. He was a prudent rather than heroic man, and there had been the business of clearing out the safe in his cabin, including one envelope that particularly mattered.

The *Sea Robin* was listing as he stepped aboard the waiting lifeboat. His men pulled clear, then rested on their oars to watch their ship not so much sink as settle on the sea bottom. She was in shallow water, her superstructure still visible, each swell creaming gently along her main deck.

Sighing, her captain looked around. The man next to him in the lifeboat shrugged and kept a tight grip on a string bag filled with cartons of cigarettes.

They were less than a mile offshore, close to the lights of a village. The low shape of a fishing boat was coming towards them in the faint moonlight, swinging in towards the nearest of the lifeboats.

The captain cursed under his breath. Cursed the Greek mate, fate, and the world in general.

He had a chill feeling that his troubles were only beginning. As far as some important people were concerned, the *Sea Robin* had sunk in the wrong damned place.

*

Andrew Laird wakened with a hangover made considerably worse by the way the telephone was shrilling at his bedside. Daylight was stabbing in around the edges of the tightly closed curtains of his hotel room and the world seemed a very fragile place.

Pawing at the bedside table, he located the receiver, lifted it, and managed a grunt.

"*Morgen,* Herr Laird." The hotel switchboard operator was brisk and remorselessly cheerful. "I have a call from London for you."

"Tell it to go away." Laird yawned, heard the operator chuckle, then waited, still coming awake.

His head ached and his mouth felt like the bottom of a parrot's cage. What had started off the previous evening as a quiet drink with a couple of West German detectives had kept growing until he'd wondered just how many more police there were in Germany.

He could hear traffic noise outside. The Mainz Hilton was located close to the centre of that city, almost next to the busy Theodor-Heuss bridge over the Rhine. Sighing, he managed to focus on the watch at his wrist. It was 9 A.M. Put that together with a call from London and—

"Andrew?" The pompous, precise voice on the line was exactly what he had expected. Osgood Morris, marine claims manager for Clanmore Alliance Insurance, had probably been at his desk for an hour by now. "Andrew, is that you?"

"I think so." Laird grimaced at the receiver.

"Good." Morris sounded both suspicious and disapproving. "I have the telex you sent yesterday evening. No loose ends?"

"None I know about," said Laird.

He'd been in Mainz for four days. Working for Clanmore Alliance as a marine claims investigator, he'd been sent out to examine a doubtful claim involving a valuable cargo of Japanese electronics, allegedly stolen from a Rhine barge after being transshipped at Rotterdam on arrival from the Far East.

The crated cargo had turned up hidden aboard another barge moored near Mainz. The West German importer who had made the claim was now in jail, awaiting trial. The local police had decided a celebration was in order, and the night had just grown from there. He drew a deep breath. Simply to have survived was probably an achievement.

"Quite satisfactory." From Morris, that came close to praise. There was a moment's hissing silence on the line, then a throat-clearing noise. "And fortunate, from a company viewpoint. I'm afraid there's another matter waiting—you'll have to forget any notion of coming back to London."

"Why?" Surprised, Laird elbowed up into a sitting position.

"We need you in Spain," said Morris. His voice seemed to waver a little. "We had some—ah—unfortunate news from there. Charlie Henderson went to the Málaga coast on a claim situation—"

"I know. He left the day before I flew out here." Laird frowned at the receiver, his hangover temporarily forgotten. "Some Panamanian-registered rust bucket that—"

"An insured risk called the *Sea Robin,*" corrected Morris.

"Same thing," said Laird. He was still puzzled. Henderson was one of Clanmore's most experienced claims adjusters, a cheerful, extrovert Englishman in his early forties. "What's wrong that Charlie can't cope?"

"He's dead," said Morris. "You've been out of touch, of course. It happened on his second night there—a road accident."

"Hell." Laird chewed his lip, dismayed. Henderson had been one of the first to make him welcome when he joined Clanmore, a man with a vast knowledge of the marine insurance world, willing to share it. "What happened?"

"We're still waiting a full report," admitted Osgood Morris. "Apparently he was driving a hired car. It went off the road for some reason, crashed, and caught fire." He made another throat-clearing noise, one that held regret but also a degree of impatience. "Our immediate concern was for his widow, then there were various arrangements to be made. But—well, life goes on."

"I thought it might," said Laird. "So?"

"So you'll have to take over at Málaga—we've no one else available." Morris sounded happier again, dealing with practicalities. "I'm under a certain amount of pressure from our chairman. He wants an early report on the *Sea Robin* claim."

Laird didn't answer. Clanmore's chairman was an elderly hard-nosed individual, often interfering but equally able to scoop up more insurance business during a round of golf than his staff could achieve in a month of orthodox work. When he spoke, Osgood Morris jumped to oblige. The marine claims manager lusted after a seat on the Clanmore board, no matter what it took to achieve.

"That's the situation," Morris's thin voice went on hastily. "You've been booked on a direct Lufthansa flight from Frankfurt, leaving at noon. Your ticket will be at the desk, and hopefully they'll also have an envelope for you. I'm having a photocopy of anything in the *Sea Robin* file flown out this morning."

"Right." Laird's thoughts were elsewhere. "How's Charlie's wife taking it?"

"Badly, I'm afraid. But she'll qualify for full company pension, and he was sensible about life insurance." The marine claims manager hurried back to what mattered. "I don't think the *Sea Robin* report should pose any problems. It all seems straightforward enough."

"Someone probably said that about the *Titanic,*" said Laird.

"Very amusing." Morris's voice frosted. "But I haven't time for pleasantries—I'm already late for the chairman's morning meeting. I'll put your name on the staff sheet for Henderson's wreath. You can pay me later."

The line went dead.

Slowly, Andrew Laird replaced his receiver. Then he got out of bed, his head thumping. His clothes were in a crumpled heap on a chair, another reminder of the previous night's celebration. Padding past them, he opened the curtains and let the cold, grey morning light flood into the room.

He stood for a moment, then glanced again at his wrist-watch. Above it, the face of the elaborate Chinese dragon tattoo which ran from his wrist to his elbow seemed to have acquired a mocking leer. There was another tattoo on his right arm, a stylized anchor and chain—both were permanent souvenirs of an earlier time, the kind he couldn't blame on anyone but himself.

Laird swore, softly but with feeling. Another day had begun, but nothing like the way he'd expected.

An hour later, after a shower and shave, he had eaten breakfast in his room. Only a few wisps of his hangover remained as he packed his well-worn travel bag and finished dressing.

A shade over medium height, with a stocky, muscular build, Andrew Laird was still a few months short of his thirtieth birthday. His thick dark hair was prematurely grey at the temples. Grey-green eyes and a nose that had been broken during a football game as a child gave him a face that at first glance might have seemed hard-set—except that it went with a mouth that could pucker into a sudden, almost boyish grin when least expected. He also had long, strong-fingered hands that could be surprisingly gentle, and when he spoke his voice still held a soft trace of his native Scottish accent.

He had dressed for travel. A white shirt, because it was the only clean one he had left, went with a dark-blue knitted tie and a light-weight grey suit that was old enough to be comfortable. His tan leather casual shoes had also seen plenty of mileage.

There was still a last, lukewarm cup of coffee in the breakfast pot. He poured it, lit a cigarette, then looked round as there was a light knock on the door. The room maid, a pert, attractive girl with blonde, braided hair, came in with fresh towels. The smile on her lips faded as she saw the packed bag.

"You are leaving, Herr Laird?" she asked, frowning.

"Yes. I've been moved on." He gave a mock sigh. Any time he'd seen the girl she'd been cheerfully friendly. "But if I'd stayed much longer you might have had problems."

"*Bitte*, Herr Laird . . . problems?" The maid looked at him for a moment, then deliberately, provocatively, moistened her lips with the tip of her tongue. "Would I have worried too much?"

She left him with a wink.

Shaking his head, Laird went over to the window again and looked out. The long span of the Theodor-Heuss bridge was still busy with traffic crossing the wide, fast-flowing Rhine. Below the bridge, a string of barges was being towed up-river by a powerful tug. On the down side, a trim white cruise steamer was hell-bent on overtaking a scruffy, self-propelled barge.

His mouth tightened a little. There was a small public garden beside the river, sheltered by a wall lined with relief figures of knights in armour. The evening he'd arrived, he'd met a man down there, a man who had given him a lead that had made it almost easy to expose the Japanese electronics cargo claim as a fraud.

The man had been one of Charlie Henderson's contacts.

Turning away, he stubbed out his cigarette and got ready to leave.

*

Frankfurt Airport rates as one of the largest and busiest in Europe, large enough for arriving passengers to be handed a leaflet map to prevent them becoming lost. As usual, it was a bustle of hurrying humanity, but a yellow Lufthansa ticket was waiting for Laird at the main desk. It was clipped to a large, hand-addressed envelope from Clanmore Alliance, which had come out on one of the morning flights from London.

He had time enough to find a bank and cash a cheque for some Spanish pesetas. Then, going through the inevitable queues at the passport and security controls, he reached the departure lounge as the Málaga flight was called.

It was a Boeing 747, packed with German families on their way to a holiday in the sun. But he had a window seat and the passenger next to him, a harassed father who seemed glad to be several rows away from his wife and children, dozed off almost as soon as the Lufthansa jet was airborne.

Laird ordered a whisky when the bar trolley came round. Then, sipping the amber liquor neat, he opened the Clanmore envelope and began reading the thin bundle of photocopied sheets.

Some of it had been known while he was in London, other details were new, a few mildly surprising. There wasn't any mention of Charlie Henderson, apart from the fact that he'd been allocated the claim.

Setting his drink on the fold-down table in front of him, letting it vibrate gently while the Boeing kept on a steady south-west course high above Europe, Laird quietly flipped through the pages.

The *Sea Robin*, owned by Pandion Shipping S.A. of Geneva, registered in Panama, managed by Frenton Services of London, had been covered by a standard Clanmore marine policy for just under ten million U.S. dollars. Her cargo was insured for close on another three million. Neither figure made him blink. By shipping standards, they were normal enough for an elderly ship like the *Sea Robin* and the mix of cargo she had been carrying.

The surprise was that Clanmore had been principal insurers for both hull and cargo. That kind of risk was usually split between two different companies. It still didn't mean Clanmore was on the hook for anything like that amount. In marine insurance, risk was always farmed out. Up to twenty companies could be carrying a percentage of the cover—some by arrangement, some on an automatic, mutual basis without even knowing about it unless something went wrong.

Any race-track bookmaker wanting to refine his knowledge of gambling and betting odds could have studied the system to his advantage.

But the *Sea Robin* had yet to be declared a total loss. Settled on her keel in the shallow water off the fishing village of San Ferdinand, she was comfortably bedded on a soft, sandy bottom. There might be a chance to refloat her. Two salvage tugs were at the scene and assessing the chances.

Frowning, Laird skimmed through the next couple of pages. They amounted to a cargo manifest. But he paused at the next, his grey-green eyes hardening as he read the first paragraph.

"The salvage tugs *Scomber* and *Beroe,* now in attendance, will investigate salvage feasibility, with Captain H. Novak, of *Scomber,* in command. Any salvage operation which may be mutually agreed on will be carried out on standard contract. Captain Novak is well known . . ."

He was. Setting down the file, Laird took a long drink of his whisky and looked out thoughtfully at the white fantasy of clouds far below the Boeing's cabin window.

Not for the first time, Osgood Morris had played his cards craftily. He'd made no mention of Harry Novak being involved—because he'd known well enough that Laird and Harry Novak usually came together like two pieces of coarse sandpaper.

Laird had to admit the captain of the *Scomber* was a skilled towmaster and salvage man. But, even by the tough standards of the salvage game, Novak also rated as a vicious, ill-tempered bully of unpredictable moods. Laird had suffered them at first hand over several months as the *Scomber*'s radio operator.

There had been other ships after that, before he'd left the sea and gone to work with Clanmore Alliance. It had been inevitable that he'd meet up with Novak now and again, and it happened. He shrugged to himself. If Novak decided the *Sea Robin* could be salvaged, then the odds were it would happen.

But on a personal level, Laird wouldn't have trusted Harry Novak to give him the right time of day.

*

Two and a half hours after take-off the Lufthansa Boeing creaked down through the clouds and came in over a high range of snow-tipped mountains. A narrow ribbon of blue running between the peaks was the Río Guadalhorce, the horizon ahead a deeper blue which was the Mediterranean.

Still losing height, the jet cast a fast-moving shadow over arid hills and dried-up streams. Then her passengers had a glimpse of a large, modern town along the shoreline before the final approach, a wide turn over the sea and in low over the smooth fairways of a golf course.

After touchdown, the Boeing stopped close to a glass-and-concrete terminal building flanked by palm trees and edged by bright banks of flowers. It had a rooftop balcony, crowded with sun-bronzed spectators. They waved enthusiastically, a previous batch of holiday-makers from Frankfurt, the Boeing's passengers for the return flight.

As usual, Laird let the majority of people aboard struggle for the exit doors before he left his seat. Then he walked unhurriedly down the aircraft steps into the heat of the sunlight, the strong tangy scent of cactus meeting his nostrils.

One of the Lufthansa stewardesses was ahead of him in the immigration hall. The uniformed officer at the desk smiled and waved her through, then glanced at Laird's passport. He hesitated for a moment and signalled to someone on the far side of the barrier before stamping the passport and motioning him on.

"Mr. Laird?" Almost immediately, a plump man with thinning fair hair stepped in front of him. "I'm Francis Edwards, from the British Consul's office. We heard you were coming out."

They shook hands. Edwards' grip was light and damp. The consular official, in his late thirties, wore a blue suit with a striped shirt and a faded regimental tie. His main concession to the climate was the floppy white hat he was carrying.

"Any special reason for meeting me?" asked Laird with a guarded curiosity. As a breed, consular officials usually preferred to stay behind a nice, safe office desk.

"Yes and no." As he spoke, Edwards began guiding a way through to the baggage hall. "Your London office telexed about you. But I'd already arranged to be here."

The first luggage from the Lufthansa flight was beginning to spill into the hall. Waiting for his bag to appear, Laird nodded.

"Maybe you can help me," he said slowly. "Exactly what happened to our last man?"

"Henderson?" Edwards pursed his lips. "There isn't much to tell. According to the local gendarmerie, it was a simple case of a stranger driving too fast by night, on a damned dangerous road." He shrugged. "Then he ran out of luck and road, went over the edge of a ravine—and the car burned out."

"Who found him?"

"A priest on a motor cycle—he saw the flames." The consular official frowned. "I know the road, Laird. It's a mountain track, the kind that even scares me in daylight."

"What was he doing up there?"

"I've no idea," confessed Edwards. "The police might know, I suppose." He glanced deliberately at his wrist-watch. "Mainly I've been involved in getting the body released. When a foreigner dies in Spain, the result is red tape by the mile. However, we cut through most of it—that's why I'm here. The coffin is going out on a British Airways flight to London." He hesitated. "Do you—ah— want to see it?"

Laird shook his head.

"Good." Edwards didn't hide his relief. "A box is a box—and when I say that car burned out, I mean it. You understand?"

"I understand," said Laird. His travel bag had emerged in the hall. Elbowing forward through the crush of other waiting passengers, he retrieved it and returned. "What about Henderson's personal effects, papers?"

"Burned, if they were in the car. The police should have made arrangements about anything in his hotel room, but I've still to check about that." Edwards shuffled his feet, obviously anxious to move. "Henderson based himself at San Ferdinand. Are you heading there?"

"Yes." Laird hefted his bag. "Straight away."

"Good. Then you've got a lift arranged." Edwards gave a surprising wink. "Enjoy it. You're in luck."

Beckoning, he led Laird straight past the customs barrier, with a familiar nod to the men on duty. On the far side, in the main terminal lobby, a small, fat, dark-haired man in a khaki shirt and slacks removed a cigarette from his mouth and came to meet them.

"This is Vicente. He'll be driving." Taking an extra step forward, Edwards spoke to the man in Spanish, then turned and grinned.

"He says the lady is outside. If I were you, I wouldn't keep her waiting."

"The lady." Laird raised an eyebrow. "What lady?"

"An executive-type Pandion Shipping female." Edwards' grin stayed in place. "I must go. But if you've any problems that need consular help, get in touch." He hesitated, then looked slightly embarrassed. "One small matter, old man. Slightly delicate, not really consular business—"

"But?" Laird wondered what was coming.

"This damned ship causing all the fuss." Edwards gestured his annoyance. "I know she's not British-registered—"

"More a multinational," agreed Laird. "So?"

The man frowned. "Clanmore is a British firm. The Spanish authorities—well, they can be temperamental. These days, Britain isn't exactly their favourite nation. Of course, diplomatically, everyone tries for an amicable relationship—"

"You mean we've got problems?"

"Indirectly, yes—one, at any rate." Edwards sighed. "Part of this ship is still above water—you know that. So some locals have been going out and doing a little looting. The Pandion Shipping people kicked up hell, particularly when they found the local police took a fairly tolerant view. We—well, my consul wouldn't like a British company to get involved in the fuss."

"Then tell him to relax," said Laird, relieved it was nothing worse. Any inshore wreck attracted an armada of scavenging boatmen, ready to carry off anything available. He imagined that the fishermen of San Ferdinand probably regarded the *Sea Robin* lying off their doorstep as a heaven-sent gift. "We don't worry if a few fittings disappear."

"I'm glad. There could be other problems, of course, but they can wait." Edwards drew a deep breath. "I'll tell my consul. He was concerned, quite concerned."

He bobbed a nod of farewell and hurried off. Laird turned to the waiting driver. The man gave a lazy nod, put the cigarette back in his mouth, and led him towards the terminal's exit doors.

Outside, the large, dusty parking area was a hot clutter of agency buses, hotel coaches and taxis. New arrivals were being hustled and loaded by shouting porters and couriers waving clipboard lists.

Vicente ploughed through it all with disdain and brought Laird to a large white Mercedes-Benz station wagon parked in the shade of a cluster of some straggling palm trees. He took Laird's travel bag, then opened the rear door and stood back.

"Welcome to the Málaga coast, Mr. Laird," said an attractive woman, smiling out at him from the broad passenger seat. Her voice was pleasant, friendly, and slightly husky. "Did you have a good flight?"

"As good as they come." Laird got in, settled beside her as the door closed, and looked at her again. She was slim, in her late twenties, with short, jet-black hair. "You're from Pandion Shipping?"

"I'm sorry. Introductions first." She grimaced apologetically. "I'm Laura Cero. Janos Cuvier, the company president, sent me to collect you. You'll meet him when we get to San Ferdinand."

"I didn't know he was involved." Laird didn't hide his surprise. That hadn't been in the Clanmore briefing and it should have been, for several reasons.

"He flew in from Switzerland with a management team the day after the sinking," said Laura Cero. In front, Vicente had got behind the wheel. Starting the engine, he glanced back at them through the rear mirror. She nodded and turned to Laird again as they began to move. "I'd forgotten. Any contact we've had with your London office has been through Paul Raynal, the group shipping manager. He's here too. In fact, there are about half a dozen of us."

"Thanks for the warning," said Laird mildly.

He took a moment to study her while the car murmured clear of the parking area. Laura Cero had dark-brown eyes, a good bone structure and strong, regular teeth. She also had an air of quiet self-assured confidence and was dressed to match—she wore a simple but probably expensive black silk shirt, a lightweight pleated black-and-grey plaid skirt, and black leather pumps.

They got free of the parking area and Vicente slotted the Mercedes into the steady flow of traffic on the road beyond. As the station wagon began accelerating, Laird took a last glance at the airport, then settled back again.

"Door-to-door delivery," he murmured. "In the insurance game we usually ask why."

"I can imagine." Laura Cero's husky voice cooled for a moment. She nodded at the slim black executive case that lay between them on the seat. "First, we had to send a car to the airport anyway—Mr. Cuvier wanted a package collected. And second—" She paused, frowning, then sighed. "Well, this isn't an ordinary situation, is it? The way your colleague Henderson died—"

"Yes." He nodded. "I'm here to pick up the pieces. You met Charlie Henderson?"

"Yes. I liked him." She thawed again. Opening the executive case, she took out a bulky envelope and handed it over. "I thought this might be useful. It includes copies of statements by the *Sea Robin*'s captain, mate, and chief engineer. Plus a list of the people on our management team—who we are, what we do."

"That'll certainly help." Laird tucked the envelope in an inside pocket while she snapped the case shut again. The car had settled into a smooth, fast pace, and they had joined a main through highway. As Vicente filtered his charge over to the outer lane, Laird turned to Laura Cero again. "Does your boss usually turn out at the head of his troops?"

"He likes to see for himself," she said. "Janos Cuvier has an established reputation for doing his own trouble-shooting."

"Complete with travelling firing squad," mused Laird. "What's your speciality?"

"Loose ends, usually." A wisp of amusement entered her voice. "I'm a lawyer. Pandion Shipping is a Cuvier subsidiary. I work for the parent company, Cuvier Corporation of Geneva."

"I see." He digested the information for a moment, glancing out at the road. To the right, the landscape was rocky and barren with a hazy backcloth of mountains. On the other side, the Mediterranean was about half a mile distant, with a scatter of fields and the pampered fairways of a golf course in between. "How long have you been with them?"

"About two years now." She gave a slight, puzzled smile. "Why?"

"Plain curiosity," admitted Laird. "Where did you study law?"

"London, then California—I took an extra business degree out there."

"So if there's any kind of legal problem—"

She nodded, amused. "You talk to me, Mr. Laird."

They were passing a road junction. A sign said TORREMOLINOS and pointed down towards the high-rise concrete skyline of the Costa del Sol's best-known playground. Laird had been there once, briefly—and briefly had been long enough. It had been high season, which meant packed beaches, crowded streets and a jungle of neon signs.

Laura Cero followed his glance and seemed to guess his thoughts.

"Do you know San Ferdinand?" she asked.

He shook his head.

"It's different. They're just beginning to know about tourists. The place will be swallowed up soon, I suppose. But for the moment, most people there are just simple fisherfolk." She chuckled. "Or maybe not so simple—we've had the odd problem."

"I heard," said Laird. He had his own raw memories of tangling with other fishing communities in different parts of the world. They followed an almost universal pattern—practising the art of pretending to be simple and innocent until it came to practical things like talking money. "Your Mr. Cuvier seems to be annoyed at San Ferdinand treating his *Sea Robin* like a welfare benefit."

"True." She brushed back a strand of her jet-black hair and pursed her lips. "He's a man of very definite opinions. You could find that out." Reaching for the case again, she opened it, took out a file, then gave him an apologetic glance. "I've some work to catch up on. You don't mind?"

Laird shook his head. While she began reading he took out his cigarettes and lit one. Hopefully, the *Sea Robin* claim was still uncomplicated. But if there were snags, he had a feeling that Pendion Shipping's first line of legal representation was an efficient presence.

He took another glance at Laura Cero. Frowning slightly, she was using a pencil to mark one of the typed sheets. One thing about her did puzzle him—her voice. There was an accent there, faint yet positive, that he somehow knew yet couldn't place, except it didn't come from any Swiss mountainside.

There would be time to find out. He settled back. Up front, their tubby driver slouched behind the wheel, looking half asleep. He had the car radio tuned to a football broadcast, the volume down low, the Spanish commentary an excited mutter.

Beyond Torremolinos, still following the coast, the road skirted a whole series of smaller resort towns, marina harbours and beaches. Offshore, small flotillas of wind-surfers darted and tumbled among the waves while the sails of their larger brethren, sails of every colour, showed bright in the glare of the sun.

It was hot. Laird wiped beads of sweat from his forehead and Vicente had the car fan on full, churning air to the interior. But Laura Cero worked on, slowly turning pages, occasionally glancing up and around and repeating that same, apologetic smile as her eyes met Laird's.

They reached Marbella, the last westerly town of any real size on the Málaga coast. The road ran through its centre, a hooting, noisy, traffic-clogged collection of shops and bars, hotels and tourist banks.

On the far side, a large Seat truck with a Málaga firm's name on the doors blocked the roadway. The driver stood beside the cab, making frantic apologetic gestures to two stony-faced uniformed gendarmerie. The police car, the rear badly dented, was still almost under the truck's radiator grille.

Vicente crawled the Mercedes round the obstacle, grinning. Then, suddenly, his grin died and he stared.

"That damn truck, Señorita Cero—it's one of ours." He frowned round. "Will I stop?"

"No." Firmly, she waved him on. "Keep going. *Es urgente* we get to San Ferdinand. Señor Cuvier is waiting."

The man shrugged but obeyed. As the station wagon cleared the bottleneck and increased speed again, Laird looked back at the truck. Its platform was empty.

"What was that about?" he asked.

"We've hired some trucks. We've started bringing off some of the *Sea Robin*'s cargo." She saw his expression. "Something else you didn't know about?"

"That's right." Laird was beginning to wonder just how little he did know. "When did that start?"

"A couple of days ago." She hesitated, then chuckled. "Don't worry. We're not thieving our own cargo or trying to pull a fast one on insurance. There is an arrangement."

"What kind?" asked Laird.

"Janos Cuvier can tell you." Putting the file away, she snapped her case shut. "He knows more about it than I do."

He left it at that.

They travelled on. The road still ran close to the long curve of the shore, and they passed two fishing villages which seemed to be in a transitional stage to becoming tourist resorts. Each had a thin scatter of hotels. Some yachts were among the craft in their harbours. But after that, the coastline became almost empty of life, while in the far distance, the Rock of Gibraltar began to take shape as a barely discernible pimple on the horizon.

At last, Vicente flicked the turn indicator and the Mercedes left the main highway. It began travelling down a narrow, pot-holed side-road, wheels raising a plume of dust and sending gravel spitting.

A crossroads came up. They overtook a plodding donkey pulling a cart loaded with firewood, an old woman perched on top of the load, an unlit stub of cheroot clamped between her lips, wrinkled face expressionless. For another short distance, the pot-holed road ran through thin, stunted scrub, then it emerged close to a rocky stretch of shore.

Winding and twisting, their route followed the shoreline close to the water. One jolt, worse than the rest, threw Laura Cero sliding across the rear seat. She grabbed Laird's arm for support—then she gasped.

An old grey van had bounced out onto the road, little more than a stone's throw away, and was heading straight for them.

Tyres howling, the station wagon braked hard, lurching as Vicente wrestled to avoid the approaching vehicle. The van driver, a pale blob of a face, was doing his desperate best to swing clear. Shuddering, the Mercedes skidded and stopped broadside on, totally off the road.

The van, untouched, had stalled with one wheel in a ditch. A door flew open and the driver came scrambling out.

"Mother of God," said Vicente fervently. Slumped back in his seat, his swarthy face grey, he looked round. "That damn fool—"

"Could have killed us." Laura Cero finished it for him angrily. She glared at the other driver, who was hurrying over, then almost groaned. "Him. I might have guessed."

The stranger, a lanky, bearded man in a faded sports shirt and wrinkled khaki trousers, reached them as she wound down her window. He peered in, eyes blinking anxiously behind metal-rimmed spectacles.

"*Hola. Está* . . . oh—" He swallowed as he saw who was aboard and lapsed immediately into English. "Anyone—well, hurt or anything, Miss Cero?"

"No, by a small miracle," she told him icily. "Not this time."

"I'm sorry—really sorry." He shuffled his feet awkwardly. "I wasn't thinking. I just was—"

"Day-dreaming?" she suggested curtly. "Do you fancy that as your epitaph?"

"It won't happen again." The bearded face wrinkled miserably, then the man glanced at Vicente and Laird. "I'm glad no one was hurt."

"So are we." Deliberately, Laura Cero began to wind up her window.

"Wait." The man gestured hastily. "What about me? I mean I'm in that ditch—"

"Your problem, Mr. Warner," she said sweetly. "Goodbye."

The window closed. Grinning, Vicente sent the Mercedes reversing back onto the road, flicked the gear lever, and they started off again. The bearded man stood open-mouthed.

"A friend of yours?" asked Laird, looking back at him through a cloud of dust.

"His name is Adam Warner, he's a college lecturer, and he also happens to be a pain in the neck," said Laura Cero. "He's here with a bunch of students. We had more trouble with them than with the locals."

"About the *Sea Robin?*"

She nodded. "Until they were warned off."

A few minutes more travel brought them round a point of land to a wide, curving bay and their destination. Offshore, the upper works of the *Sea Robin* rose starkly from the gentle blue swell of the Mediterranean. He recognized the big salvage tug lying astern. She was the *Beroe,* her captain a competent but unimaginative individual. Two smaller craft, workboats of some kind, were bobbing close in beside the sunken cargo ship.

San Ferdinand was located halfway along the curve of shore. It was slightly bigger than he'd expected, with a small, stone-built harbour backed by a close-packed huddle of a village. The beach was sandy, giving way to a worn white limestone rock. Inland, the countryside was flat and featureless until, inevitably, the mountains began their dramatic barrier. Leaning forward in his seat, narrowing his eyes against the bright sunlight, Laird reckoned the *Sea Robin* to be less than a mile offshore, slightly more than that east of the fishing village.

"Mr. Laird—" He realized it was the second time Laura Cero had spoken. She smiled patiently. "I asked where you planned to stay."

"Anywhere there's a room." He shrugged. "Where did Charlie Henderson go?"

"The Mercado—a *hostal* near the harbour. There's not much choice."

"It'll do," agreed Laird. "Where are your people located?"

"The company rented a villa, the Casa Turo." She glanced at her wrist-watch. "We're going there first."

Laird mustered a half-smile and nodded. He was being treated like a package marked "Express Delivery." For the moment at least, he'd nothing to lose.

Located in a patch of secluded pinewood on the fringe of San Ferdinand, the Casa Turo was located in grounds surrounded by a high brick wall. The main gate had stone pillars, topped by bronze shields which had an eagle coat of arms. Beyond the gate, a driveway led through more pine trees to a rambling two-storey villa set in an expanse of garden. The house was built of cream stone and topped by a pink roof of clay tiles.

The Mercedes drew up beside two other cars, a small red Seat and an old black Ford coupé. Vicente got out first, then made a lazy pretence of helping his passengers to alight.

It was warm, the air was clean and pine-scented, and insects buzzed among the flower-beds. Laird saw a swimming pool and, next to it, a tennis court which only lacked nets. Thick bougainvillaea in full purple flower clung to the walls of the villa, climbing from its veranda to the balcony windows of the upper floor. There was no sign of human life.

"Come on in," said Laura Cero briskly. "Leave your bag. Vicente will keep an eye on it."

The front door lay open. Inside, Laird could hear a woman singing somewhere at the back of the house. She was slightly off-key but sounded happy.

He followed Laura Cero along the cool shade of a wood-panelled hallway, their footsteps loud on polished marble.

"Here." She stopped at a door, tapped on it, and waited. A moment passed, then it opened. The man standing in the doorway was tall, stringily thin, middle-aged, and totally bald.

"Good. You arrived safely, Mr. Laird." He spoke in a surprisingly deep voice and held out a bony hand. "I am Janos Cuvier. Thank you for coming straight here."

Laird took the offered hand. Cuvier's grip was dry and hard, like clasping a parchment claw. That formality over, Cuvier waved Laura Cero on ahead, then ushered Laird into the room. It was large, furnished Spanish style with deep leather armchairs, dark wood, and a scatter of goatskin rugs. Two men were waiting at a big open fireplace over by the far wall. Like Janos Cuvier, they were casually dressed in open-necked shirts and blue denim trousers.

"Two people who also want to meet you, Mr. Laird," said Cuvier, leading him over. "This is Captain Van Holst, of the *Sea Robin*. And my shipping manager, Paul Raynal."

They shook hands. Van Holst was in his late fifties, a bulky, heavy-faced individual with small, nervous blue eyes. Raynal was a small man with dark, wavy hair, sharp features and a slight lisp.

"A drink first, eh?" suggested Cuvier. He indicated glasses already lying on a side table. "We didn't wait—my apologies. But you can catch up. What will you have?"

"A beer would be good," said Laird gratefully. "Cool as you've got it."

Laura Cero chuckled and went over to a drinks cabinet. Laird heard glasses clink, but his attention was on Janos Cuvier. First impressions could be dangerous, but they always mattered.

The owner of the Cuvier Corporation and the head of Pandion Shipping didn't come from any normal executive mould. Corporation presidents, the successful kind, didn't usually appear both lean and hungry the way this one did. He looked in his early fifties and might be older, but he moved with a young man's restlessness.

He had also been out in the sun too much. The skin stretched tight across his skull was red and broken, the thin beak of a nose was peeling badly.

"Before we say anything else." Cuvier touched him lightly on the arm. "You must have known the original Clanmore representative who came here, Mr. Henderson?"

"Yes." For a moment, Laird felt all three men were watching him. "I did, pretty well."

"I can only express our sadness." Cuvier pursed his lips. "A difficult situation for you, too. Did he file any kind of report before —well, before it happened?"

"No." Laird took the glass of beer Laura Cero brought over. It felt cold and moist against his fingers. "I'm starting more or less from scratch."

"We'll help all we can," promised Cuvier. He indicated one of the leather armchairs. "Sit down, please. You may feel tired from travelling, but I thought a brief meeting straight away would be best."

"A good idea," agreed Captain Van Holst quickly. "I think—" He saw Raynal frown at him and stopped there, then found a seat like the rest. Only Laura Cero remained standing. She went over to the window and stood with her back to the view.

"Now." His thin face attentive, Cuvier leaned forward in his chair. "Tell me the position as you see it, Mr. Laird?"

"So far?" Laird took a first sip of the chilled beer. "The insured cover documents don't have any problems, hull or cargo." He glanced towards Laura Cero. "I've got the copy statements, there are some other claim details to assemble. We'll have to consider the suggestion of a salvage attempt."

"Depending on the salvage master's report." Cuvier nodded. He pursed his thin lips. "We should have that tonight. I understand that Captain Novak is an expert."

"He is," said Laird stonily. "But the final decision depends on the underwriters."

"That *Sea Robin* is a good ship, Mr. Laird," began Van Holst warily. "Not young, but still sound. Maybe—"

"Maybe we should wait and listen," said Cuvier. His deep voice lost its edge again as he turned back to Laird. "I'm not a person who cares particularly about ships and the sea. I run a business, Pandion is part of that business—plus and minus signs, bottom-line results. Your people in London are probably the same."

"They make it a religion." Laird took another swallow of beer, watching the man. "They also pay me to worry about things, like when I hear you're unloading insured cargo."

Cuvier exchanged an almost amused glance with his shipping manager.

"But we have their approval," he said, showing his teeth in a brief, reassuring smile. "You weren't advised?"

"No."

"It was agreed with your chairman. The paperwork still has to be prepared but is incidental." Cuvier gestured that aspect aside. "I came here, I saw the situation, and I telephoned London—I have met your chairman a few times. We talked about the cargo, among other things. He agreed it would have to be treated as a total loss, for insurance purposes, but he hoped some of it might be salvaged. Except, unfortunately, there was no way to handle the situation locally."

"So you came to an arrangement," said Laird flatly, inwardly cursing all meddling senior executives, particularly the type who took their own decisions. "What kind?"

"Pandion Shipping isn't involved by name—that wouldn't be

totally ethical." Cuvier showed his teeth again, briefly, and indicated Raynal. "But Paul is handling the details. We're landing what we can, moving it to warehouse storage near Marbella. Later —well, Clanmore and my organization should both benefit a little."

"Or more than a little?"

Cuvier shrugged. "We're only talking of some of the cargo, Mr. Laird—a modest amount." He saw Raynal wanted to speak. "Paul?"

"There's another reason, Mr. Laird, a practical one," lisped Raynal softly. "If there is to be an attempt to salvage the ship, any way we lighten it now makes the job fractionally easier. Captain Novak agrees and—ah—so does Captain Van Holst."

Pleased to be included, Van Holst nodded vigorously.

"So it's legal and practical," summed up Laura Cero, coming over from the window. She smiled down at Laird. "Satisfied?"

"Question asked, question answered." Laird nodded, still wondering what kind of deal had been arranged.

"Good." Cuvier stirred. "Laura, has Mr. Laird a place to stay?"

"Not yet." She shook her head. "But the Mercado will have a room. I'll telephone them."

"Do that." Cuvier paused, then turned to Laird again. "Will you join us for dinner tonight? Captain Novak will be here." He took Laird's agreement for granted. "Wait here while Laura telephones —I'd like a moment alone with you."

He waited until she had gone, Van Holst and Raynal close behind. Then, as the door closed, he got to his feet and came across.

"I'll speak plainly, Laird." His voice was slow, a deliberate murmur. "I can only give Pandion Shipping so much of my time, even when something like this happens. But before I leave, I want any negotiations about the *Sea Robin*'s loss to be completed. Detail matters are incidental." He pursed his lips. "There has been delay already, due to the death of your colleague. I believe he was married?"

"Yes." The change of tack took Laird by surprise.

"Then his widow would welcome a practical gesture of sympathy." The bony hands came together, almost in an attitude of prayer. "It could be a generous one, I guarantee. But it would depend on circumstance."

"I'll bear that in mind." Laird fought down a surge of anger. The deliberate, cleverly indirect bribe being dangled in front of him was by its nature hard to dismiss. He abandoned what was left of his drink and got to his feet. "Anything else?"

"No. But I hope we have an understanding." The thin, bald-headed figure walked with him to the door, opened it, then leaned against the wood. "Ask for any help you need—ask Laura or Raynal or come to me direct. I hope two, three days at the outside should be long enough for you to finish."

"I can try," said Laird.

Cuvier nodded. "We eat around eight. I'll have you collected." The door closed.

It seemed a longer walk than before to get back out into the sunlight. The hallway was empty, all Laird could hear was the same distant off-key voice still singing. Outside, Vicente was propped against the front of the white Mercedes. The tubby driver came lazily to life as Laird approached.

"Finished, señor?" he asked.

"Just starting," said Laird bitterly, and got aboard.

He looked back at the Casa Turo as the Mercedes began to move. Laura Cero was at one of the balcony windows. She waved, and he raised a hand in reply.

Then he settled back, his grey-green eyes cold and angry.

Janos Cuvier had tried to put him over a barrel. Maybe he had even succeeded.

But the real question was why.

CHAPTER 2

The Hostal Mercado was a modest three-storey building located a couple of minutes' walk from San Ferdinand's harbour. It had a flat roof and cracked, cement-finished walls long overdue a coat of paint. Facing the sea, it was separated from the beach by a road and a patch of waste ground that included an exposed sewage pipe.

Initial impressions inside weren't encouraging. Most of the front area was a drab, ill-lit bar with greasy tables, shabby curtains and an apparent lack of customers. A half-hearted attempt had been made to brighten things a little by draping some old fishing nets across the ceiling. A few brass lamps from a long-forgotten ship decorated the bar counter. Behind the bar, flanking a notice that the management didn't give credit, several enlarged photographs of fishing boats had been tacked to the woodwork.

"My son Roberto took these, Señor Laird. He is an artist with a camera," beamed the small, extraordinarily fat woman who had been waiting for Laird when he arrived. Señora Isabel Vegas, owner and apparently most other things concerning the Mercado, had a dark wrinkled face and long, greying hair. She wore a shapeless blue dress, damp with sweat under the armpits, carpet slippers, and a man's grey trilby hat. *"Maravilloso* . . . they look good, eh?"

"They give the place character," agreed Laird politely. But the photographs were good. He noticed something stir up among the fishing nets, then a cat looked down at him. He cleared his throat. "About the room, Señora—"

"Mamá," she corrected him, showing a set of blackened teeth. "Mamá Isabel is what everyone calls me. How long will you stay?"

"A few days. I can't be sure," admitted Laird.

"Yo comprendo." A fat, work-calloused hand gestured in understanding. "I charge five hundred pesetas a night. Suppose you pay five nights in advance? If you stay six, the extra night is free." Mamá Isabel winked. "I got the idea from a tourist magazine."

"Fine." Laird counted the money into her hand. "I've got some laundry."

"Laundry is extra." She stuffed the money somewhere under the neck of her dress. "Your friend Señor Henderson had our best room. It is still empty." Turning, she raised her voice. "Roberto—"

Her son ambled out from a curtained doorway at the rear of the bar. Like his mother, Roberto Vegas was small and dark and fat. But he had a cheerful, grinning face and was smartly turned out in a white shirt, red bow tie, tight black trousers and platform-heeled black shoes.

"Mamá?" He gave Laird a friendly nod.

Mother and son spoke briefly for a moment. Then, giving Laird another smile from under the brim of her hat, Mamá Isabel left.

Picking up Laird's bag, beckoning him to follow, Roberto led the way through another curtained doorway at the back of the bar.

From there, they went up a creaking stair to the top floor. Opening the second door along, Roberto ushered Laird in ahead of him.

It was a modest-sized room, sparsely furnished, but the walls were white, recently painted. There was clean linen on the large bed and the faded green carpet on the floor had been carefully darned. The view from the window was out towards the Mediterranean. A small metal crucifix was on the wall above the bed and another of the fishing-boat photographs decorated the opposite wall. It was a study at sunset, one that caught atmosphere in a way that wasn't easy.

"Your mother is right," said Laird. "You know how to handle a camera."

"Thank you." Roberto beamed. "Is the room okay, Señor Laird?"

"Fine." Laird prodded the bed and almost winced. "Do you have many guests?"

"People come, people go." The young Spaniard put the bag on a chair. "We had an American couple, but they left this morning. There are a few other people." He shrugged. "San Ferdinand is not as well known as Marbella."

"Be grateful," said Laird drily. He loosened his tie. "So this was Henderson's room?"

"Sí." Roberto's smile faded. "He was a nice man."

"What happened to his luggage?"

"The Guardia Civil have it, señor. Ramón García—Sergeant García of the Guardia collected all there was the day after the accident." Roberto hesitated. "The bathroom is next door. Do you wish anything else?"

Laird shook his head and Roberto left.

Once the door had clicked shut, Laird took off his jacket and went over to the window. The harbour was to his left, a few boats lying along the small quayside. Though he could only see part of the village, he had a view of a long sweep of coastline and the window also looked almost straight out towards the pathetic silhouette of the *Sea Robin* and the small assortment of craft clustered around her.

It was a practical enough location. Opening his bag, Laird dumped his grubby shirts and other laundry in a pile on the floor

beside the battered dressing tab
the rest of his few belongings ar
the bed. As he'd expected, it was
worn sag in the middle.

Lying back on it, hands behin
hairy-legged spider was prowlir
for a moment, then let his eyel
let his mind rove over the situa
had a feeling that, despite his ε
to be smooth and simple.

Suddenly, he heard an ang
outside. One of the voices was Engiisn.
crossed to the window, opened it, and looked out.

Down in the road below, almost outside the Mercado's door, a
heavily built Guardia sergeant stood frowning. He had his thumbs
hooked into his revolver belt. Facing him, talking fiercely, wag-
ging a finger in indignant emphasis, the lanky, bearded Adam
Warner looked in danger of exploding. A couple of paces away,
leaning against the side of Warner's old van, a girl with tousled sun-
bleached fair hair regarded both men with a look of resigned
tolerance. She was in her twenties, wore a blue T-shirt and white
shorts, and her feet were bare.

Warner finished. The Guardia sergeant, his tricorn patent
leather hat glistening in the sunlight, shaped an expressive shrug
towards the sun-tanned girl. Slowly and deliberately, he brought
up one hand and poked Warner in the chest. Then he spoke for a
moment in a low, unmistakably warning voice.

"It's still a damned lie." Warner's voice carried loudly and his
bearded face flushed. "What's the matter, Sergeant? If you really
believe any of it, why don't you arrest me?"

The Guardia sergeant shrugged again and released Warner.
Then, giving the girl a casual salute, he turned and walked away.

"As far as I'm concerned, Cuvier can go to hell," shouted Warner
after him.

The Guardia sergeant didn't bother to look back. Coming over,
the girl laid a hand on Warner's arm and spoke to him. Eventually,
they disappeared together into the Mercado.

Curiosity roused, Laird left his window, waited a moment, then
left his room and walked down the two flights of stairs to the
hostal's bar. Warner and the girl were sitting at one of the tables.
Mamá Isabel was behind the bar and the only other customers

ermen playing a noisy game of dominoes at
tables.
said Laird as Warner looked up.
ier gave a scowl of recognition. "Right, if you're here
nd of message from Cuvier—"
t even work for him," said Laird, grinning. "Cool down."
—" Warner hesitated. "—but you were in his car."
eing given a lift." Laird saw Mamá Isabel padding diplomati-
ly towards them. "Can I buy you a drink?"

"Yes," said the girl cheerfully. "Then maybe my brother will tell
me who you are."

"I don't know his name," said Warner sulkily. He gestured towards her. "This is my sister, Helen."

"He said graciously," murmured the girl. She chuckled.
"Friendly as a bear, isn't he?"

"I'm Andrew Laird." He smiled at her and took the empty chair
opposite them. Helen Warner had a deep suntan, blue eyes, a snub
nose and high cheekbones. But she also had a warm vitality about
her, a striking, lively air of being totally able to handle most situa-
tions—and her brother. "I—uh—met Adam on the way here."

"When that damned fool Vicente almost killed me," said
Warner.

"Maybe it looked different from where they were—I know the
way you drive," said Helen Warner. She looked at Laird. "But you
don't work for the Cuvier Corporation?"

Laird shook his head. "I'm with Clanmore Alliance—marine
insurance."

Mamá Isabel was waiting. Helen Warner ordered a glass of
chilled white wine, both men asked for a beer.

"We met the Clanmore man who was killed," said Warner slowly
as Mamá Isabel left. He pursed his lips, unrepentant. "The way he
died was damned bad luck—tragic. But if you're with them,
doesn't that mean you're part of the Cuvier circus?"

"Not the way I see things," said Laird mildly. "I heard you
disagreeing with the local Guardia. Are you having a war with
Cuvier?"

"Not from choice." Grimly, Warner took off his spectacles, polished the lenses on a loose fold of shirt, then replaced them. "And
all I did was tell Garcia what I thought."

"Which was pretty stupid," commented Helen Warner. "You
could have been dragged off to a dungeon." She shook her head at

Laird. "Brother Adam has the happy habit of being his own worst enemy."

"I'd call it self-defence," retorted Warner indignantly.

"Would you?" said the girl quizzically. "I don't think Andrew even knows what you're talking about."

"I don't," admitted Laird. He stopped as Mamá Isabel returned with their drinks, paid for them, then smiled as she padded back to the bar again. "But I'd like to hear what's wrong."

"Cuvier has got hold of the notion we're robbing him." Warner took a swallow of beer, then wiped froth from his small, sandy-coloured beard. "Either that, or he wants rid of us. We annoy him."

"Us?" Laird raised an eyebrow. "You or your students?"

"You heard, then." Warner sniffed derisively. "I won't ask how. I've got twelve students here, and Helen to help me. It's an international exchange camp—plenty of colleges run them. We mix students from different countries."

"The kind who couldn't afford any kind of vacation on their own." Helen Warner looked at her brother with a sudden affection. "Finding the money, putting it together, isn't easy."

"I enjoy it." Warner looked embarrassed. "Anyway, we're here."

Late teens to early twenties, a few of them girls, Scandinavian and Dutch, French and German, two from his own college—lumped together as a group for a month. Adam Warner's manner became enthusiastic as he explained the rest. They had a tight budget. They were living under canvas close to the beach, on ground belonging to a friendly farmer. Ground not far along the shore from Janos Cuvier's temporary headquarters at Casa Turo. They'd been there almost two weeks when the *Sea Robin* had sunk off San Ferdinand.

"No trouble till then?" asked Laird.

"None," said Warner emphatically. He wrapped both hands around his drink, frowning at the glass. "All right, my kids are students—not angels. But the locals tolerate them. Anyway, we're all busy enough most of the day."

"Explain," prompted Helen Warner.

Warner shrugged. "To get the money for a camp, you've got to have some kind of educational project. My subject is history, Laird —they're all history or archaeology students. We're looking for a ship, or what's left of one."

"You mean a wreck?" Laird showed his surprise.

"Yes. But a lot older than your cargo ship. I'm talking about a

French three-decker—a naval ship from the Napoleonic wars."
Warner's eyes glinted enthusiastically behind the spectacles. "She
was blown ashore in a gale and broke up. Some of her timbers
were used to build houses in the village."

"Waste not, want not," murmured Helen Warner. "It's an old
Spanish custom."

"She was the *Emeraude.*" Warner ignored the interruption. "I
heard about her years ago, when I came along this coast on a
walking tour. She was a perfect project idea." He showed sudden
alarm. "Not that she was a kind of treasure ship or any damn fool
thing like that."

"So you came back." Laird rubbed a finger on the greasy table-
top, leaving a clear mark. "Had any luck?"

"Enough to keep everyone happy." Warner scowled and sat
back. "Then the damned *Sea Robin* business began. Some of the
youngsters went out to the wreck a couple of times—"

"By night," said Helen Warner. "With kitbags." She chuckled
and took another sip of wine. "The things they collected—"

"But we didn't know till afterwards," said Warner anxiously.
"Not till Cuvier's people caught them, knocked them about, then
tried to have them arrested."

"And that's what it's all about?" Laird hid his amusement. "You
can't blame Cuvier too much."

"For that, maybe not." Warner's bearded lips closed tight for a
moment. "But there have been—well, incidents ever since."

"Like?"

The other man shrugged. "Everything and anything, things stolen or lost, things that go wrong—we're blamed, the police are
told. But Cuvier can go to hell. I'm not moving."

Laird believed him. Beneath that awkward, almost nervous exterior, Adam Warner could obviously be a remarkably stubborn,
and probably infuriating, character.

"We have to go." Warner finished his drink and pushed back his
chair. "Helen—"

"I know." She glanced apologetically at Laird. "We told Adam's
private army we wouldn't be long." She rose, then suggested,
"Come out and visit us."

"His friend Cuvier wouldn't like it," said Warner. "But come if
you want, Laird—I don't mind."

"Thanks," said Laird. He winked at Helen Warner. "I'll wave a
white flag."

The fishermen at the corner table stopped their game to watch brother and sister leave. Their interest was Helen Warner's long, tanned legs. One man whistled his appreciation while another gave a mock growl and slapped his forearm. Warner's walk became an angry stalk, but Helen looked round deliberately and laughed as she went out.

Left on his own, Laird finished his drink, then knew what he had to do next. Osgood Morris always felt happier when he knew that his staff had arrived where they were supposed to be.

There was a pay telephone next to the bar, inside a cabinet of solid wood which had a tiny porthole window just big enough to allow the outside world to check that the user was still alive. He went over and the telephone was modern enough. San Ferdinand had international trunk dialling.

Closing the door, Laird fed coins into the slot, then dialled Clanmore Alliance in London. Thirty seconds of electronic chirping later, the London switchboard answered and he was put through to Osgood Morris.

"How's your weather?" asked Morris.

"Spanish," said Laird. "Osgood, why the hell didn't you tell me Pandion Shipping had a squad of head-office people down here— including the boss?"

"Because I didn't know." Clanmore's marine claims manager made an apologetic noise over the wire. "The chairman only told me this morning—and remember, Henderson didn't file any kind of report. Ah—have you met Janos Cuvier?"

"Yes," said Laird flatly. "He claims he has some kind of understanding with us about shifting cargo from the *Sea Robin.*"

"He has." Morris sounded even more uncomfortable. "I've only just heard about that too. I'm not sure of what's planned, but—"

"He's doing it now."

"Oh." Morris was silent for a moment. When he spoke again, his voice was lower, cautious. "I think Cuvier made the suggestion and the chairman just—ah—thought it was sensible."

"You mean he was talked into it?"

"He approved." Morris's manner chilled. "The Cuvier Corporation put a lot of policy business of different kinds our way, not just marine. Pandion Shipping is almost a sideline."

"So be nice to Cuvier?" asked Laird wearily.

"Exactly." Morris was firm. "I'm glad you understand. Just keep in touch."

The line went dead. Laird hung up, struggled with the heavy door, and left the booth. Mamá Isabel had gone from behind the bar and her son had taken over.

"*Hola,* Señor Laird." Roberto's fat face split in a friendly greeting. "Settling in okay?"

"So far," said Laird.

"*Bueno.*" The glass being polished took an extra rub from Roberto's cloth and he leaned over the counter. "Well, any help you need, like maybe photographs with my camera, just ask."

"I'll remember," nodded Laird. A thought struck him. "Did you take any photographs for Henderson?"

"All the things he asked." Roberto gestured with the towel. "The ship, the crew—mostly the crew."

Laird frowned. "Did he say why?"

Roberto shook his head. "Just that I was to be discreet. That was easy. I have a good telephoto lens."

"I'd like to see them," said Laird slowly, puzzled. Photographic evidence wasn't a regular part of a claim report. But if Charlie Henderson had wanted photographs, he had had a reason.

"I have the negatives but no prints, Señor Laird." Roberto hesitated. "When Señor Henderson died—"

"I'll take care of what you're owed," promised Laird.

The plump face brightened. "I have my own dark-room. I can make prints tonight."

*

Outside, there was still plenty of heat in the late afternoon sun. A dog barked half-heartedly from a patch of shade as Laird left the Mercado and walked towards the village.

San Ferdinand was bigger than he'd expected. Most of it was crammed into a tight tangle of narrow streets. Here and there an open doorway gave a glimpse of a cool, dark interior or a tiny inner courtyard bright with flowers. The people he saw were all busy on errands of their own. An occasional motor cycle rasped past, and there were a few cars and delivery vans.

He reached a small square in what looked like the oldest part of the village. It had a fountain memorial to the dead in the civil war. The fountain didn't work. Someone had spray-painted a Falangist slogan on the wall behind it, someone else had over-sprayed that message with a hammer and sickle. Four old men sat on a bench, a line of faded dark suits and black berets, arguing about football.

Another narrow street brought Laird to the harbour. It was small, built of hard grey granite and protected by a narrow finger of breakwater. There were no yachts along its quayside—San Ferdinand was very much a working place. Great swathes of nets hung drying or being repaired. Two fishing boats were unloading their catch, silvered torrents of sardines being shovelled into boxes and heaved ashore.

There were other boats, some empty and creaking gently at their mooring ropes, almost all fitted with big gasoline stern lamps for night fishing. Laird glanced at them, but was more interested in another vessel. She was a big, grubby, flat-decked workboat with a crane mounted aft, and she was berthed in isolation out near the breakwater. A gang of men were unloading her and a large truck was parked on the quayside just above. He recognized the truck. It was the same vehicle with the Málaga plates, the one he'd seen stopped by the police.

The crane clanked to life and a large crate was lifted into the air from the workboat. It swung in towards the quay, then was lowered beside others on the truck's platform. More crates were stacked on the quayside.

Load unhooked, the crane clattered busily and swung inboard again. Guessing what was going on, Laird walked towards the activity and, beyond the fishing boats, came to where a rope had been slung like a barrier between two iron posts.

He stepped over the rope, neared the truck, and saw the way in which the crates aboard were stained and wet, some still dripping water.

Half a dozen men made up the shore end of the gang, and there were about the same number aboard the workboat. Nodding casually to the nearest of them, Laird went closer and looked at the blotched stencilling on the sides of the crates.

"So what the hell are you nosing at?" demanded a hoarse Cockney voice. A heavy hand gripped his left arm like a vice and swung him round. The hand's owner, a tall, thin, unshaven seaman, bared his teeth in a snarl and shoved Laird hard back against the nearest packing case. "No rubbernecks allowed. *Vamos.* On your way, fancy boy."

"I don't believe it," said Laird with mock awe. "I've found a talking ape!"

The seaman's mouth dropped open. Then his free hand swung, aiming a blow at Laird's head. Except that Laird wasn't there.

Ducking, he broke free from the grip on his arm and heard the man's fist thump hard against the wood of the packing case.

Grunting, sucking his bruised knuckles, the man came forward again, eyes glittering.

"I'm goin' to take you apart for that, fancy boy," he promised fervently while the rest of the shore gang gaped.

It had happened to Laird before, and he'd learned. The only rule was that there were no rules. The truck was at his back. As the man rushed in, he braced his hands behind him, against the truck's side, and brought his right foot up in a pistoning kick. His heel connected with the other man's stomach as if it had met a slack drumskin. There was a retching gasp and his unshaven opponent fell to his knees on the damp stone of the quay.

But the man wasn't finished. Still gasping, shaking his head, he hauled himself up again. Then his right hand closed around the haft of a knife at his belt.

"Cool it," rasped a new voice. "Francey, cut that out or I'll break your neck. What the hell's going on?"

A burly figure in faded overalls, fair hair cropped close to his skull, came scrambling up from the workboat. He reached the truck, glared at the seaman, then swung to face Laird. "You. What the—" His voice died and he stared. Then he grinned. "I don't believe it—Andy! What brings you here?"

"Work." Laird returned the greeting with a grin and some relief. "Hello, Jingles." He thumbed at the thin, angry seaman. "One of yours?"

"Yes. Not from choice." Jingles Reilly, a man in his forties, was mate and chief diver aboard the *Beroe,* the salvage tug working beside the *Sea Robin.* But before that, like Laird, he'd served on the *Scomber* until Harry Novak's calculated brutality had become too much. Chuckling, he clapped Laird on the shoulder, then glanced back, shaping a scowl. "Francey, get your greasy paw off that blade. I'm talkin' to a friend."

"He called me an ape," said the man sullenly.

"He was wrong," said Reilly solemnly. "An ape is a noble animal. You, Francey, are a useless flea-bitten thing like an organ-grinder's monkey. And I'm the organ-grinder around here, so shove off." He waited until the man slunk away, then faced Laird again. "Are you all right?"

"Fine," said Laird amiably. "I owe you a drink."

"Who doesn't?" Reilly gestured the other men back to work. "Here about the *Sea Robin*?"

Laird nodded. "From the insurance angle. How does she look?"

"That depends on your view." Reilly gestured towards the sea. "On the *Beroe*, we're strictly hired help. It's still Captain Weller in command, and he's happy as long as he's paid. Novak and his *Scomber* are runnin' the show."

"I heard," said Laird. "Where is Novak?"

"On his way back from Gibraltar. He took the *Scomber* there to collect some extra gear."

"While you haul cargo ashore," murmured Laird.

Reilly shrugged. "Mostly deck cargo. Novak says he wants room to work, seems to think he can refloat her."

"Do you?" asked Laird.

"Me?" Reilly frowned. "I've been down an' seen that hull damage. Hell, Andy, if you've time and money, you can refloat anything. But I don't know if it's worth it." He shrugged again. "Still, that animal Novak usually knows what he's doing."

Laird nodded and looked out across the harbour. The sun's glint on the water made him narrow his eyes.

"How about the cargo? Who checks what comes ashore?" Laird saw Reilly's reaction and made a quick, soothing gesture. "I'm just curious."

"Nobody's fiddling anything, Andy—at least, not here," said Reilly positively. "We keep a tally of what comes ashore. The truck drivers sign for each load, and there's a Spanish customs officer lurkin' in the harbour office who inspects each truck as it leaves."

"So everyone's playing it by the book?" Laird allowed just a trace of sardonic disbelief in his voice.

Reilly grinned a little. "Sorry, but you've got to believe it. Anyway, there's nothing glamorous in the stuff we're bringing in. You've seen the cargo manifest?"

Laird nodded.

"Then you know what I mean."

A shout came from behind them. Another crate, bigger than the rest, was being hoisted up from the workboat. Coming in towards the quay, it was swinging wildly.

"Watch it, damn you!" Reilly howled the warning and gave Laird a quick, despairing glance. "That drink can wait, right? I'll be around."

He plunged towards the men struggling with the crate. Laird

watched until the chaos ended, then turned and headed back towards the village. He had passed the barrier rope and was level with the first of the fishing boats, when a bulky figure ambled out from the shade of a high stack of fish boxes.

"*Buenas tardes,* Señor Laird." Sergeant Ramón García looked hot but his grey-green Guardia Civil uniform was immaculately buttoned and his tricorn hat was set square on his head. "I saw you have a little trouble out there. Is it settled?"

"I think so." Laird considered the man's large, comfortably confident face. He had a feeling that García was the kind of cop who probably made a habit of waiting to see how things worked out. As a philosophy, it could certainly make for an easier life. "Thanks for asking."

"It did not seem right to intrude." Hooking his thumbs into the holster belt which spanned his ample stomach, García fell into step beside him. "I know about you, of course. You are comfortable at the Hostal Mercado?"

"Everything's fine," said Laird drily.

"Good." García nodded to a fisherman watching them from the deck of the nearest boat, and ignored the way the fisherman scowled. "Mamá Isabel and I are related, so if there is a problem, let me know." He hummed under his breath for a few more paces. "*Sí . . .* and if I can help officially in any way—"

"Maybe you can," Laird told him. "I'd like to hear how Charlie Henderson died."

"*Es muy triste . . .* very sad." The Guardia sergeant shrugged. "The report is at my office, if you have time. We also have his luggage. His room was paid in advance, but there is some money due on the car hire and other small matters—"

"I'll take care of them," said Laird stonily. "Cash against receipts, Sergeant."

They left the harbour and walked a short distance into the village, García exchanging an occasional greeting with some of the people he passed. A few gave him a cheerful reply but the majority contented themselves with a cautious nod.

"The uniform," explained García unperturbed. "The Guardia Civil still has a certain reputation—from the old days. Now, of course, we are a democracy, more liberal."

"Nobody gets shot any more?" suggested Laird.

García gave a chuckle. "It is *prohibido,* Señor Laird. Except, of course, during working hours."

San Ferdinand's *estación de policia* was just off the central square Laird had walked through earlier. A police car and two motor cycles were parked outside the small, shabby building. They reached it as another Guardia officer, wearing a white crash helmet, climbed aboard one of the motor cycles and rode away.

Inside, it was dull but cool, with a faint smell of stale perspiration mingled with cheap disinfectant.

A young policeman looked up from behind the public counter, gave Laird a bored glance, then went back to reading his newspaper. A few flies buzzed around the bulletin board behind him, the squashed remains of others stained its posters.

García's office was a small room at the rear. Grunting, he removed his hat and wiped some sweat from his forehead. He had thinning grey hair, cropped in a close crew cut.

"Sit down, Señor Laird." He produced a hard-backed wooden chair from a corner and placed it beside his desk. Then, unfastening his tunic, he went over to a cupboard and brought out a battered suitcase with airline luggage tags attached to the handle. Bringing the suitcase over, he dumped it on the desk. "This is everything your friend Henderson had with him."

"Thank you." Laird didn't particularly like the task, but it had to be done. As García went round to his own side of the desk and slumped into a battered swivel chair, he opened the case and frowned for a moment at its contents.

"Mamá Isabel packed for me," explained García. "That seemed more suitable."

Laird nodded. The neatly folded clothing showed a woman's touch. Charlie Henderson's notion of packing had always been pretty much like his own—stuff everything in, then hope the case would close. He rummaged down through the layers. There were no papers, no documents of any description.

"I have some travellers' cheques and his passport," volunteered García. He watched Laird for a moment, then made a sympathetic noise. "There are pleasanter tasks."

"And worse." He had found Henderson's spectacle case, the familiar wire-framed glasses with their half-moon reading lenses nestling inside it. Henderson had seldom worn them, had always complained they made him look senile. Laird put them back. Then, finished, he shut the suitcase and pushed it to one side. "Nothing from the crash?"

"Nothing you would want to recognize, señor." García shook his head firmly. He opened a file lying in front of him on the desk. "You asked about the accident report. Of course, that was a task for the gendarmerie."

Laird nodded he understood. The Spanish three-layer system of policing was fairly rigid in its rules. The Guardia Civil came top of the pecking order, taking their orders from central government. Traffic work was usually handled by the gendarmerie, who wore grey uniforms and were controlled by the civil governor of each province. The third group, the blue-uniformed municipal police, were mostly confined to towns and cities.

"All I want is an outline," he suggested. "My people will put in a request for a full translation later, but that can wait."

"Yo comprendo." García sucked his lips. "Your friend Henderson hired the car locally that day. He made an afternoon trip to Marbella—we know that, because he got a parking ticket. Later, he had his evening meal at the Hostal Mercado, then went out again." He paused and looked up. "That's almost all we know."

"Almost?" Laird raised a questioning eyebrow.

"The gendarmerie are thorough, in their own way." García shrugged. "They now say that about eleven that night Henderson stopped at a little bar called El Águila—that's on the same mountain road where he crashed, high up. He had one drink, a beer, stayed maybe twenty minutes, then left."

"Alone?"

García nodded. "Then half an hour later a local priest, Father Sebastian, came along the road on his motor cycle—he had been called to a sick parishioner. He saw flames at the bottom of a gully." He paused and shook his head. "Father Sebastian climbed down, more than I would have done alone, in the dark. But it was a waste of time."

"He tried." Laird chewed his lower lip for a moment. "But what was Henderson doing up there?"

"A good question," admitted García. Opening a desk drawer, he took out a half-smoked stub of black cheroot, then flicked a kitchen match to life with his thumbnail. He lit the cheroot stub with care, drew on it, then leaned back. "Unfortunately, we don't know. But it is a damn dangerous road, Señor Laird. One mistake and good-bye."

A few moments later he showed Laird the road on a map, a thin squiggle reaching laboriously up one side of the Sierra Blanca ridge, linking a couple of villages, then petering out. The same puzzle nagged at Laird's mind—what had taken Henderson there less than forty-eight hours after his arrival?

A meeting of some kind might be a possibility, a meeting with someone who hadn't shown up. But why—and what had gone wrong? He felt a chill sense of something being wrong. Yet he had nothing positive to justify the feeling; no real reason to challenge what everyone seemed prepared to accept. He gave a slight shiver, the thought a growing tendril of doubt in his mind. But it was a doubt it was wiser to keep to himself—at least for now.

He left a few minutes later, García escorting him through the outer office to the door of the police station.

"How long will you be here, Señor Laird?" asked García.

"Everyone asks that," said Laird unemotionally. "A few days. Until the job is done." He looked out at the drab, dusty street with its sun-faded paintwork, still thinking of Henderson and that mountain road. "Thanks for your help. That ship must have brought you a few problems."

"*Sí.*" García grimaced in the bright light. "Some *muy triste,* like your friend's death. Others just trouble—I will be glad when things get back to normal." He lowered his voice. "Have you met Señor Cuvier?"

Laird nodded.

"An impatient man." García sighed to himself. "Impatient—but also rich enough to be important, which makes it worse."

*

A small shop near the harbour was San Ferdinand's nearest equivalent to a ship's chandler. It had binoculars in stock, all second-hand, and Laird bought a battered pair of bridge glasses with German lenses and Spanish naval markings. He walked along to a spot near the harbour, then focused them on the distant half-submerged outline of the *Sea Robin.*

Work was still going on as before. The cargo recovery under way seemed concentrated on the forward hold, and he could make out the tiny figures of two scuba divers who were using one of the smaller craft as a diving platform.

He studied the scene for a spell, thinking more of the ship than its cargo. In the Mediterranean, currents could be strong but tidal action was a minimal factor. In some other parts of the world, the tidal range between high and low water might be an incredible fifty feet. But the almost land-locked Mediterranean's average was seldom more than two feet. That ruled out some of the more basic methods of salvage, using the tide itself to help refloat a ship— though the other side of the coin was a more stable working environment.

If an attempt was going to be made to refloat the *Sea Robin*, it might likely come down to making temporary repairs to her ruptured hull, sealing off whole sections, then forcing the sea out and new buoyancy in by using powerful compressors.

But Jingles Reilly was right. It could be a long, difficult and costly job. He wasn't sure that a small, middle-aged cargo ship was worth the cost and effort.

A slow-moving speck in the distance caught his eye. Laird tightened the focus on the lenses and the speck became the tiny shape of another salvage tug.

He recognized her easily enough. The *Scomber*, broad-beamed and with a distinctive single cut-away funnel, was on her way back from Gibraltar. He shrugged. Harry Novak would be aboard. Harry Novak's assessment of the *Sea Robin* would carry a lot of weight with Clanmore's marine department.

But at the end of the day that wouldn't be enough. Accountants would take practicalities and possibilities, reduce them to computer-calculated risk projections, and the computer would decide.

He stuffed the binoculars back in the leather case which had come with them. Laird still preferred humanity to computers, even when humanity meant Novak.

Soon afterwards, he went back to the Hostal Mercado. There were more customers in the bar, but the barman was a stranger who simply nodded a greeting as he walked through. He went up to his room. His laundry was back, washed, ironed, carefully folded, even a couple of buttons sewn on to one of the shirts.

It was a homely touch, one that softened the smile on his lips. Mamá Isabel might never make it to any listing of five-star hotels. But, in her own way, she offered a welcome.

Then the tendril of doubt came back into his mind again. What had happened to Charlie Henderson? Why had he gone up that ridiculous mountain road? Somehow, he was going to have to find out.

*

Outside, day gave way to dusk. Laird showered and shaved, put on a clean shirt, and was knotting his tie in front of the mirror when he heard a knock at the room door. Going over, he opened it.

"Mind if I come in?" asked Laura Cero, standing in the hallway. She chuckled. "Mamá Isabel wasn't too happy about me coming up here. I think she has some solid, old-fashioned ideas about stray women in her establishment."

"She's keeping an eye on my moral welfare," said Laird solemnly. He beckoned her in. "I didn't expect you."

"Vicente's having the night off." She looked around the room with curiosity. "I said I'd collect you."

The glare of the unshaded overhead light glinted on her jet-black hair and caught the bright glitter of a small diamond pendant at her throat as she moved around. She was wearing a white wool stole over a pastel-green cocktail dress. It was sleeveless, with a scooped neckline that accentuated her small, firm breasts.

"It seems reasonable." She finished her inspection. "How do you like it?"

"From here, everything looks pretty good," said Laird. "Including the room."

"Thank you, Mr.—all right, Andrew." She smiled a warning. "But I work for Janos Cuvier and tonight is business."

"Strictly business," he agreed. "I'll try to remember."

He joined her over at the window. The village had become a glowing pattern of lights in the gathering darkness. At the harbour, some of the lights were moving as boats set out for a night's fishing and other craft came in.

"The *Scomber* is back," she said absently.

He nodded. The salvage tug had come into harbour about half an hour earlier. She was berthed near the breakwater end of the quay, big enough to dwarf the local boats.

"Captain Novak says he knows you." She turned, close enough for their arms to brush. "He says you sailed with him."

"At the time, I didn't have much choice," Laird told her. He didn't move, enjoying her nearness. "Will Cuvier let you off the leash after dinner?"

"Tonight?" She shook her head regretfully. "There's work waiting—he's been on the phone to Geneva most of the afternoon. One of the other companies has a problem."

Laird grimaced. "Does he ever let up?"

"Not often." Her shoulders shaped a shrug under the white wool stole. "But that's his way. Do you know how he started?"

"I'll listen." Reluctantly, he went across to the bed and collected his jacket. "I know he's Romanian by birth, but came west."

"Walked west," she corrected. "He got to Switzerland with not much more than the clothes he wore."

Something in her voice surprised him. "You knew him then?"

"I was still at school. But my father gave him a job as a truck driver. He even lived with us for a spell, using the spare room. Then—well, he moved on. He got a truck of his own, started his own business—"

"It happens," said Laird. "And now he's the Cuvier Corporation. How many people got trampled along the way?"

"A few," she admitted. "That's inevitable, isn't it? But he kept in touch with us—and helped pay me through law school." She glanced at the tiny gold watch on her wrist. "Ready? He doesn't like people being late."

The white Mercedes was parked outside the Mercado, next to an old farm truck that smelled of manure. They drove through the village, where the cool of evening was bringing people into the streets, then out beyond. Darkness had arrived, with the moon a slim crescent in a star-cluttered sky. Then the station wagon turned in at the same driveway, reached the front of the Casa Turo, and Laura Cero cut the engine.

"Andrew." She laid a warning hand on his arm. "Be diplomatic if there's a problem. I don't want us on opposite sides."

They got out and walked towards the brightly lit villa. Crickets were chirping in the darkness and Laird could hear the low, distant murmur of the sea in the background.

A Spanish maid opened the door to them, gave Laura a friendly smile, then took them to a large reception room which had large oil paintings on the walls and polished silver gleaming on side tables. The half dozen people already in the room couldn't even make it look half-occupied.

"Good—our guest." Janos Cuvier strode forward to meet Laird. He wore a white dinner jacket, a colour that seemed to emphasize his thin, stringy build, and his bald head gleamed under the chandelier lights. "How many times have you had a lawyer as chauffeur, Mr. Laird?"

"Not often, but I could get used to it," said Laird.

Cuvier chuckled. He signalled another maid and she brought over drinks on a tray. It was a champagne cocktail, with no choice. Laird took one dutifully.

"Now, come and meet some people," said Cuvier.

Two of the group he'd met before—Raynal, Pandion Shipping's sharp-faced manager, and Van Holst, the bulky captain of the ill-fated *Sea Robin*. A plump, smartly dressed woman, middle-aged, with henna-dyed hair, was Marda Nord, who was Cuvier's personal secretary. Next to her were two younger men, quietly dressed, carefully polite, one dark-haired and the other fair.

"Hans Botha and John Vasco, two of my management staff," said Cuvier casually. "I call them my utility twins—they possess a variety of talents, from accountancy onward." He let the two fade into the background again and steered Laird towards the last of the group, then said drily, "I think you know Captain Novak."

"That's right." Laird had been aware of Novak from the moment he'd entered. He looked squarely at the broad-shouldered, thick-waisted figure of the tug master, and spoke flatly. "Yes, we're old shipmates."

Novak gave a loud laugh. In his mid-forties, with dark shaggy hair, he had a heavy, ill-tempered face on which a scar, running from cheek-bone to eyebrow, seemed as if it should be there. He was in shore-going rig, a dark-blue suit with a crumpled white shirt and a stringy black tie. He gave the briefest of nods.

"So you're still in your comfy shore job, Mister Laird." There was a sarcastic emphasis on the "Mister," but behind it there was a wariness. "Haven't tired of it yet?"

"Not yet," said Laird quietly. "I hear you've been busy."

"That's my way. Or maybe you've forgotten." Novak turned to Janos Cuvier. "Anyone works for me, he earns his keep. Whether he likes it or not."

"A sound principle," murmured Cuvier, watching them both. "Would you agree, Mr. Laird?"

"Within reason." Laird sipped his drink, still woodenly polite, but old memories came flooding back as he'd known they would, memories as deep as that scar on Novak's face.

The scar was part of them, yet they began earlier than Novak.

They started when a young Andrew Laird, a farmer's son, had been a final-year medical student at a Scottish university. The future had been bright, until his mother had been condemned to endure a suffering without hope. Eventually, calmly, she had asked him for the only help that could be given. He had loved her too much to refuse.

Even if the crime lay in being caught, the medical profession set its own standards. Nothing could be proved, but there had been no final examinations. Afterwards, initially, he had taken a job as a deckhand on a tramp steamer. Then, with some deep-water time behind him, he'd trained as a radio operator.

"Did you serve long with Captain Novak?" asked Cuvier with a studied innocence.

"Long enough—maybe for both of us," said Laird.

The *Scomber* had been his first berth as a radio operator. Novak paid top rates but treated his salvage tug crew like animals. Finally, inevitably, there had been a day when a berserk deckhand carved a gash down Novak's face with a broken bottle. Andrew Laird had used a blunt needle and a strand of fine radio wire to stitch the wound while Novak whimpered and quivered, never asking how his radio man came to have medical skills. But from then on he had maintained a grudging respect towards Laird. Harry Novak was always wary of anything or anyone he didn't totally understand.

Andrew Laird had moved on to other skippers, other salvage tugs, until he'd left the sea for the marine insurance job. The reason had been a girl. He'd thought they were going to marry, but it hadn't happened.

An elbow jostled his side and brought him back to the present. Van Holst had joined them. From the thickening slur in his voice and the glazed look in his eyes, he'd already had enough to drink.

"You go to sea wit' a man, you never forget him, right?" The Dutch captain gestured in a way that almost spilled the small amount of liquor left in his glass. "I know, Mr. Laird. I had a good ship an' a good crew. Now—they're both gone, eh?"

Novak grunted his lack of interest. Beside him, Janos Cuvier showed a frown of displeasure. But Laird nodded.

"What happened to your crew, Captain?" he asked.

Van Holst sighed but it was Cuvier who answered, almost curtly.

"We shipped them home. Flew them out on the charter flight that brought us down." He shrugged. "They've been paid off—not much else we could do. I suppose we were lucky that we didn't have casualties."

"Excep' for my damn fool of a first officer," said Van Holst gloomily.

"Poor man." Laura had been listening in the background. She chuckled. "He gets ashore intact, then falls on the quayside and breaks a leg. He had to stay on in hospital in Marbella for a few days."

"Damn fool," repeated the Dutchman. He turned ingratiatingly to Laird again. "But I don' blame him for what happened to my ship, Mr. Laird. It was nobody's fault. When an engine dies, a ship dies, right?"

"We all know what happened, Captain." Janos Cuvier's thin face showed a cold expression, close to angry impatience. "But there are other matters to discuss, matters that don't concern you."

"Sure." Van Holst flushed, forced a grin, and shuffled his feet awkwardly. "Sorry. Time I left anyway. I'm still okay for that lift to Marbella?"

Cuvier nodded. Muttering good-night, the Dutchman wandered off.

"Going out on the town?" asked Novak, grinning.

"His affair." Cuvier shrugged his lack of interest, then turned to Laird. "I prefer to eat before I talk business. Would you agree?"

"I do—and he will," said Novak.

Then he turned and looked around for another drink.

CHAPTER 3

The dining room had dark wood panelling and an oval table decorated with more of the Casa Turo's silver. A grey-haired Spanish major-domo, helped by a younger man, served a meal that began with a cold consommé.

"I bought a package deal," explained Cuvier while they ate. "Staff as well as the house—all in. The place belongs to a politician who has to stay close to things in Madrid." He gestured around. "Obviously he is reasonably wealthy but—"

"But he can always use the extra rent?" Laird looked along the table towards his host. Cuvier was at one end and had placed Laura at the other. Probably by design Laird had found himself exactly opposite Harry Novak. Both of the "utility twins" had made their excuses and left, but Paul Raynal was seated beside Laird while Novak was paired with Cuvier's plump, henna-haired secretary. She was working hard at making the best of it. "Well, it gives you the simple comforts."

"Exactly." Cuvier nodded amused agreement. "Plus privacy—which has its own value."

The consommé was followed by tiny strips of fish in a red wine sauce, and they in turn preceded a main course of *pato con aceitunas,* which turned out to be duck with olives, served with a saffron-flavoured rice. Cheese took the place of a sweet. Even though he had to listen to Harry Novak's noisy eating, Laird enjoyed the meal.

Any conversation was casual, kept deliberately that way by Cuvier. Their bald, thin-faced host seemed to take each remark, assess where it might lead, then if necessary steer a course to a different subject.

Laird let it happen. But part of the time he was thinking about the injured first officer kept in hospital in Marbella. His time there could have overlapped Charlie Henderson's afternoon visit to the resort town. Suppose Henderson had visited the man? Could the result have been the reason that had taken Henderson on that other, fatal journey?

Outwardly, he tried to give no sign. He joined in conversation like the rest, and made appreciative noises about the food. Coffee was served, accompanied by glasses of a dark Spanish brandy. The large decanter was left on the table as Cuvier dismissed the major-domo and his assistant. A moment later, Cuvier looked pointedly at his secretary. She rose, made a murmur about dictation still waiting to be typed, and went out.

"Now." Cuvier carefully cut and lit a cigar. "Mr. Laird, I think we should begin."

Elbows propped on the table, Novak grunted agreement. Raynal leaned forward a little, pursing his lips, while Laura laid a small notebook and pen beside her glass.

"I'm ready," nodded Laird.

"Good." Cuvier watched him closely, as if ready to gauge his slightest reaction. "I've spoken again to your chairman, by telephone. I've suggested a possible course of action he seems inclined to accept—although he made it clear he'd need your report and other assessments before a final decision."

"I see." Laird mentally cursed Clanmore's chairman for his continued meddling involvement. "A deal. What kind?"

"Paul." Cuvier turned to his shipping manager. "You can explain."

"We want at least an attempt to refloat the *Sea Robin*." Raynal's lisping voice was slow but positive. "I understand Captain Novak believes it possible."

"Does he?" Laird made it a direct question across the table.

Novak hesitated, then nodded. "I go along with 'possible.' At this stage, anyway."

Novak's caution, the mere fact he had doubts, told Laird a lot. He faced Raynal again.

"You know you could go for a total loss claim?"

"Yes." Raynal frowned unhappily. "But Pandion Shipping is geared to a five-ship operation. Without the *Sea Robin*, we're down to four—operationally bad, costly. We'd have to replace her."

"And?" Laird waited.

"Our hull insurance may not have been totally adequate," admitted Raynal reluctantly. He gave a wary glance towards Cuvier. "I warned about that, some time ago."

"Meaning that you'd lose money at insured value, that replacing her would mean extra finance?" Laird suddenly saw where they were heading. He felt almost amused. Plenty of shipping operators tried to keep down overheads by restricting insurance costs to an acceptable minimum. Trouble only arrived if a ship became a total casualty. He wouldn't have described the *Sea Robin* as drastically undervalued, but Cuvier's people had obviously done their sums. "Hard luck—but that's not Clanmore's worry."

Raynal nodded gloomily.

"But Clanmore would certainly benefit if the ship could be refloated," murmured Laura from her end of the table. She considered Laird shrewdly. "Suppose it was possible, Andrew. It would be less expensive than paying out on a total loss claim—or it might be. Your people would save money, Pandion Shipping would save money." She paused, then added an extra weapon to her argument. "Under the terms of insurance, we've a right to propose salvage."

"But we take the final decision," he countered, thinking fast. Insurance companies were usually the side pressing for an attempt at salvage, shipowners the people holding out for total loss payment. "You're talking about a gamble, a gamble that could go wrong—"

"Then you'd be back at a total loss payout," agreed Laura frankly.

"Plus the bill for trying to salvage," reminded Laird. He nursed his brandy glass, frowning. "All right, I know we agreed to a survey. But we haven't even had Novak's report."

"You've got it now," snapped Novak. He pulled an envelope from an inside pocket and tossed it across the table. "Pandion have their own copy."

"Right." Laird picked up the envelope but left it unopened. "What does it say?"

"Maybe yes, maybe no—but that my vote would be give it a try," said Novak. He grabbed the brandy bottle and filled his glass again, the room light accentuating the scar across his face. "I put divers down, went down myself. She's sitting on reasonably firm bottom sand, which is good. The damage—well, from what I can see there are two main gashes on her underside, like someone went wild with a helluva big can-opener."

"So you'd start with a patch job?"

"As the easy part." Novak knew he had an audience and enjoyed it. "Then the real work—we'd bring in lift pontoons, attach them to the hull by cables, get the cables under the hull by pressure-hosing through that sand. At the same time, we'd be preparing every compartment aboard ship. Then it comes down to knowing how to use a helluva lot of compressed air."

Battleships had been raised from the dead that way. It needed skill, determination, and luck, down to the exact location of the giant hollow pontoon cylinders, first flooded, then returned to their tremendous buoyancy. Laird had seen it happen often enough—seen it fail as well as succeed.

"How about equipment?" he asked quietly.

Novak shrugged. "I can get all I want from Gibraltar—no problem."

"Cost?"

"Let's say you're not talking about any kind of fixed-price operation." The man grinned sardonically across the table. "Sorry—shipmate."

"The expert—your expert—says it could be done." Janos Cuvier used two bony fingers to drum a brief tattoo on the table. "Do you agree?"

"It might," said Laird. "But it would cost—not to mention the bill for a refit."

"Admirable caution," said Cuvier with a sarcastic edge. "But you'll accept that there's a possibility that must be totally explored, that at least some preliminary work could be done?" He added softly, "I believe the results could be rewarding—in ways we both care about."

The subtle blackmail hint from the afternoon was there again, close to the surface. Laird felt a cold anger, but fought it down.

"What's your immediate plan, Novak?" he asked quietly.

"On a go-ahead?" Novak rubbed his chin. "Pressure-hose a couple of trial tunnels through the muck under her bottom. Get a better look inside her, if I can. My divers won't like that, but what the hell?"

Laird sat silent, letting them wait. For the moment, what was being asked was practical. In addition, he had his own reasons for avoiding a breakdown situation—different reasons from the one that Janos Cuvier might imagine.

"Andrew?" Laura was watching him, an uncertain frown on her face. "It seems fair to me."

"Yes." He nodded slowly. "We'll go for the final picture. Then London decides."

"Thank you," said Cuvier. A strange flicker of relief crossed his thin face, then had gone, replaced by a sudden smile. "Captain Novak, I think you should pass that brandy round the table. A drink seems in order."

*

Laird left a little later. Paul Raynal was giving Novak a lift back to the harbour, where the *Scomber* was lying, and offered to take him as well. But he turned down the chance. The night was still warm and dry, with only the faintest of winds, and he felt like walking.

He managed to talk to Laura on her own on the way out. She went with him to the front veranda of the Casa Turo, then stopped.

"You can be awkward, can't you?" In the moonlight, her eyes held a twinkle of amusement. "There was a moment when I thought you were going to turn us down."

"I nearly did," he admitted. "You looked like you were ready for it."

"I was." She nodded. "I could have made noises about maritime case law. Then we had something else in reserve—but I'm glad it wasn't needed."

"That makes two of us." He grinned. "What kind of secret weapon did you have in mind?"

"It'll keep. Just in case we need it another time." She went down the veranda steps with him and stopped at the edge of the garden. "You've made Janos Cuvier happy."

"For now." Laird took a deep breath of the night air. The crickets were still chirping somewhere in among the shadows, the world suddenly seemed pleasantly peaceful. But he wondered. Something strange was lurking out there, something uncertain yet dangerous. "Have you still got to go back and work?"

Laura nodded ruefully, then touched his arm. "I'm sorry. Maybe tomorrow—"

"Your friend in there permitting." He said it with an easygoing humour, then went on casually. "That character who broke his leg, the *Sea Robin*'s first officer—"

"Constantinos." She nodded. "What about him?"

Laird shrugged. "He still might have some kind of claim for compensation. When did he leave hospital?"

She frowned. "Three days ago, I think. Yes—that's right. Paul Raynal got him a flight home to Athens."

"Maybe we'll hear from him." Laird dismissed it casually. But three days back meant the morning after Charlie Henderson had died. "Did he travel on his own?"

"No. Sam Grant, the chief engineer, was still around—so he went with him." She looked at her wrist-watch and wrinkled her nose. "I'd better get back, Andrew."

"Tomorrow," he reminded her.

"Yes." Quickly, unexpectedly, she kissed him lightly on the cheek and Laird felt that soft, raven-black hair brush his face. Stepping back, she smiled at him. "Thanks for not being stubborn."

Then she went quickly up the steps and disappeared into the villa.

Laird stood for a moment, not particularly proud of what he'd done. Then he shrugged to himself. The ways things were, he hadn't had much option. He might be totally wrong, he might not. But until he found out, he would have to play it that way—even with Laura Cero.

A few minutes later he was clear of the Casa Turo's grounds and on the coast road, walking back towards San Ferdinand. There was only a slight breeze, the sea was very close, and he could hear the piping sounds of unseen birds, night-feeding along the shoreline.

Then he heard voices, voices singing to a guitar accompaniment. Puzzled, he reached a bend in the road, then saw the glow of a fire not far ahead. Getting nearer, he saw the fire was burning on some open ground on the shore side of the road. Several figures sat around it, and the glow also silhouetted some small tents.

It had to be Adam Warner's student camp. Leaving the road, Laird crossed the rough, scrub-littered ground towards the glow. He wasn't seen until almost the last moment. Then the singing died, a tall, red-haired youngster with a guitar struck a last, random chord, and for a moment there was a silence broken only by the crackle of burning driftwood.

"Just visiting," said Laird cheerfully, stepping into the edge of the firelight. He saw Helen Warner among the group. She was sitting on a box, two younger girls at her feet, and he made towards her. "You said I could, remember?"

"Yes. You're welcome." She rose to her feet, smiling, and came over. She was in a long-sleeved shirt, worn loose over dark trousers, sandals, and a red kerchief tied bandanna-style at her throat. "Join the party, Andrew." Glancing round, she signalled the nearest of the students. "Frank, drag Adam from his tent. Tell him Andrew Laird is here."

The youngster went off. Beside the fire, the guitar player plucked a few notes. But the faces all around showed an odd mixture of suspicion and wariness, even as Helen Warner made a quick roll-call of introductions. Laird counted ten students, which meant a couple were absent.

"Did you come from the village?" asked Helen Warner.

"No." He lowered his voice and winked at her. "I've been consorting with the enemy—I was at Cuvier's place."

"Oh." The fair-haired girl grimaced. "We won't shout about it, all right?" She left it at that as Adam Warner appeared, combing his beard with his fingers, his spectacles glinting in the firelight. "Adam—we've a visitor."

"I can see him," said Warner almost peevishly. Then, apologetically, he became more friendly. "Sorry, Laird. I was having a snooze. That doesn't leave me at my best." He paused. "After dark isn't a good time if you're here for a guided tour—"

"It can wait," said Laird easily. The atmosphere around the camp-fire was thawing a little. The guitar player, a Norwegian named Jan, was trying to coax a new tune from his instrument. One of the girls was singing the words under her breath. Laird was surprised to recognize it, one of the old student protest songs that had been popular back in his own time. "I just thought I'd get some exercise."

"Why not?" Helen Warner rummaged in a cool bag and handed him a can of beer. "Share a box for a minute."

He sat beside her, her brother content to squat beside them. After a moment or two Adam Warner gave a frown.

"Where are Tom and Piet?" he demanded of the group at large. He turned to his sister. "Helen—do you know?"

She shook her head and looked puzzled. "I thought you did. They were gone when I got back from that trip to the village."

"How long have you been back?" Warner chewed a stray tendril of beard and looked worried.

"An hour." She winced. "Oh hell, not again!"

"Doesn't anyone know?" demanded Warner again.

No one answered. The guitar player gave an awkward grin. Suddenly, Warner seemed to remember Laird again.

"Is that the reason you're here?" he demanded shrilly. "Have you come spying?"

"Don't be an idiot, Adam," said Helen defensively. "How would —" She broke off.

Laird heard the sounds a moment later, footsteps crunching over shingle, coming towards them. Then two figures reached the camp-fire's flickering light. They were young. Their grins died as they saw Adam Warner, and they came forward reluctantly. Both of them had wet hair, although the shirts and shorts they were wearing looked dry.

"Where were you?" rasped Warner angrily. He held up a hand before they could answer. "Don't bother. I can damned well guess, can't I?"

"Hey, Adam," said the taller of the two uneasily, his eyes on Laird. "Now look—"

"You look." Warner cut him short. "I warned both of you. I told you what would happen. I—" He stopped as the guitar player gave a sudden, warning shout.

The others swung round in time to see a car's headlights sweep towards them from the road. It bounced over the rough ground towards them, the blue police lamp on its roof blinking furiously.

Warner swallowed hard and looked helplessly at Laird.

"You two—" Laird glanced quickly at the delinquent pair. "Answer fast. You've been at the *Sea Robin*?"

They exchanged a quick glance, then nodded. "Where's your gear—scuba lungs, whatever you had?"

"Down at the beach, beside the boat." The same student as before swallowed unhappily. "We hid the stuff we brought back—"

"Then shut up, sit down at the back." Laird switched his attention to the startled guitar player. "You. Make some kind of music with that thing. The rest of you, try and look happy."

The guitar began a ragged throb as the police car skidded to a halt. The two culprits had melted among their companions as two uniformed figures came stalking over. The one in the lead was Sergeant García.

"*Buenas tardes,* everyone," said García in a loud sarcastic voice. He was clutching a large baton between his massive hands. Behind him, the other Guardia officer also carried a baton but had his right hand resting against his pistol holster. García saw Warner first, and bared his teeth in a cold greeting. "So, Señor Warner, and how is your little *familia* tonight?"

"Fine, Sergeant." Warner nervously signalled the guitar to stop and rose uncertainly. "Is something wrong?"

"*Sí.*" García signalled his companion. "Miguel—count them." He faced Warner again. "Trouble again, Señor Warner—does that surprise you?"

"Well—" Warner hesitated.

"Sergeant." Laird got to his feet and ambled over, nodding cheerfully. "Good to see you again. What's the problem?"

"Señor Laird." García stared at him and didn't hide his surprise. "Why are you here?"

"Just visiting." Laird stepped closer, then murmured in his ear. "Peacemaking, Sergeant. Like you, I want to keep Señor Cuvier happy. *Comprende?*"

The Guardia sergeant blinked, looked blankly at him for a moment, then gave a wary nod of understanding.

"So what's happened?" asked Laird briskly.

"More thieving at the ship." García scowled again. "It was seen from the tug anchored out there—too late for them to do anything, but they sent a message ashore. Two men in skin-diving suits, Señor Laird. They escaped in a rubber boat, heading this way." He jerked his head towards Adam Warner. "These people have skin-diving suits—and rubber boats."

"But they're all here, aren't they?" murmured Laird.

"Eh?" García's eyes widened.

"And I've been here for quite a spell, Sergeant," added Laird.

"Miguel—" García spun round and hurried over to his assistant. They talked for a moment, then stood together, making still another head count. Then, frowning, García walked back.

"Señor Laird—" He hesitated, then gave a sound like a groan. "—you vouch for this, that none of them have been away?"

Laird nodded.

"*Gracias.*" The man shrugged. He turned to the two Warners and gave a weary salute. "My apologies."

The two Guardia Civil went back to their car, got in, and it started up. It was moving before Warner broke the total, stunned silence in the camp.

"You lied to him." He blinked through his spectacles, bewildered. "Why?"

"Does it matter?" asked Laird. He wasn't totally sure himself. "Maybe I wanted to prove something." He thumbed towards the camp-fire, and the huddle of students. "But sort out that pair of apprentice pirates. Tell them the average Spanish jail doesn't win tourist rosettes."

"I will." Warner nodded grimly. "Right now, believe me."

He stalked off towards the pair. For the moment, Laird found himself alone with Helen Warner. He also discovered he was still clutching the unopened can of beer she'd given him before things started to happen.

"Well." He grinned at her, looked at the can, then set it down on one of the boxes. "Another time. I'll get on my way—your brother may not want an audience."

"What you did mattered to him," she said quietly. "Sponsors don't like trouble at a camp. A bad report could have finished him for next year." She paused, the flickering firelight playing shadow tricks around her snub nose and high cheek-bones, her blue eyes considering him thoughtfully. "Thank you."

Laird could hear Adam Warner talking angrily, his voice getting louder by the moment. Helen Warner came with him as he retreated from the campsite, and they stopped in the darkness just clear of the tents.

"You're sure you want to walk back?" She indicated the old van, parked nearby. "I could give you a lift."

"Walking might be safer," he said drily.

"All right." She chuckled, then kissed him—not on the cheek, like Laura Cero had done earlier, but squarely and firmly on the lips, in no hurry to finish it. But as Laird's hands touched her shoulders she broke the contact and stood back, smiling but shaking her head. "Not now—Adam has enough problems."

Laird nodded, then, reluctantly, walked on towards the road.

*

It was close on midnight when he walked into the Hostal Mercado, but the bar was noisy and busy. Mamá Isabel and Roberto were both working hard at the counter, their customers apparently locals, with a thin sprinkling of seamen from the salvage tugs. The air was smoke-filled, the conversation loud and the drinking serious, but none of the faces were familiar.

Laird took the stairway up to his room. It was hot and stuffy and he opened the window wide, took off his jacket and loosened his tie, then noticed a large brown envelope lying on the bed. When he opened it, it held about a score of large black-and-white photographs which still had the slightly sticky feel of brand-new prints.

Spreading them out along the bed, he examined them carefully. Roberto's collection began with a couple of flash shots, taken by night, which showed some of the *Sea Robin*'s crew coming ashore from their lifeboats. Then came a few daylight photographs of the crew and their captain plus some good studies of the ship, showing how she had settled. The latter seemed to have been taken from a fishing boat and there were other boats around, men from them exploring the *Sea Robin*'s decks and superstructure in a way that Janos Cuvier wouldn't have appreciated.

Grinning, Laird turned to the rest. After a moment, he felt puzzled. Almost all had the blurred foreground or background appearance of being taken by a hastily focused telephoto lens. There were several faces he knew—all members of the Cuvier management team, including Cuvier and Laura Cero—but whether there were two, three, or more people in a photograph, they all had one thing in common. The face of a stout, middle-aged man of average height, a man with dark, curly hair balding on top, was there in every one. He was casually dressed, had fleshy, taciturn features, and one photograph, in which he filled most of the frame, showed a silver medallion on a chain round his neck.

He was a mystery. But if Charlie Henderson had wanted him photographed, then he was a mystery that mattered. Listening to the sounds still coming from the bar below, Laird knew it would still have to wait until morning.

There was one thing more to do. He took out Harry Novak's envelope, opened it, and read the curt, badly typed yet concise survey report on the *Sea Robin*. It matched what Novak had said at the Casa Turo, gave a mention of cargo being moved "in part to facilitate future operations" but was cautious in its conclusions. Novak was being careful, very careful. Refloating was a possibility, a probability—it wasn't Novak's usual style.

Whatever happened, whatever decision was made, right or wrong, Harry Novak wasn't going to be on the losing team.

*

He slept well that night and woke with sunlight pouring into the room from a cloudless blue sky.

It was going to be a warm day. Laird dressed in an open-necked shirt, light-weight trousers held at the waist by an old favourite braided leather belt with a seaman's heavy brass buckle, then went in search of breakfast. He found it being served in the bar, where Roberto was on duty on his own. The few other guests were finishing and the bulky, sleepy-eyed figure of Sergeant García was slouched against the bar counter, drinking coffee.

García gave a casual nod but stayed where he was as Laird took a table near a window. Roberto brought a breakfast of coffee, fresh bread rolls, goat's butter and a thick, sweet strawberry jam, but was too busy to do more than murmur a greeting. A little later, García rammed his tricorn hat on his head and left. The other guests began to drift away.

At last, there was only Laird. He waited until Roberto came over with the coffee-pot, let him refill his cup, then stopped him.

"Got a minute?" Laird indicated the vacant chair opposite his own.

"*Gracias.*" The fat young Spaniard settled thankfully, using the sleeve of his clean white shirt to wipe perspiration from his plump face. "Were the photographs okay, Señor Laird?"

"Very okay," Laird assured him. "Now tell me about the man in most of them. Who is he?"

"Señor Henderson pointed him out." Roberto shrugged with a degree of indifference. "I was to take pictures, but he was not to know. It wasn't too difficult."

"Does he have a name?" asked Laird patiently.

"Sí." Roberto hesitated. "When will I be paid for the photographs, Señor Laird?"

"Right now." Laird brought money from his hip pocket and counted several peseta notes onto the table. "All right?"

"He was the chief engineer on the *Sea Robin.*" Roberto beamed, scooping up his payment. "Señor Henderson said his name was Sam Grant—until he went away he stayed with the shipping people at the Casa Turo."

"Do you know why Henderson wanted the photographs?"

Roberto shook his head. "All he told me was to use my camera."

Laird gave up and thought for a moment. Charlie Henderson had wanted photographs of Grant, then Grant had left immediately after Henderson's death. He was past the stage of feeling any surprise. What mattered now was to assemble his own priorities yet at the same time maintain at least a token display of normal activity.

"I'm going to need your help," he said slowly. "Can you get some time off?"

"Sí." Roberto nodded cheerfully. "You want me to take more photographs?"

"No. But maybe to deliver some of those prints." He smiled slightly at the young Spaniard's disappointment. "Have you got wheels?"

"*Mamá* has a car—I can borrow it."

"Good." Laird let the rest of the pattern shape in his mind. "I'll let you know when. Right now, I want you to tell me where I find Father Sebastian"—he saw Roberto's eyes widen—"yes, the priest who discovered the accident. And I want to hire a car."

*

Ten minutes later he left the Mercado and walked down towards the harbour. The *Scomber* had gone from her berth and he could see her out beside the other salvage tug, both lying close beside the foundered *Sea Robin.*

The harbour was quiet, only a handful of fishing boats moored along the quay. The sun warm on his back, Laird looked around hopefully for a boatman, then spotted a small launch getting ready to leave. His luck was in. It was from the *Beroe*, and the man aboard was Jingles Reilly.

"Jingles—" He hurried along towards the boat. "Any chance of a lift out?"

Reilly beckoned him down. There was an iron ladder set in the stonework of the quay, and a moment later Laird swung in beside the salvage tug's mate and chief diver. The launch engine was already spluttering and Reilly cast off the single mooring line.

"Earn your keep," he suggested, thumbing Laird towards the controls. "I'm not in the mood."

Laird took over, opened the throttle, then turned the launch's head towards the harbour mouth as they began moving. He glanced at Reilly, who had settled himself thankfully on the stern thwarts. The burly, fair-haired man looked tired and grey.

"What's wrong with you?" Laird asked. "Too many rough nights?"

"Like hell," said Reilly gloomily. "It's my guts—bad booze or somethin' I ate. We've a damned cook who should be barbecued." He watched critically and in silence until they cleared the harbour, then, as the launch met the light swell of the open sea, an occasional fine curtain of spray damping aboard, he began to look slightly happier. "Did you meet Novak last night?"

Laird nodded, easing the launch round a fraction to meet the swell.

"And?" Reilly managed a quizzical grimace. "What happened?"

"He still thinks it could be a refloat job." Laird shrugged without looking at the man. "What about you, Jingles?"

"As long as I get paid, should I worry?" asked Reilly. "You're the character who decides if she's worth it—though I wouldn't bother." He huddled lower in his scanty shelter. "No diving for me today—not the way I feel."

Glancing round, Laird grinned at the misery on the man's face.

"You'll live," he said drily. "I heard you'd some excitement last night. What happened?"

"Just a couple of thieves with scuba gear." Reilly couldn't have been less interested. "One of our hands on deck watch heard them on the *Sea Robin*, used a spotlight, and they took off." He gave a sigh that was close to a groan. "Look, Andy, you used to know a thing or two about doctorin'—"

"For you, I'd call a vet," said Laird easily, then gave in. "Try no booze and a light diet for a couple of days—but drink plenty of water."

"And if that doesn't do it?" Reilly was worried.

"See a doctor. And I mean it."

"Here?" Reilly scowled at the shore. "You're jokin'."

"You know how the first decent medicine got to Europe?" asked Laird gently. "The Moors brought it over here to Spain from North Africa while we were still living in caves."

"So what's wrong with a cave?" demanded Reilly.

The launch muttered on, nearing the two tugs and the handful of smaller craft clustered round the *Sea Robin*. At close hand, the cargo ship was a pathetic sight. There were men aboard her, wading only ankle-deep in places as the swell barely creamed along her decking. The *Scomber* was anchored close alongside, using the derrick boom she mounted aft, swinging cargo from the casualty to a waiting workboat.

The *Beroe* was positioned on the other side of the *Sea Robin*. Laird could hear compressor pumps rasping busily on both salvage tugs, could see the thick hoselines suspended over their sides, the muddy colour of the sea around them. Down below, divers must be using high-pressure hoses to carve the new tunnels Novak wanted in the silt under the cargo ship's hull.

A dead fish, a big, silvery mullet, floated past the launch. He'd noticed one or two others on the way out, and there were more dead fish floating here and there as he steered in towards the *Scomber*. Fish often died around wrecks—at first, at any rate. Later, when conditions stabilized, they might use the same wreck like an apartment block.

Reilly rose and took the controls again, throttling back, nosing the launch in. Laird indicated the fish.

"You didn't eat them?"

"With the cook we've got, who knows?" countered Reilly. "He's the boiled-eggs type."

Laird grinned, remembering the hallowed piece of nautical doggerel that condemned all galley staff. He said it aloud.

" 'What's yours, gents?' asked cookie, pensively picking his nose.

'Hard-boiled eggs' was the chorus,

'You can't stick your fingers in those—' "

"And we've got the original," said Reilly feelingly. He cut the engine and let the launch bump against *Scomber*'s massive rope fenders, close to an accommodation ladder.

"Thanks," said Laird. He swung himself onto the ladder and glanced back. "About that drink I owe you, Jingles—it'll be milk."

Reilly growled an obscenity in reply, then gunned the launch clear, heading for the other tug. Grinning, Laird climbed the ladder and reached the *Scomber*'s deck, back aboard what had once been familiar territory.

The men working on her deck were strangers who ignored him —Harry Novak's crew kept changing. But the salvage tug was still as always, an impressive, compact workhorse of a little ship, dirty, needing paint, yet not in any way neglected in terms of her equipment.

He heard Novak before he saw him. Even above the wheezing beat of the compressor engine, the man's loud, rasping voice was unmistakable and angry. The noise came from aft and Laird followed it, then saw what was wrong.

The *Scomber*'s derrick boom had jammed. A pulley block had seized and a large metal container, lifted from the *Sea Robin*, was left swaying and jerking in mid-air between the salvage tug and the waiting workboat.

"I told you both, didn't I?" Novak, legs wide apart, scarred face furious, had a grip of one terrified deckhand by the collar of his jersey and was shaking him like a rabbit. A second man cowered against the derrick winch. "You useless garbage, I warned you about that damned block—didn't I?"

"Skipper—" The man he was shaking, face pale with fright, licked his lips. "Wait, skipper—"

Novak used his free hand and gave the man a deliberate cuff across the face. Then he threw him tumbling back beside his companion.

"Get the bo'sun, tell him I want that sorted out," he snarled. Swinging on his heel, he saw Laird and his scowl deepened. "And what the hell do you want?"

"Your survey report," said Laird. He ignored one of the deckhands who went scuttling past. "I want to talk about it."

"Now?" Novak growled under his breath and thrust his hands into the pockets of his grimy overalls. "Why?"

Laird shrugged. "Yes or no?"

Novak hesitated, then nodded and led the way along the deck to the short iron ladder which led to the *Scomber*'s bridge. They went up. The bridge was deserted and Novak heeled the door shut as they entered. Looking past him, Laird could see the cramped space of the radio compartment at the rear and remembered for a moment how it had been.

"Well?" demanded Novak curtly.

"That report," said Laird. "It's not your usual style, Captain. Either there's something worrying you or something you don't like—or both. Want to tell me about it?"

Novak stared at him. "So now you reckon you're some kind of bloody salvage expert?"

"No." Laird waited.

"There's nothing worrying me, mister—and the only thing I don't particularly like about this job is you." Novak leaned his elbows on the dull brass of the compass binnacle, almost grinning. "I said I needed more time, you said okay. What's wrong? I thought Clanmore Alliance liked the cautious approach."

"But you're sitting on the fence?"

"Uh-huh." Novak was unperturbed. "Letting other people do the worrying."

Laird turned away. The salvage tug's bridge gave a clear view along the full length of the luckless cargo ship, from empty lifeboat davits and blank-eyed portholes to small details like a length of green weed trailing from a companionway and a small, scummy patch of oil leaking from somewhere aft.

But he had seen still worse and seen it salvaged—if the cost was justified.

His attention switched to the men working on her foredeck. They had built what looked like a small coffer-dam of sandbags and canvas round the edge of her main hatchway and had a pump working, spouting water from the hold in a steady stream.

"Interested?" Novak came over to join him, suddenly talkative and almost friendly. "We're getting the water level down in that for'ard hold—enough to haul more of the cargo out. Your pal Jingles Reilly did a pretty hairy spot of diving work in there."

Laird nodded. "How about on the bottom?"

"Everything looks okay so far. I've three divers down hosing through the silt." Novak shrugged. "If the pilot tunnels under her hull work out, then that means we'd be in a 'go' situation to slip hawsers under her for the lift pontoons." He paused, then added slyly, "If we go ahead."

"I'd like to go over," said Laird.

"Now?" Novak hesitated, then nodded. "Go ahead. I've plenty to do here."

Laird left him and went down to the *Scomber*'s deck. A small boat was working like a ferry across the narrow gap to the *Sea Robin*, and the seamen crewing it rowed him over without comment.

Trousers rolled up above his knees, socks and shoes stuffed into the belt at his waist, Laird stepped aboard the cargo ship moments later and splashed through the ankle-deep water towards the nearest companionway door.

From there, he made his way upward, through deserted but dry companionways, past empty cabins and compartments, noticing a rat scurrying for cover, then reached the *Sea Robin*'s bridge.

Looking around, he gave a wry grimace. The whole bridge area had been systematically looted. Lockers lay open, anything portable seemed to have been removed. Even the steering wheel had been unbolted and was gone.

But that happened, and San Ferdinand's fishermen, not to mention Adam Warner's junior-league pirates, were only following what was almost time-honoured tradition.

He left the ransacked bridge, went back down to the deck, and splashed his way along to the men at the hatchway. They were taking a break, though the pump was still throbbing, and they eyed him with a mild curiosity.

"Watch how you go," warned one of them, a young, freckle-faced man wearing a rubber wet-suit, his scuba mask and harness lying beside him. He thumbed towards the gaping mouth of the hold. "You get wet down there."

Laird nodded and straddled the edge of the makeshift cofferdam, looking down into the black, lapping water several feet below. The freckle-faced diver joined him.

"Not much to see, is there?" He grinned at Laird in a friendly way. "We're just hauling stuff out, like we were unloading groceries."

"Any special kind of shopping list?" asked Laird.

There seemed to be a pattern to the clearance under way, exposing a metal half-deck leading aft. Some of the heavy crates remaining already had cargo slings attached.

"Too right, we have." The young diver indicated the half-deck below. "Novak"—he hesitated—"are you a pal of his?" He relaxed as Laird shook his head. "Novak wants a way cleared to a store compartment. You know what's in it? Wine—bulk tanks of best French rotgut from Marseilles. Not that we're likely to get as much as a sniff of it."

"Hard luck," sympathized Laird. "And after that?"

"Who knows?" The youngster shrugged. "I don't particularly care, friend. This is my last trip with our beloved captain. I've got myself a job on one of the North Sea oil rigs—and after the *Scomber*, that's going to seem like a holiday."

A clatter came from across the water, then a warning shout. The salvage tug's derrick boom, working again, came swinging over and the large tackle block on its end narrowly missed Laird's head. Novak grinned at him from the *Scomber*'s deck and gave a sardonic wave.

*

A little later, one of the workboats heading back to the harbour with a load of crates gave him a lift ashore. From there, Laird walked back to the Hostal Mercado. At the door, sitting in an old armchair in the hot sunlight, Mamá Isabel stirred as he approached. Her dark eyes considered him from under the shady brim of her trilby hat, a plump hand stopped him from going past.

"You wanted a car, Señor Laird." Producing a set of keys from a pocket of her shapeless dress, she handed them over. "It is round the back, in the shade. Roberto gave you directions to Father Sebastian?"

Laird nodded.

"Bueno." She spoke quietly, but with an underlying note of concern. "My son also says you want his help. What kind of help, Señor Laird?"

"Nothing that's going to get him into any kind of trouble, Mamá Isabel," soothed Laird. "That's a promise."

"I hope so." She sighed, shifted her ample frame, and looked directly up at him. "I think we have trouble here already. That fool of a cousin of mine, Ramón García, may be a Guardia sergeant—but he could have a war going on under his nose and not know about it." She paused. "Those photographs that Roberto took—are they part of what is wrong?"

"They might be," said Laird slowly. "So I don't want them talked about."

Mamá Isabel nodded, oddly satisfied. "You had a visitor while you were out. Señorita Cero, from the shipping people, and she was looking for you."

"Did she say why?"

"No." Mamá Isabel made a noise like a chuckle. "When a pretty girl comes looking for a man, I don't ask." She settled back in her chair again, eyes half-closing under the hat brim, then added quietly, "Go carefully, Señor Laird. For a *hostal* to lose too many guests is bad for business."

Going in, Laird checked the change in his pockets, then went to the telephone booth. He needed an operator's help to obtain the British consul's number in Málaga, but once he'd been connected his luck was in. Francis Edwards answered his extension and made suitable noises when he heard who was calling.

"I need some help," said Laird bluntly, cutting him short. "The unofficial kind—but it could maybe save you some diplomatic hassle later."

"I see." He could almost hear the man's expression change behind the words. "Uh—what kind, Mr. Laird?"

"A Greek named Constantinos, from the *Sea Robin*, was in hospital in Marbella. I want to know if Charlie Henderson visited him the day before he was discharged—and then if a man called Sam Grant, the *Sea Robin*'s chief engineer, was with Constantinos when he flew to Athens the next day."

"Can I ask why?" The consular official's voice was frosty with suspicion.

"No. You'd stay happier that way," said Laird. "The Spanish may not love you as a brother later, but they certainly won't declare war." He had an afterthought. "But while you're checking, keep clear of Janos Cuvier's people."

"I'm not sure we should get involved," said Edwards unhappily over the line. "I mean—"

"Can you do it?" asked Laird.

"Yes." The man sighed. "I suppose this is something to do with Henderson's death?" He didn't wait for an answer. "All right—I'll take it on trust. What about the police?"

"Later," promised Laird. "I want to know what I'm talking about."

"That makes two of us," muttered Edwards. He sniffed, then added sarcastically, "Any other way in which Her Majesty's Government can help?"

"Just one," said Laird. "I want to get some photographs back to my London office. If I have them delivered to the airport—"

Edwards sighed. "That's easier. Have them handed in at the British Airways desk. I—uh—know some of the girls there." He paused. "Maybe I should say something to the Consul—"

"I wouldn't," said Laird. "Why spoil his day?"

He hung up, then went to his room to collect the photographs, his jacket, and the binoculars he'd left there.

Ten minutes later, three of the best of Roberto's photographs were in an envelope addressed to Osgood Morris in London. Sam Grant's face was circled in every one, with a question mark. He'd scribbled a quick covering note. Roberto was out on an errand for his mother, but Mamá Isabel took the envelope and promised he'd leave for the airport the moment he got back. Laird had another of the photographs in a pocket of his jacket.

The car waiting behind the hotel was a battered little blue Seat 850 with sagging upholstery and pedal rubbers worn smooth with use. But it started first time and the fuel gauge read full.

As Laird drove it out to the main road, Adam Warner's van went past. Helen was behind the wheel, saw him, and hooted her horn. Laird waved in reply, then set the little car moving again.

He was going on a hunt. His lips tightened at the thought—and at what the result might be.

*

The chapel was an ancient, tiny building in the foothills, about ten kilometres north-east of San Ferdinand. The chapel house, even smaller and almost as old, was located at the other side of a walled graveyard at the rear. Laird parked the blue Seat, and as he got out, he heard a male voice singing lustily somewhere near. The voice stopped, he heard the clatter of tools, then the singing began again.

The sound led him to a wooden shed in the back garden. The door was open and the singer, a tall, thin man in his sixties and wearing overalls, was working on the engine of a motor cycle. Laird reached the doorway and saw the clerical collar just visible under the overalls.

"Father Sebastian?" he asked loudly.

The singing stopped and the priest glanced round. Laying down the spanner he was holding, rubbing his grease-stained hands on the front of his overalls, he came over and gave a cheerful nod.

"*Sí* . . . and I know about you, Señor Laird. Mamá Isabel telephoned me." Father Sebastian had grey hair, thin features and friendly blue eyes. As he spoke, he came out into the sunlight and the smile on his lips became sympathetic. "You want to talk to me about your friend Henderson."

"Yes." Laird took the offered, more or less clean hand. Father Sebastian's grip was light yet firm. "If you can spare the time."

"I can." Father Sebastian rubbed a hand along his chin, leaving an oily mark. "For whatever good it will do. I told the gendarmerie anything I know, which is little enough."

"But you were there," said Laird.

"I was." The priest gestured at the high peaks that formed a solid backcloth in the distance. "My parish has almost as many mountains as people, Señor Laird. That is why I use a motor cycle, though my bishop does not totally approve—two wheels can use tracks where four wheels would be useless." He gave a quick apologetic grimace. "All of that is incidental. How can I help you?"

"Tell me about it," invited Laird.

"Easily done." The keen grey eyes saddened at the memory. "I had been visiting the sick—an old woman, dying for more years than I can remember. *De acuerdo* . . . I was coming down the road, I saw the fire—" He shook his head.

"You didn't see any other traffic?"

"No. The gendarmerie asked me that." Father Sebastian looked at him oddly. "Have you a reason for that question, my son?"

"I don't know," admitted Laird.

"It's a lonely road." Father Sebastian sucked his lips for a moment. "Have you seen it?"

Laird shook his head.

"Then maybe you should," said the priest thoughtfully. He gave a slight smile. "There's a slow way and a quick way—can you ride pillion?"

"If that's the quick way," said Laird.

*

They set off as soon as the priest had changed his overalls for a set of black motor cycle leathers and a white crash helmet. He also produced a spare helmet for Laird, then wheeled out his motor cycle, a powerful light-weight Suzuki.

Rasping away from the chapel house, they took a narrow track that led through olive groves and some sheep pastures towards the hills. The track led to a road, they left the road after a short distance for another track, and all the time the Suzuki was climbing. Once or twice they passed an isolated farm and someone waved a greeting. Farther on, a tiny village clung to the side of a steep slope and, beyond it, they plunged through a forest of pine trees, bouncing along a path with scrub clawing at their legs.

"I forgot to ask," shouted Father Sebastian. "Are you a Catholic, Señor Laird?"

"No." Laird clung to his grip as the Suzuki shuddered over some broken rock. "Why?"

"I've had passengers who started praying," said the priest cheerfully. "I usually recommend a saint or two—it sometimes helps."

Laird was more interested in holding on. They left the forest, joined a road, left it for another track, then suddenly, the stark, bleak rock of the mountains was all that was ahead. Far below, a small lake was a glint of blue. High overhead, little more than black specks in a harsh blue sky, hawks were circling.

Still the Suzuki kept climbing—through a high valley where a few brown goats were grazing close to a solitary house, over a ridge beyond that.

Then Laird saw the road ahead, a winding, twisting ribbon of tarmac that had no apparent right to be there at all. They reached it, the Suzuki's engine note steadied, and Father Sebastian gestured ahead.

"Almost there," he shouted encouragingly. "We have saved a lot of time, believe me."

They kept climbing. Laird saw the sheer, unprotected drop that lay in wait at almost every bend. Then, at last, the motor cycle slowed and halted. He dismounted stiffly and waited while Father Sebastian propped the machine on its stand. They had stopped in the middle of a sharp bend.

The world seemed empty. He could hear the wind, the occasional spitting crackle as the Suzuki's exhaust cooled, and the distant bleating of a goat. But the road was deserted, looked as though it had always been that way.

"Over here," said Father Sebastian quietly, beckoning.

They walked a few paces to where the road verge, a coarse mixture of gravel, pale red earth and weeds, had collapsed. The gully below them was deep and steep. At the bottom, the burned-out wreck of what had once been a car lay among a jumble of broken rocks.

"You can see how it happened." Father Sebastian watched Laird as he spoke and, probably without realizing it, fingered the crucifix just visible under his leather jacket. "It was at night. If your friend didn't know this road—" He shook his head sadly. "I'm sorry. There was nothing I could do."

Laird looked down the gully, thought of the priest climbing down that treacherous slope in a darkness lit only by the flames from below, and bit his lip.

"You tried." He considered the slope again, seeing the gouges made by the falling car, the other marks which showed the route used to bring Henderson's body up later. "I'd like to go down for a moment."

Father Sebastian nodded but said nothing.

It was a difficult enough scramble in daylight, a scramble that dislodged small torrents of dusty gravel at almost every step. When he reached the wreck, close-up, it was worse than anything he could have imagined.

The car seemed to have landed nose-first, then to have rolled on its roof. What was left was twisted, flattened metal, with one wheel and some sections of bodywork hurled some distance from the rest of the vehicle. Fire had totally gutted the interior, leaving seats that were mere ash and metal springing. Almost every vestige of paint had been flaked or burned from the exterior. Two tyres had been reduced to residual ash and black blobs of melted rubber.

He walked round the wreck, the acrid odour of burning still clinging to the air. Then he looked inside again, using a piece of metal trim to stir the broken glass and ash. Something small, twisted and blackened caught his eye, and he hooked it out with the metal trim.

It was a man's belt buckle. Sickened, he threw it away among the rocks, then turned and toiled his way back up to the road. Father Sebastian was waiting, and held out a hand to help him on the last step.

"He would know little, if anything. At least, we can pray it was that way." The priest spoke with a mixture of sympathy and understanding. "But—well, I think you still had to see for yourself. Am I right?"

"Yes." Laird moistened his lips. There was still one more thing he had to do. "Father, this road—on the map, it doesn't seem to lead to anywhere."

"True." Father Sebastian nodded drily. "It was built by the army, a long time ago. Armies build roads that way."

"But there's a bar somewhere farther up—"

"Yes." The priest nodded. "Called El Águila. A small place, about three kilometres from here. I heard your friend was there that night."

"I'd like to talk to the people there," said Laird slowly. "I want to show them a photograph, ask if they recognize a face."

Father Sebastian frowned at him for a moment.

"It matters?"

Laird nodded.

"I see." The priest gave a long sigh. "A husband and wife run that bar. They are—well, wary of strangers, but they know me. Perhaps, if I went alone—"

"I could wait here." Laird produced the folded photograph he'd brought from San Ferdinand, and pointed to the face of the *Sea Robin*'s chief engineer. "This man."

"Very well." Father Sebastian tucked the photograph away, then went over to his Suzuki. "It won't take long."

The motor cycle throbbed away, then vanished round another bend in the road.

Left alone, Laird took out his cigarettes, lit one, and stood with his back to the gully, looking at the road.

A car coming down the short straight towards the bend would have had to slow and slow drastically to round it safely. Otherwise, at any kind of speed—he stopped it there, shaking his head. Charlie Henderson had been a reasonably cautious driver. Even if he had been pushing on, there should have been time to try braking —yet there were no skid marks on the rough tarmac.

The same black doubt gnawing at his mind, he began walking along the empty road, glancing back every now and again towards the bend, trying to gauge how it would have shown.

Then, about two hundred yards from the gorge, he stopped short. The sun was glinting on a small dark patch of ground on the weed-and-gravel verge. He went over, bent down, and touched the sticky surface where oil from a car's sump had dripped down, spreading before it soaked into the coarse soil.

Rising, Andrew Laird looked around carefully. There were faint traces of tyre marks on the soft verge—too faint to be identifiable in terms of tread, but distinct enough to show that two cars had stopped, one behind the other. He found an indistinct footprint, then another.

There was no way anyone could tell when the cars had stopped or why, whether they had been together or separate. But they had been there, sometime within the last few days.

He swore bitterly under his breath. Even the most sceptical of individuals would have found it hard to dismiss that kind of coincidence.

Yet, in terms of evidence, it would get nowhere.

*

It was another twenty minutes before Father Sebastian's Suzuki came rasping down the road again and coasted to a halt. The priest dismounted, spent a moment removing his white crash helmet, then rubbed a hand through his iron-grey hair and looked puzzled.

"I saw them," he confirmed. "I showed them the photograph."

"And?"

Father Sebastian produced the photograph and unfolded it carefully.

"This man you wanted to know about." He pointed. "You know his name?"

Laird nodded. "Sam Grant—he's English."

"They know nothing about him. They've never seen him." Father Sebastian paused, then pointed again. "But the man beside him—yes, they remember him. He was in the bar earlier that evening, had a drink, bought some cans of beer, then left. That was about an hour before your friend Henderson arrived."

Laird stared at the photograph. It was one of the group shots taken by Roberto.

The man Father Sebastian's finger indicated was young, smartly dressed, serious-faced, and had dark hair. He was Hans Botha, one of Janos Cuvier's "utility twins."

CHAPTER 4

"*Gracias,* María," said Father Sebastian firmly. "I am going to be busy with Señor Laird. Perhaps for a little time." He smiled at his housekeeper, a small, elderly woman dressed in black. "Should anyone come, unless it is life or death, I am *ocupado.*"

The woman placed the tray she had brought to the priest's study exactly in the middle of Father Sebastian's desk. It held two glasses of wine and a plate of small, plain biscuits. Then, with a quick, birdlike glance in Laird's direction, she reluctantly allowed herself to be shooed from the room.

"An excellent woman," said Father Sebastian wryly as the door closed. "An army would not get past her. But she has an awesome interest in all that happens—I may have a problem with her once you are gone." He handed Laird a glass of wine, offered the biscuits, then sighed. "Well, Señor Laird, what now?"

Laird sat silent for a moment, letting a first sip of the wine wash some of the taste of dust from his throat. Before the return journey from the mountain road, he had shown the priest the trace of oil and the car tracks. He had seen Father Sebastian's quick understanding, had admired the deliberate way the priest hadn't asked a single question.

But Laird had told him a little, just enough. Then they had climbed aboard the motor cycle and the little Suzuki had rasped its way back to the chapel house.

Father Sebastian's study was a small, cool, plainly furnished room. A hand-carved crucifix hung behind his desk There were two old armchairs and a well-filled bookcase in which religious works fought for space with books on subjects as varied as motorcycle maintenance and amateur gardening. A framed photograph showed the priest as a much younger man, in football kit. He was grinning at the camera and clutching a silver cup.

"A small personal vanity," murmured Father Sebastian, following his gaze. He settled in the armchair opposite Laird, nibbled at one of the biscuits, then nursed his own glass. "I asked you something. But if you feel it is not my business—"

Laird shook his head. "That's not my problem."

What had begun as a doubt, a doubt that had grown into first suspicion, then a possibility, had now become something very much stronger. At least one of Janos Cuvier's men had been on that mountain road the night that Charlie Henderson had died.

The threads were beginning to come together. But into what kind of final pattern?

"Can I help?" asked Father Sebastian.

"You can remember what you saw." Laird sucked his lips for a moment. "But I didn't come here to cause you problems."

"Mostly, Señor Laird, my job is about problems," mused Father Sebastian. A troubled note entered his voice. "I have one question. I am prepared to trust your answer. Are any of my people in danger?"

"Not that I know about," said Laird carefully. "But then, there's a lot I don't know." He sat silent for another moment, letting the peace of the room steady his thoughts, aware of the thin, grey-haired figure opposite waiting patiently. "Whatever is happening, it centres on San Ferdinand and the *Sea Robin*. I've very little to go on. How would you rate the local Guardia in that kind of situation?"

"Sergeant García is a man of somewhat limited imagination," said Father Sebastian drily. He sipped his wine. "According to my housekeeper, he is also of somewhat limited honesty in everyday affairs—though I could imagine that changing to a saintly purity in any matter where he felt his superiors might be involved."

Laird nodded. The judgement matched his own. It also meant he could look for no immediate help from that quarter.

"Have you heard any kind of talk about the *Sea Robin*—anything you can tell me about?"

"Without compromising my position as a priest?" Father Sebastian gave a mild, understanding chuckle. *"Lo siento . . .* I'm sorry, no. Not even of the compromising kind. Just gossip that the shipping people take a firm line with—ah—allegedly innocent but uninvited visitors to their property."

"I'd heard." Laird glanced at his wrist-watch. The time was well after noon, later than he'd realized. "Could I use your telephone?"

"In the hall," nodded the priest. He added pointedly, "Beside the poor box."

Laird went out into the little hallway, where the smell of polish blended with the perfume from a vase of freshly cut flowers. Lifting the receiver, he dialled the consular number in Málaga and, a few moments later, was connected to Francis Edwards.

"I thought it might be you," said Edwards gloomily. "All right, I did what you asked."

"And?" demanded Laird.

"You were right," admitted the plump Englishman. "Your friend Henderson did visit the hospital at Marbella that afternoon—it's a small enough place for them to remember. He spent about half an hour with this fellow Constantinos, then left." He paused, then sounded puzzled. "It seems that straight afterwards Constantinos announced he was discharging himself, that he wanted to get home to Greece."

"Did he have any other visitor after Henderson?"

"One—after he made a phone call. A man arrived and stayed a few minutes. The hospital people don't know who he was." Edwards paused again and sniffed deliberately. "However, you were totally wrong about the airport situation. Constantinos did fly out to Greece next morning—some of the Pandion Shipping people took him to the airport. But this man Grant you talked about didn't go with him on the flight—no one named Grant was on any flight that day."

Laird tensed. "You're sure?"

"In the consular service, we make it a rule to be sure," said Edwards huffily. "Maybe you've got your dates wrong."

"Maybe." Laird decided not to argue. "Thanks. You've helped a lot."

"In what?" The voice over the line sounded almost petulant, and Laird could picture the peeved expression on the man's round face. "Didn't you tell me Grant was chief engineer on the *Sea Robin*?"

"That's right," agreed Laird.

"Then I"—Edwards hesitated—"no, I won't ask. But I hope to God you know what you're doing. I told you, the Spanish authorities can be sensitive—"

"So can I," said Laird in a flat voice. "I'll be in touch."

He hung up.

At least part of the story Laura Cero had told him had been a lie, whether she'd known it or not. But if Grant hadn't flown out with Constantinos, where had he gone? And what kind of pressure had Charlie Henderson put on the *Sea Robin's* first mate in one short visit, pressure that seemed to have been enough to send him scurrying?

Thoughtfully, Laird fed some money into the slot of the wooden box placed conspicuously beside the telephone. Then he returned to Father Sebastian's study.

"Finished, Señor Laird? Sometimes I wonder if the devil had a hand in inventing telephones. If I want a number, usually it is engaged or a case of *no responden.*" The priest paused, then added softly, "You have the look of a man who has just heard something he doesn't like. If you want to stay, and talk about it over lunch—"

Laird shook his head. "I want to get back to San Ferdinand. Maybe another time."

"Another time." Father Sebastian nodded and came over. "*Sí,* I think there will be, Señor Laird."

*

The mid-day heat shimmered from the tarmac road as Andrew Laird drove the blue Seat back towards the coast. He mopped his brow, felt his sweat make the steering wheel damp and sticky, and gave up thinking about anything except driving.

There was little other traffic. An occasional car or motor cycle passed him, heading in the opposite direction. Then, as he neared San Ferdinand, a large truck appeared ahead. It lumbered east, both vehicles having to slow to a crawl to squeeze past each other on the narrow road, and Laird grimaced as he saw its load—a selection of crates from the *Sea Robin.*

A little later, he was on the coast and could see the sunken cargo ship and the smaller craft working around it. He was near Adam Warner's student camp and, on an impulse, he slowed as he glimpsed the tents near the shore, then swung the steering wheel.

The little car bounced over the rough ground and he parked beside Warner's van. Getting out, he found the camp deserted, but hearing voices, he walked on towards the beach. A rough path led him through a patch of scrub, then he stopped. In front of him, a group of Warner's students were hard at work, digging a long, shallow trench in the sand and shingle. A little way out, two small inflatable boats bobbed in the sparkling water. They were moored but empty.

"Hello, Laird."

The voice made him turn. Adam Warner was climbing out of the trench. The thin, bearded college lecturer was wearing only khaki shorts and sandals, but his eyes were bright behind his metal-rimmed spectacles and he looked happy.

"Come to volunteer?" asked Warner, reaching him.

"No, thanks." Laird grinned at the sweat trickling down Warner's scrawny chest. "Just sightseeing."

"After last night, you're welcome." Warner flicked at a fly that had landed on his arm. "Well, you can see what we're doing. Want me to explain?"

"It would help," agreed Laird gratefully.

"Right." The man gestured at the trench, then at earlier trenches which had been cut across the same stretch of beach at regular intervals. "We're doing a straightforward grid search. Digging here, checking the sea bed further out. That French three-decker I told you about—"

"The *Emeraude*." Laird nodded.

"You remembered." Warner was pleased. "Well, we know she came ashore about here. Which meant wreckage, a lot of wreckage. That's what we're looking for, and finding. No trace of the main hull yet, but it could be here—or anywhere."

Laird followed him along the trench. Taking a rest from their labours, one or two of the students grinned at him. Warner stopped beside two of them, one the guitar player of the night before.

"Show him, Jan," invited Warner.

The youngster stepped back. A blackened length of broken timber lay half exposed in the damp sand at his feet.

"Teak—probably part of a deck rail," explained Warner. "Given time, the sand covers most things above tidal level. Here's what we found beside it."

Stooping, he lifted a piece of sacking lying at the edge of the trench. An old glass bottle and a twisted metal plate lay side by side, with what looked like two small, badly rusted cannon-balls joined by a short, equally rusted length of chain.

"Chain-shot," explained Warner. "For smashing an enemy's rigging. Then they had another little variation called grape-shot— musket balls packed in a bag round a core, for killing people." He gave a slight shudder at the thought, dropped the canvas back in place, and rose. "All right, Jan. Go carefully."

The student nodded and resumed work. He was scraping round the edge of the wood with a small trowel.

"What about out there?" Laird gestured towards the moored boats. A figure wearing scuba gear had just surfaced beside one of them and was leaning on its side, resting.

"Same thing, but strictly a sea-bed search." Warner narrowed his eyes against the glare. "We're not going to find anything that is going to startle the world of marine archaeology—no chance, Laird. But it's a damned good student project." He shrugged. "Any real find, if it happens, will belong to the Spanish authorities. That's part of the agreement I had to sign. Still, I'll show you something."

He led the way back over the shingle, then across towards the tents. Lifting the flap of one of the largest, Warner waved an invitation.

Going in, Laird stopped and stared. In front of him, the long barrel of an old cannon lay across two wooden trestles.

"We found that just a stone's throw from the shore," said Warner proudly. "It was one hell of a job getting it in."

The cannon was about ten feet long, metal deeply pitted, encrusted in marine growth from muzzle to breech, a weapon of war from the past. Laird touched it with his fingertips, the metal cold to the touch. For a moment he wondered about the men who had used it, the ship they'd served aboard, the action she might have seen.

"Valuable?" he asked.

"Not particularly." Warner shook his head. "Cannon come pretty much ten a penny these days. Scuba divers turn them up anywhere there's a recorded wreck of any real age." He pursed his lips. "A gun like that could have had a range of over a mile—well over a mile. Like to imagine the power of a full broadside at close range?"

"Nasty," said Laird.

He looked around. Other trestles in the tent supported plank tables with more souvenirs of the dig. He saw a sword hilt, the remains of a musket, a small collection of coins, labelled pieces of wood, the bric-à-brac of a past tragedy.

"Shouldn't do it, of course," murmured Warner. "Purists say leave things where you find them. But those kids aren't purists."

"So I've heard." Laird ran a hand along the cannon again, then faced him. "They're going to have to stop those raids on the *Sea Robin*. Next time, someone could end up hurt."

"Or in jail." Warner chewed a stray tendril of beard and nodded unhappily. "I've warned them all. Next time, anyone caught near that ship is on the next plane home. But that's not good enough for your friend Janos Cuvier. He wants us all out—we discovered that for sure, this morning."

"Meaning?" Laird raised an eyebrow.

"We had a visitor," said Warner grimly. "The farmer who owns this piece of ground—telling us to leave, or else. Then a weak story about how he needs this area *muy urgente* for grazing." He sniffed. "Grazing? There's not enough to keep a self-respecting goat alive, and he eventually admitted it. One of Cuvier's people had come along and made him a cash-on-the-nail offer to get rid of us."

Laird whistled sympathetically. "What can you do about it?"

"What I did," corrected Warner sadly. "I—well, I lost my temper. Told him to go to hell. But Helen's gone to see him." He flushed. "You may have noticed my sister has a more diplomatic approach." Then he stopped. Someone was shouting outside, then other voices joined in. Warner was already on his way out of the tent. Laird followed, as a young, dark-haired girl came running from the beach towards them.

"Herr Warner—" She was breathless as she reached them. "—Herr Warner, down there—"

"Slow down, Helga," Warner said quickly. "Just tell it. What's happened?"

"An accident." She swallowed. Beneath her tan, her face was drained of colour. "It is Piet—"

Warner began running, Laird loping beside him.

The trench along the beach had been abandoned, the digging team were clustered round a limp figure in a grey scuba diving suit, lying at the water's edge. Another young diver, similarly dressed, had removed the casualty's diving harness and tanks and was still stripping off his own—no, her own. As they got closer, Laird saw she was a girl with close-cut red hair.

Warner got to her first and grabbed her.

"What happened, Anna?" he asked urgently.

"I don't know—I'm not sure." She shook her head, totally bewildered. "It—he just collapsed."

Pushing past Warner, Laird dropped on his knees beside the unconscious student. It was the fair-haired boy Piet, one of the two who had raided the *Sea Robin*. His eyes were closed, he was hardly breathing.

"Tell how it happened," urged Warner. "Anything you remember—come on, Anna, think."

Nodding, Laird looked up at them. Piet's pulse was weak, as if he was in some kind of shock.

"We—we were checking one of the sections." The girl gestured out towards the sea. "Piet was looking around some rocks—I was going over to join him, he seemed to have found something. Then"—she moistened her lips—"then he just sort of fell back, made for the surface, but as if he could hardly move—"

"How deep were you working?" demanded Laird.

"Ten metres, no more." Her voice was unsteady.

"And he was just searching among the rocks?"

She nodded. "I—I couldn't get him into the boat. He—I had to swim him in."

"Thank God you did," said Warner fervently. He knelt on the wet sand beside Laird and stared at Piet. "He looks bad, Laird. But what's wrong with him?"

"Wait." An idea came alive in Laird's mind, one he didn't owe to medical school but he'd heard talked about somewhere. Grabbing Piet's right hand, opening the limp fingers, he checked the boy's palm. It was unmarked. Swearing, he tried the other hand, which already felt cold and clammy.

They were there, half a dozen tiny black marks like broken spikes, tips barely protruding from the soft skin. Instinctively, he checked Piet's pulse again. It was even weaker.

"I need some help." He looked up at the anxious faces. "Who can do mouth-to-mouth artifical respiration?"

"I've done first aid." Moistening his lips, a fat boy stepped forward. A girl joined him.

"Get started," he told them curtly.

He waited just long enough to see the way they brought Piet's head back and opened his jaw. Then, as the fat boy took first turn, mouth to mouth, and Piet's chest expanded in response, Laird lifted the young diver's left hand again.

It had to be done carefully. Using his teeth, Laird bit on the first of the black tips, drew it out, then spat it clear. It was over half an inch long, needle-pointed, and it left the puncture wound bleeding.

He repeated the process. Bite on a spike, draw it out, go for another. The only sounds around were the murmur of the sea and the harsh, forced rhythm of the mouth-to-mouth breathing.

The last spike was the smallest, and the most difficult. It came free, Laird held it in his fingers, and sat back on his heels.

"What the hell is that?" asked Warner hoarsely.

The fat boy took a rest and the girl moved in to take over. The mouth-to-mouth rhythm continued with hardly a break.

"He grabbed a sea urchin." Laird saw Warner's blink of disbelief. "Where's Piet from?"

"Holland. But—"

"Where sea urchins come civilized." Laird delicately rolled the fragment of spike in his fingers. "You get a different breed of animal in warmer waters. This is from the black urchin, which carries its own defence system—these spikes are hollow, poisonous, like a hornet sting, except worse." He shrugged. "How bad, varies from one person to the next. Piet probably felt pole-axed."

He stopped talking and tried the fair-haired youngster's pulse again. It was still weak but firming. He signalled an end to the mouth-to-mouth respiration and watched. Piet's breathing was easier, he showed a first faint sign of coming round.

"We'd better get him to a doctor," said a new voice behind him.

Laird turned. Helen Warner was back. She stood there, her short, fair hair tousled as usual, deliberately calm, a puzzled expression showing for a moment on her face as their eyes met.

"Or get a doctor here," suggested Laird. He grinned at the worried faces round about. "Piet is going to feel lousy when he comes round, but he'll be all right."

"I'll drive into San Ferdinand." Adam Warner rose thankfully. He chased some of the trench diggers to organize a litter, then faced Laird. "We—well, we owe you again."

"I'll send a bill," said Laird drily.

He stayed where he was, watching Piet again, seeing a gradual trace of returning colour, conscious of Warner talking to Helen in a low, urgent voice. Then Warner hurried off, and in a moment the grey van drove away towards the road. Getting to his feet, leaving Piet in the care of two of the girls, Laird joined Helen.

"You're useful to have around," she said soberly. "You seemed to know what you were doing."

"I read a book once." Laird took her arm and led her a few steps along the beach. "Adam told me where you were. Any luck with your farmer?"

She nodded. "We can stay. I made noises about the Spanish government liking us being here—and a few threats and promises."

"Cuvier won't be pleased," mused Laird. "You're sure there's nothing else behind this war? Your brother can stir things up."

"He didn't." She straightened almost angrily. "The only reason is the *Sea Robin*. In fact—" She bit her lip and didn't finish.

"Well?" Laird raised an eyebrow.

"I thought it was because your people—the insurance side, were causing trouble."

"Because a few kids went raiding?" Laird frowned.

"It looked that way." She bit her lip. "At least, the pressure came on at the same time as Henderson got here."

"Are you sure?" It didn't fit, not with Charlie Henderson. Behind them, Piet was being lifted onto the litter brought from the tents. The boy seemed to be conscious. His friends made encouraging noises as they moved him. Laird drew a deep breath, knowing there was another question he had to ask. "Was it before Henderson died—or after?"

"Well, he'd only been here a couple of days before—" Helen hesitated, then shrugged. "Just afterwards. But—"

"It wasn't Charlie Henderson," said Laird.

"All right." She showed surprise at his vehemence. "I'm sorry. I—I'd better go and keep an eye on Piet. Are you going to stay?"

"No need." He relaxed and smiled at her. "I'll be back. Maybe it'll be third time lucky—no crisis."

"I'll try and arrange it," she said solemnly, then looked at him steadily, deliberately. "I'd like it that way."

*

Laird left a couple of minutes later and drove the short distance into San Ferdinand. The village was quiet, even the dogs staying in the shade, and he was beginning to realize it was a long time since breakfast. Leaving the Seat parked outside the Mercado, he went in. Mamá Isabel was behind the bar, which was deserted, and produced some limp goat's-cheese sandwiches and coffee.

"Any word from Roberto?" asked Laird, taking a first bite of the strong-tasting cheese.

Mamá Isabel nodded, face inscrutable under the brim of her hat. "He telephoned from the *aeropuerto.*" Her voice carried an underlying disapproval. "He said to tell you he delivered the envelope as you asked. He should be back in another hour."

No one had come looking for him, there had been no other telephone messages. Laird thanked her, washed down the first sandwich with some coffee, then realized Mamá Isabel was still standing near.

"Señor Laird." She hesitated, scratched at the sweat-soaked front of her baggy dress for a moment, then moved her bulky body a step nearer him. "Ramón García was here earlier. He—we talked about you."

"And?" Laird eyed her quizzically. "What's the problem? Don't tell me I'm on the local Guardia hit list."

Mamá Isabel didn't smile as she shook her head.

"I did not tell him Roberto was helping you. But he thinks"— uncharacteristically, she looked away—"he thinks—"

"That I'm trouble?"

"Sí." She nodded gravely.

"Why?"

"Because Señor Cuvier's people have asked him what you have said to him, what he knows about anything you have done." She frowned. "Ramón told them. He said there was nothing to hide. But he is worried."

"And Guardia sergeants don't worry easily?" Laird nodded his understanding. "Whatever happens, Roberto won't be involved."

"Bueno." Mamá Isabel nodded slowly. "You have paid for your room, Señor Laird. You can stay. But nothing more—you understand?"

"Completely," said Laird wearily. He looked at his coffee cup. "I could use a refill—if that's allowed."

"The Hostal Mercado looks after its guests," she said unemotionally, and fetched the pot.

About half an hour later, he went out again and drove the short distance to the harbour. Several fishing boats were in, but only one, a small trawler, was landing any kind of sizeable catch. The others appeared to have got their nets wet for very little except a few boxes of squid and a handful of grey mullet.

Laird left the car and walked the quayside towards the roped-off area being used by the salvage teams. Things were different there. Two trucks were parked nose to tail, one already loaded, the other half-filled, a Spanish customs officer lounging in the shade of its cab and talking to a group of men. One was Harry Novak, cap stuck on the back of his head, thumbs hitched into the waistband of his trousers. He was grinning, gesturing towards the truck platform.

It looked as though he had reason to be pleased. The first truck held the now usual assortment of salvaged crates. But the other was carrying a number of stainless-steel metal drums—Harry Novak had reached the wine compartment off the *Sea Robin*'s forward hatch.

Laird went closer. Novak saw him, beckoned him over, and the men with him turned in his direction. One was Paul Raynal. The other, standing slightly awkwardly a pace or two behind the Pandion Shipping manager, was Captain Weller from the *Beroe*. Where Novak, as captain of the *Scomber*, had a reputation for bullying drive, Weller was almost the opposite. Plump, grey-haired, a good seaman and salvage skipper, he had a mild face and a milder manner. Behind his back, he was sometimes nicknamed "the Padre." How he could team with Novak was one of life's mysteries.

"I expected you'd come vulturing round, Laird," said Novak with sneering good humour. "You're out of luck. No free samples of this booze—not even for insurance snoops."

"You're breaking my heart," said Laird. He exchanged nods with Raynal and with Captain Weller, whom he'd met several times. Ignoring him, the customs officer had turned away and was relieving himself against a wheel. "Is this the first lot?"

"Reached them mid-morning," said Novak, slapping one of the drums with open satisfaction. "A few problems, but we got there—smooth enough, eh, Weller?"

"We've a good team out there," murmured the *Beroe*'s captain. "That always makes a difference."

"If they're kicked up the backside often enough," declared Novak caustically. "That's the real secret."

"But as far as the wine is concerned, I can't recommend the vintage," lisped Paul Raynal. His sharp features shaped an uncharacteristic grin. "Your average connoisseur would class it as mainly fit for clearing drains."

"If it's liquid, someone will drink it." Laird took a closer look at the glinting metal drums. They were two-hundred-and-fifty-litre size, and the Clanmore breakdown of the *Sea Robin*'s cargo manifest had said ten thousand gallons of *vin ordinaire* had been loaded at Marseilles. At a rough mental conversion, that meant not far short of two hundred drums to come ashore. He saw that the customs officer, nature's call dealt with, was watching him suspiciously. He winked at the man, then turned to the others. "Any more progress on the hull survey?"

The three men exchanged glances. Raynal shaped a momentary frown, then Harry Novak rubbed a hand across his scarred face.

"We'd a compressor problem on the *Scomber*," he said uneasily. "That knocked out our power hoses, Laird. We aren't much further forward on the underside work."

"Why not?" Laird raised an eyebrow. "Couldn't Captain Weller have taken over?"

"He had his own problems," said Novak flatly.

"That's right," agreed the *Beroe*'s grey-haired skipper and grimaced. "You know Jingles Reilly, don't you?"

Laird nodded.

"He's on the sick list." Weller shrugged sympathetically. "Gut trouble—fairly bad. He's in his bunk and I wanted to get him ashore, to a doctor. But he told me to go to hell. So—well, I've lost my best diver until he's back on his feet."

"Tell him I said hello. He wasn't feeling too good when I saw him this morning."

Weller nodded. His attention had strayed to the harbour entrance and a workboat that was chugging in, deck filled with more of the steel drums of wine. Some of the harbour work gang had seen it too, and were ambling along the quay for another spell of unloading.

"Want to stay and count them, mister?" asked Harry Novak sarcastically. Then he stopped, looked beyond Laird, and gave an irritated grunt. "Hell, more company. Maybe we should have sold tickets."

Jano Cuvier's white Mercedes station wagon was murmuring in from the harbour gate. It stopped at the rope barrier, but the doors stayed closed. The headlamps flashed once, and Paul Raynal set off towards the car at an obedient trot.

Laird followed at a more leisurely pace. As Raynal reached the car, Janos Cuvier got out and the two men stood talking, breaking off when Laird arrived. As usual, Vicente lounged behind the Mercedes' wheel. His other passenger was Laura Cero, sitting in the rear. She gave a smile and a nod.

"Come to see our progress, Mr. Laird? Things are going well." Janos Cuvier broke off his conversation with Raynal and greeted him briskly. The head of the Cuvier Corporation seemed in a particularly good humour. "I had a feeling you might be here."

"It's hard to stay away," said Laird woodenly.

"We both safeguard our interests." Cuvier's face showed something close to a grin. Pausing, he made a deliberate business of sniffing the harbour air, then gestured his disgust. "But it would help if these places had a better smell."

"I've known worse." The sun was glinting on Cuvier's bald dome of a head. For some reason, Laird found himself wondering briefly how the man would have looked with hair. "You know there's a hold-up on the survey work?"

"A temporary thing." Cuvier shrugged his unconcern, then took a half-step nearer. "However, I won't be here much longer. It's a matter of business priorities—other problems that can't wait. I plan to return to Switzerland tomorrow evening. Unless—" He considered Laird almost lazily. "—unless, of course, you can suggest any remaining major difficulty involving the *Sea Robin* situation."

"Not at the moment." Masking his feelings, Laird kept his voice unemotional. "You've taken care of most things."

"Good." Cuvier gave a slightly amused nod. "Paul Raynal will either stay on for a day or two or come back here later." His mood changed, and he gave a relaxed chuckle. "I do have one small, domestic problem. But maybe you could help."

Laird raised an eyebrow. "How?"

"Don't worry, Mr. Laird. I wouldn't call it a hardship." Cuvier turned towards the car, beckoned to Laura, and smiled as she got out and came over. "Laura, you still feel disappointed about tonight?"

"It can't be helped." She looked puzzled.

"I may have the answer." Cuvier grinned at her, then switched to Laird. "Would you see any difficulty in escorting a particularly attractive young woman for the evening?"

"That would depend on how she felt." Laird glanced at the girl, noting the immediate, almost angry frown on her face. "Why?"

"A promise I made," said Cuvier. "I told Laura she could see some genuine flamenco dancing while we were in Spain. I have two reservations for a particularly good presentation in Marbella tonight—but I can't go, and I can't spare anyone else." He considered Laura cautiously. "It would seem sensible to suggest you go together."

"Perhaps he doesn't feel that way." Laura Cero's mouth tightened with embarrassment. "It's not so important—"

"Of course he does," said Cuvier briskly. "Sometimes it is important to do things that aren't important. Agreed, Mr. Laird? And of course, you'll have Vicente and the car—"

"No." Laird shook his head and watched Laura. "If she'll do it, I've got transport."

"Laura?" Cuvier was slightly impatient.

"All right." She nodded, amusement mixed with her annoyance. "Why waste two good reservations?"

"Then it's settled. Make your own arrangements, eh?" Cuvier glanced at Raynal, who had been a silent spectator. "Paul, I want a word with Captain Novak. Then we have another matter to discuss."

He nodded to Laird, and the two men started off along the quayside.

"Damn him," said Laura indignantly. "Look, you can still think up an excuse—"

"No way." For more than one reason, that was the last thing on Laird's mind. "What time is the show?"

"Late. About ten—"

"I'll collect you at seven." He grinned at her. "We've got to eat first. I'll charge you to expenses."

"That makes all the difference," she said. "I like business evenings."

*

A little later, he picked up the Seat again and drove back to the Hostal Mercado. When he got there and parked outside, Roberto was sweeping the front porch with a brush.

"Señor Laird." The brush paused and Roberto's fat young face smiled a slightly shame-faced welcome. *Mamá* tol' me she spoke to you. I'm sorry. She had no right—"

"She had. You're her son," Laird told him gently. "Any problems at the airport?"

Roberto shook his head. "I delivered the photographs, like you asked. The girl at the desk said okay, they'd be in London by this evening. *De acuerdo?*"

"Couldn't be better," Laird assured him. "Tell your mother I'll be out tonight, back pretty late."

"Okay." The brush took a flick at a stray cigarette end, then faltered. "You don't need me for anything else?"

"*Gracias,* no—not right now."

Roberto nodded gloomily. "I wondered, with these two men being here."

"Which two?" Laird blinked.

"Two of the men in my photographs. They are in the bar, having a drink." Roberto looked hopeful.

"Have they asked anything?"

The fat youngster shook his head.

"Then stay clear of them," advised Laird. "Whoever they are—but let me know if they do quiz you."

He left Roberto, went into the shabby bar area, and took a quick glance around. There were about half a dozen customers at the tables. Behind the bar, Mamá Isabel was too busy washing glasses to notice him. But Roberto was right. Dark-haired and fair-haired, quietly dressed as ever, the two men Janos Cuvier called his "utility twins" were at a corner table. Each had a beer in front of him.

The dark-haired Botha saw Laird, nudged his companion, and Vasco turned slowly. They smiled, nodded casually, then looked away again.

Laird thought of the mountain road, of the fact that Hans Botha had been there the same night Charlie Henderson died, and fought down an instinctive desire to go straight over.

It would do no good, not yet.

He went up to his room, took his second-hand binoculars from their battered case, and went over to the window.

Out at the *Sea Robin,* they were still salvaging cargo. As he watched, he saw yet another of the glinting metal wine containers swing out on the end of a derrick boom and settle on the deck of one of the waiting workboats.

He lowered the glasses slowly. In not much more than twenty-four hours, Janos Cuvier would be leaving. It was like being given a deadline, a deadline Laird knew it was going to be almost impossible to meet.

But he could try. Beginning with Laura Cero, even though he wasn't sure whether he'd be glad or sad if she couldn't help.

Taking the Clanmore claim file on the *Sea Robin* from its dressing-table drawer, he went over to the bed, sat down and began to read the whole thing again from page one onward. There might be something in it somewhere.

And he desperately needed any kind of a lead, no matter how tenuous.

*

About an hour later, Roberto slipped up to the room. Botha and Vasco had left. They'd kept to themselves, had tipped well when they paid for their drinks—that was all.

Laird went back to the file once Roberto had gone. He worked on it for about another hour, until the close-spaced typing began to blur, then gave up. The things he needed to know were the things that weren't in it. Things like more background on the Pandion Shipping operation, the same kind of background on the *Sea Robin*'s captain, Van Holst, and his officers—particularly his vanished chief engineer.

He could have phoned London. But knowing Osgood Morris, it wasn't necessary. The moment the marine claims department manager received that envelope of photographs, his nostrils would begin twitching. Give Morris the slightest hint that something might be wrong and, though he might break into an immediate cold sweat, he'd start digging—for once; digging first, then telling the chairman later.

That way, Osgood Morris could be on an each-way bet. Either because he found dirt that could stick, or, just as valuable from a personal viewpoint, he could take the credit for killing false rumour.

Laird gave a lopsided grin at the thought. Every successful firm needed an Osgood Morris. But it was a pity that other people had to work under them.

Both salvage tugs were still working beside the *Sea Robin* when, at about six, he treated himself to a shower and the luxury of his second shave of the day. He dressed carefully, choosing another clean shirt and a dark-red silk tie, spitting on his shoes and rubbing some sort of polish to the scuffed leather with a handful of toilet tissue.

Still with time to kill, he went down to the bar and was almost glad to see the bulky, Guardia-uniformed figure of Sergeant García elbowed up at an otherwise deserted part of the counter.

"Señor Laird." García gave him a token nod. The man's large hands were wrapped round a brandy glass, his tricorn hat was lying on the counter. "I hear you saw Father Sebastian today."

"That's right." Laird signalled the barman to bring the Guardia sergeant another brandy and one for himself. "You seem to hear most things, Sergeant."

"My job is to listen—or ask." García poured what was left of his drink into the new glass, took a gulp, then wiped his mouth with the back of one hand. "How much longer are you staying?"

"Mamá Isabel already asked me," said Laird. "I don't know yet. Does it matter?"

"To me?" García shrugged. "Not particularly." He scowled at his hat. "Let's say I won't weep when all of you have gone—you, Señor Cuvier and his people, the man Warner and his young pirates."

"Better get used to strangers," said Laird. "The concrete is coming. Another couple of years and you could be up to your neck in tourists."

The man swore under his breath. "Then what happens? Every fisherman running about pretending to be a waiter, or running a bar instead of a boat? *Eso duele . . .* you expect me to like the idea?"

"No." Laird sipped his own drink for a moment, mentally revising one part of his opinion of the man. "What's worrying you, Sergeant? Anything in particular?"

"A certain Captain Alvarez, at District Headquarters," said García. He scowled at the thought. "He wants to know why the British consul at Málaga has shown a sudden apparent new interest in the death of your friend Henderson."

"I see." Laird took another sip of the brandy and let it burn its way down. It was a harsh, local spirit, probably weeks rather than months old. "What did you say?"

"That I didn't know." García slammed his glass on the bar counter, hard enough for the liquor to slop over. "Any more than I could have told him why other things seem to be happening I don't understand—with most of them coming back to you, Señor Laird."

"Me?" Slowly, Laird shook his head. "I wish I knew what you meant, Sergeant. Or that I could tell you anything that helped."

"*Gracias,*" said García bitterly. He swallowed what was left of his brandy at a massive gulp, picked up his tricorn hat, and rammed it on his close-cropped head. "For the drink, at any rate. For the rest—go to hell."

He marched out, shouldering his way past two startled fishermen who chose that moment to amble in from the street. They gaped after him as he left, exchanged a philosophic shrug, then began laughing at some private joke.

Sighing, Laird stayed at the bar for a few more minutes, then abandoned the rest of his drink and went outside.

*

Prompt on seven, he drove the little blue Seat up to the Casa Turo and swung in beside the other cars parked on the gravelled driveway. Before Laird could switch off the ignition, Laura appeared at the door of the villa, waved, then came over.

She was smiling as she reached the car and Laird opened the door. Her jet-black hair brushed high and back from her forehead, she was wearing a white organza blouse, scoop-necked, cape-styled, layered with lace, and teamed with a calf-length black organza skirt, hemmed in black lace.

"You're prompt." She got aboard in a froth of skirt. As before, her only jewellery was the small diamond pendant, and she was carrying a small black handbag. Her perfume had a light, subtle fragrance, exactly in character. As Laird got behind the wheel again, she asked, "You don't feel like you've been hijacked?"

"Call it part of the Clanmore service." He winked at her, and set the little car moving.

The setting sun was behind them on the dusty coast-road drive to Marbella. They talked a little, easily, casually, and after a spell Laura kicked off her shoes and sat with her feet resting on the dashboard in front of her.

"I don't think I want to go back tomorrow," she said suddenly, almost fiercely. On their right, the sea had begun to take on a golden glow as the sun began to touch the horizon. Inland, the mountains took on a sharper silhouette.

"But?" Laird waited until they had overtaken a lumbering truck, then gave her a sideways glance.

"But." She nodded a wry agreement. "That's how it is."

They came into Marbella along the Avenida Ricardo, got caught up in the web of narrow streets that led to the town centre, and looked for a parking place. The pavements were busy with tourist holiday-makers, they nosed along in traffic made up of cars with registration plates from every part of Europe. Neon signs challenged the gathering dusk, cafés were noisy with music.

At last, Laird found a parking spot beside a public garden.

"I don't believe it," said Laura, as he locked the Seat and joined her on the pavement.

She pointed. The street name, on a plate, read "Avenida Carlos Mackintosch." It seemed a reasonable omen, and a little farther along they found a small restaurant that didn't have a neon sign but looked busy.

There was time for a drink at a tiny bar before they could get a table. The menu was handwritten, the candle decoration on the table smoked every time anyone went past, but the food was good. Laura settled for a veal dish with *"Moros y Cristianos"*—black beans and rice; Laird chose a fish course that came with lemon and red peppers, and they shared a half-bottle of wine. Their waiter, who didn't hide his delight in hovering near Laura, also gave them directions to the flamenco venue.

They lingered over coffee, the candle's flame catching a flickering sparkle from the tiny diamond pendant at Laura's throat.

"You know what's wrong?" she said suddenly. "I feel guilty. I'm the only one on the Cuvier team who isn't working tonight."

"I wouldn't let it break your heart," said Laird whimsically. "What's the panic about?"

She frowned and hesitated, one finger drawing a pattern on the table-top. "I could say that's classified."

"So you're a loyal employee," agreed Laird. He shrugged. "Forget it."

"There's no harm in telling you a little." She grimaced at him across the candle flame. "A little is about all I know anyway—it's financial, not legal, and the way Janos Cuvier works, you only hear when he thinks you need to know. It's some kind of cash-flow problem."

"Bad?"

"Awkward." Laura shrugged. "The way the Cuvier Corporation is structured, if one company goes sick, at least another couple can start shivering."

"If he really needs money—"

"There's the *Sea Robin* claim?" She was ahead of him. "No, he still doesn't want to go for a total-loss situation. He's determined to press for a salvage attempt."

"Why?" persisted Laird. "All right, he says the ship was underinsured. Maybe it was, but—"

"It would be hard cash," she agreed. "But he doesn't want to know. He's not always easy to understand."

"I've noticed," said Laird sardonically. He brought out his cigarettes, offered the pack, and she took one. They shared a light from the candle, then he sat back. "Were you involved in the way he tried to have Warner's students thrown off their campsite?"

She surprised him.

"I suggested it." Her dark eyes met his own calmly, unrepentantly. "He asked me what he could do, legally. It didn't work, but it was worth a try."

"Did you want to see them thrown off?"

"Me?" She blinked. "No. Why should I?" She drew on her cigarette for a moment. "Andrew, he doesn't like them around—it's as simple as that, and he can be pretty ruthless."

He hesitated, other questions in his mind, questions about Henderson's death, then decided that might be going too far, risking too much.

Laura Cero mistook his silence.

"Look." She reached across the table and touched his hand. "I don't always like what I have to do. Isn't it sometimes that way with your job?"

"Yes." He signalled the waiter for their bill. She was still watching him, something close to worry in her eyes. He smiled and squeezed her fingers. "Lousy, isn't it?"

*

It was dark outside as they walked the short distance from the restaurant to the night-club where the flamenco show was located. There was a pale crescent of moon overhead, but it had competition. The resort's night-life attractions meant flashing neon signs, headlights, brightly lit windows, and the rasp of exhausts as young, leather-clad motor-cyclists weaved through the traffic.

Some of the bikers, most of them, were ordinary kids. Others were the Costa del Sol's equivalent of mugging squads—travelling in pairs, ready for a kerbside handbag snatch from a moving machine, then off at full-bore acceleration. When that happened, the odds were against them being caught. If any were caught, they were liable to produce a spring-blade knife and be ready to use it.

Laird kept Laura on the inside as, arm in arm, they followed the directions they'd been given. After a few streets, they escaped the crowded pavements. A church was their marker point. From there, along the Avenida Valdez, they reached a white building with narrow windows protected by decorative ironwork.

A sign on the night-club door said "Closed" in several languages. But it opened when Laird knocked, and Janos Cuvier's reservation got them in to a darkened cavern of a room with a handkerchief-sized stage. They had a tiny table near the front, and every seat around was taken as the house lights dimmed and the stage spots came up.

The beginning was low-key. Tape-recorded music began sobbing from two amplifier cabinets as the first dancers took the stage. Tall, statuesque women, they performed what could have been a ballet routine with flouncing skirts, impassive grace, and a slow, exact clicking of castanets.

The applause was polite as the tapes gave way to a single guitar on stage. But then the mood changed, becoming faster, bouncier as the *canto chico* part of the programme began. A man dressed in black, his shirt open to the waist, joined the women. More musicians appeared. The evening exploded to life, the stage quivered to the staccato of pounding heels, handclaps, high-pitched cries.

One set of dancers left, another group stormed on. Their presentation was the more emotional *canto jondo* . . . as a small, dark-haired woman sang of love and death in piercing style, the dancers weaved new patterns to a rhythm as deliberate as a heartbeat.

Then it changed again. Flamenco, ancient and Moorish in origin, swamped its audience in a tidal wave of colour and emotion, of colourful folk-art and sheer physical endurance. Castanets clicking, heels pounding, sweat running down their faces, the dancers seemed oblivious to anything outside the tight boundary of their little stage-world.

The show lasted two hours. At last, it was over. The flamenco group took a final bow and departed, the house lights came up, people began making for the exits.

"Well?" Laird looked at Laura.

"It was wonderful." Her eyes were still bright with excitement. "Andrew, I—"

"Thank your boss, not me," he reminded drily.

They left the night-club and began walking back to where they'd left the car. It was still warm. Humming under her breath, Laura stopped to try a quick, heel-tapping step, then laughed and caught up with him again.

The next street was quiet, residential, lined with parked cars, and empty of life. They were halfway along it when Laird heard the motor cycles start up. He glanced back, then froze.

There were two machines, crawling down towards them under the street lights. Each rider carried a pillion passenger. All of them wore hoods that covered their faces. He heard another machine and swung round. It was coming towards them from the other end, at the same unhurried pace, again with a rider and pillion passenger. He heard Laura draw a quick intake of breath—and the three machines came nearer, deliberate in their menace.

"What will we do?" asked Laura in a low, tense voice.

He shook his head, fingers loosening the belt at his waist. It was his only weapon. They were cut off, couldn't even run.

CHAPTER 5

He had the belt held loose in his right hand, the heavy brass buckle swinging gently. It had been styled for this kind of work as much as for decoration; there had been times before when he'd needed it, his back against a wall. But never like this, with a girl at his side, a girl like Laura Cero.

"Stay close," he told her softly, watching the riders close in. "If we can talk our way out of it—"

The hope was feeble. One machine was on the pavement, still creeping nearer. The other two, level with them, stopped, but the riders kept their engines revving. The pillion passengers slid from their seats, the crude hoods on their heads making them faceless horrors in the glow of the street lights. A spring-blade knife clicked open. Another tapped a stubby baton against his side.

"*Hola, señor,*" said the tallest in a hoarse young whisper of a voice, while the motor cycles revved on in the background. "No one wants the lady to get hurt, okay?"

Laird took a quick, sideways glance at Laura. Her face was pale, her handbag clutched tightly. Suddenly, her mouth started to shape an urgent warning and he turned just as the pillion rider with the baton made a dive forward. Laird swung his belt. The heavy buckle, on the end of a short length of leather, smashed into the hooded face and brought a howl of pain.

There wasn't time to avoid the next one, the tall leader. He had a knife, he used it in a vicious arc, and Laird felt the sharp steel slice through the cloth of his jacket, then felt a stinging rake on his upper arm. Cursing, Laird grabbed his attacker's thin wrist, saw the third hooded figure coming in, swung the belt back-handed to try to fend him off, heard it connect, then, too late, looked round for the first man.

A kick took him behind one knee and he staggered. The baton smashed against his shoulder. Still gripping the tall knifeman's wrist, twirling the belt and its deadly buckle like a flail, he forced the others to retreat a step. But they came in again, together. One yelped as the buckle connected, then both smashed into him.

Laird fell, dragging one figure down with him. He tried to struggle, saw a knife glint over his face, jerking for a downward strike. Then, instead, something white flickered at the edge of his vision. There was a solid thud, a crunch that might have been breaking teeth, and the knifeman lurched back, scrambling clear, the knife abandoned, both hands clutching his hooded face.

His two companions had backed off, hesitating. Laird realized Laura Cero was standing over him, the front of her white organza blouse ripped, her face tight with angry resolution. She held her handbag like a club in one clenched fist.

The men still hesitated. Then a harsh shout came from one of the waiting motor-cyclists. Another revved his machine urgently. As Laird got to his feet, the three ran back, jumped on their pillion seats, and the machines roared away.

Arm still stinging where the knife tip had raked, blood trickling from the wound, Laird looked around. A house door had opened farther down the street. Light poured from the open doorway and several people were coming out, a party ending. Talking, laughing, oblivious to what had been happening, the group spilled out onto the roadway.

"No." Laird caught Laura's arm as she started towards them. "It's over. No need."

"But you're hurt." Bewildered, she stared at him. "The police—"

"For what? Those characters are far away by now." Laird scowled in the direction the motor cycles had vanished, made an awkward job of fastening the belt round his waist again, then gave an involuntary grin. "And I'll mend. But what the heck do you pack in that handbag—a sledgehammer?"

"It was a present from my mother, last Christmas." She paused, looking almost embarrassed. "She worries about me."

"Give," said Laird drily. He took the bag, felt its surprising weight, fingered the thick, rock-solid base, and made a guess. "Lead?"

Laura nodded. Her face was still pale, but her voice had steadied.

"It—well, it's the only black bag I own. That's why I had it—"

"Tell your mother I love her," declared Laird, returning it. Blood was still trickling down his arm, staining through the ripped cloth of his jacket. He saw the abandoned spring-blade knife lying on the roadway, picked it up, closed it, and slipped it in his pocket. He waited while Laura tidied the torn front of her blouse as best she could, then drew a deep breath. "Let's get out of here."

She nodded and they set off, close together. The party-goers were still exchanging farewells and getting into cars, and one of them called a greeting as they passed.

"Smile," murmured Laird.

She did, and he waved cheerfully with his good arm.

The next street was brightly lit and busy, and from then on there was no problem. The rented blue Seat was parked as he'd left it near the Avenida Carlos Mackintosch and they got aboard. Suddenly, Laird felt himself start to shake, from sheer reaction. He could have been killed back there, killed—or at the very least, disfigured for life.

"Andrew—" Laura said his name quietly, anxiously, and he fought his way back to something approaching a relaxed grin.

"I'm fine." He grimaced at his blood-stained left sleeve. "Like to help me do something about this?"

With her help, he removed his jacket. The sleeve of his shirt had also been ripped, but the wound below it, a three-inch gash on his upper arm, was shallow and not much more than superficial. Laura cleaned it with a handkerchief from her bag, a handkerchief soaked in eau de cologne, which stung in a way that made him yelp. Then, using the spring-blade, she cut the sleeve from his shirt and used it as a bandage.

"Not too bad." She inspected her handiwork critically, then allowed her fingertips to stray down to touch the tattooed dragon below it. She gave a grave smile. "He looks fierce."

"Because he happens to be a she—or that's what the man told me." Laird grinned at her. "Thanks. That's fine."

"Then get in." Laura opened the passenger door as she spoke. "I'm driving."

"But—"

"Please. I need something to do."

He nodded, glad because of the way his arm was still throbbing. Coming round, she got behind the Seat's wheel, then sat there for a moment, not touching the controls.

"Those men back there—"

"Anyone can get mugged. Anywhere. Maybe they were high on drugs."

"Maybe." She bit her lip. "But it was as if they—well, they wanted to kill you."

"They lost the place," soothed Laird. "That happens too."

But he wondered, as Laura started the car and set it moving. The same thought had been lurking in his mind since the first moment of the attack. That hooded squad, six strong, had been more like a team operation than a casual targeting. Equally significant, they'd shown no interest in Laura—in fact, once she'd made her surprise move, a positive reluctance to tangle with her.

Otherwise, even with those party-goers appearing on the scene —yes, they could have easily taken him back there. Taken him out permanently.

Or was that what they'd wanted?

He glanced at Laura, her attention firmly on the road, her torn blouse gradually working loose again, and his mouth tightened.

Because that thought led to another. If the whole thing had been planned, it had to come back to Janos Cuvier.

*

They talked very little as the car travelled on through the night, meeting the occasional headlights of another vehicle, mostly on a road that was deserted and empty. Laura asked for a cigarette and he lit one for her, then placed it between her lips. She had to brake once, hard, to avoid a startled hare which appeared almost under their wheels. Farther on, their lights were reflected from a pair of bright-green eyes in a patch of roadside scrub. Some four-legged predator was on the prowl, but hunting for a different kind of prey.

At last, they turned off on the narrow coast road that led to San

Ferdinand. Soon they were running close to the shore and then, without warning, Laura flicked the Seat's gear change into neutral and let it coast to a halt.

"I want to stop for a minute," she said quietly. "Get out, walk— all right?"

Without waiting for an answer, she switched off lights and engine and left the car. Laird stayed where he was, watching, until she walked a short distance, to stand silhouetted against the faint moonlight and facing the sea. Then he got out quietly and joined her.

"What's wrong?" he asked gently.

"I don't know." She shook her head. "I think I suddenly realized how scared I was back there."

"Then that makes two of us," he told her quietly. "Take it easy."

He put his arm round her shoulders. She turned, her body pressed against his, holding him tightly, her head against his chest.

"Laura." He made her look up. "It's all right."

She nodded, and he kissed her. The kiss lingered, a tension building between them. Then she looked at him again, almost shyly.

"I have to leave tomorrow." She put a finger against his lips, stopping his reply.

Then she took his hand, and they went down towards the shore.

*

It was close on 3 A.M. when Andrew Laird got back to the Hostal Mercado. He parked the Seat in the yard at the rear, draped his jacket carefully over his bandaged arm, and walked round to the front.

The door had been left on the latch, a single light had been left on to guide him across the silent, empty bar to the stairs. He went up quietly, reached his room, and opened his bag to get the small first aid kit he always carried.

Lifting it out, he stopped short and his mouth tightened. The kit was a small leather case with two locking catches. The left-hand catch was faulty, had been since the day he'd bought it second-hand from another medical student. The trick was to have the catch in the locking position before it was closed.

He'd left it that way. Now it hung open.

Inside, nothing had been taken. But there were small signs that someone had carefully checked the contents.

Sooner or later, he'd expected it to happen. Laird spent a few moments going round the rest of the room, noticing other small signs, like the way one of the shirts ironed by Mamá Isabel now had fresh wrinkles on its previously smooth front. But nothing was gone. Even the Clanmore file was where he'd left it, in the bottom drawer of the dressing table.

He grinned. There was nothing in the file to worry any outsider, and Roberto's photographs, those that remained, were safe. Laird left his room, went along the corridor to the small bathroom, and made sure they were still where he'd put them, hidden in the crack of space between wall and back of the toilet cistern.

Back in his room, he examined the spring-blade knife he'd collected in Marbella. It was plain, with a black bone handle and a viciously sharp blade. A factory somewhere probably produced them by the thousands.

Shrugging, he tossed the knife onto the dressing table. Removing the temporary bandage, he looked at the cut on his arm. He'd been lucky. It was a shallow gash, the kind that should heal quickly. Using the first aid kit, he cleaned the wound again and covered it with an adhesive dressing. He put the blood-stained shirt and jacket at the bottom of his travel bag, then got ready for bed.

Naked, feeling the night still warm, he went over to the window and looked out. The sea was still a dull silver in the faint light of the crescent moon. Nothing seemed to be moving, the only sound was the murmur of the waves.

But he wondered how much was really happening.

*

Andrew Laird slept badly that night, wakened twice because he'd rolled over on his injured arm, and lay for a spell each time with his mind a restless jumble of thoughts and uncertainties. All that did come through to him was that something had to happen soon. Just by being in San Ferdinand he was acting almost as a catalyst, causing events and changes without being certain why.

Which couldn't go on.

At eight in the morning, when he got up, the weather had changed. There were grey clouds in the sky and the wind had altered, coming in from the south-west. The air felt heavy, as if a storm was on the way.

Laird shaved and dressed, wearing a long-sleeved shirt to cover the adhesive plaster on his arm. Tucking the shirt into his trousers, he heard a knock at the room door. It opened, and Mamá Isabel waddled in.

"*Teléfono*, Señor Laird." Under her hat brim, her sharp eyes made an impassive inspection of her guest and the room. If she saw the spring-blade knife on the dressing table, or wondered about it, she gave no sign. "There is a call for you downstairs, in the bar—from London, a Señor Morris."

She turned and had gone before he could thank her.

Laird went down. Two of the Mercado's guests, a man and woman dressed like tourists, were at one of the tables and being served breakfast by Roberto. Going past them, Laird went into the old-fashioned telephone booth and closed the door. The telephone receiver was lying off the hook and he lifted it.

"Can I ask exactly what the devil you're trying to stir up out there?" asked Osgood Morris without preamble the moment he heard Laird's voice on the line. "Those photographs, queries, apparently unfounded allegations—has the sun got to your head?"

"It's cloudy today." Laird drew a deep breath. When the Clanmore marine claims manager was in that kind of a mood, things could be difficult. "Osgood, the man in those photographs—any luck in identifying him?"

"No, at least, not yet." He heard Morris sniff. "Charlie Henderson's funeral was yesterday afternoon, and I only got your package when I returned. But—"

"I think it matters," said Laird forcefully. "There's something wrong out here."

"Because an owner wants to salvage his ship?" Morris didn't hide his impatience. "If it saves money, our shareholders won't see things that way. What's more, we're starting to get pressure from another direction. The Spanish authorities are making noises. They say San Ferdinand is a potential future tourist resort and the last thing they want is a wreck spoiling the view. They want her moved; they don't care how."

"All right." Laird bit his lip. Governments could deliver that kind of ultimatum—or do the job themselves, then send the bill. "Osgood, suppose I told you Charlie Henderson's death may not have been an accident?"

"You mean—" Morris broke off, a gulping noise came over the line. "Now damn it, look—"

"That's why the photographs matter," said Laird, cutting him short. "There's something else you can tell the chairman when you hold hands with him this morning. Cuvier is heading back to Switzerland. He's in some kind of financial jam."

"Who told you?" Morris's manner changed.

"Someone who knows a little."

"I see." The marine claims manager became cautious. "But if that's true—" He paused, and Laird could almost hear him thinking. "I've told you before, we do a lot of policy business with the Cuvier Corporation."

"Which should make it easier to find out," countered Laird flatly. "But the photographs matter most."

"Yes." Osgood Morris was adept at mental somersaults, particularly when Clanmore money was at stake. "All right, we'll work on it. If necessary, there's a certain assistant commissioner at Scotland Yard who owes me a favour. Any police involvement at your end?"

"Not yet."

"Better keep it that way, until we're beyond wild guesses." Morris sounded gloomy. "But there's one thing you've forgotten, or didn't know about."

Laird raised an eyebrow at the receiver. "Like what?"

"Henderson's funeral," said Morris. "It was a cremation service."

The line went dead and Laird replaced the receiver with the sick feeling he'd won one round but lost another. Opening the door of the booth, he went out and almost collided with the burly figure outside. Sergeant Ramón García looked in a surly mood.

"I'm finished." Laird gestured towards the telephone.

"I was waiting for you, Señor Laird," said García with a scowl. He had cut himself shaving that morning. From his expression, he would have been happier if it had been Laird's throat. "Why did you lie to me?"

"About what?" Laird was caught off guard.

"Two nights ago, on that beach, with Warner's people." The Guardia sergeant's lips tightened. "You said you had been with them for some time. I talked to Raynal, the shipping line manager. He said you were with Señor Cuvier most of the evening."

"Then I made a mistake." Laird shrugged. "Sorry."

"You think that enough?" García's voice rose in its anger. The couple at the breakfast table glanced round, then looked away again quickly. If the Guardia sergeant noticed, he ignored them. "You are a trouble-maker, Señor Laird. Nothing more, nothing less

—and I know a good way to deal with your kind, a way you wouldn't like."

Laird frowned. "That almost sounds like a threat, Sergeant."

"No, a promise." The sergeant grabbed him by the arm, fingers digging in through the shirt, hitting the dressing over the wound beneath in a way that made Laird wince. "Do you understand?"

Laird looked at García's hand, still gripping his arm, then at García, saying nothing. But there was something in his eyes, his expression, for García to read and the man did. García let go, moistened his lips, and stood back.

"Get off my back, Sergeant," Laird told him softly. "I've enough problems."

García stiffened, his face flushing with a new anger. Then, with a major effort, he controlled himself. He gave a curt nod, turned on his heel, and marched out of the bar. As the door closed behind the man, a clatter of crockery came from behind the bar as Mamá Isabel deliberately thumped down a tray. She looked at Laird with a frown of disapproval, then turned away.

Her son was less inhibited. He came over as Laird took a seat at one of the tables near the window.

"*Buenos días*, Señor Laird." His round face split in a grin. "Hey, I thought maybe you were going to be arrested."

"Too early in the morning." Laird ordered orange juice, coffee and rolls, then stopped the young Spaniard leaving. "How were things here last night?"

"Last night?" Roberto was puzzled.

"Here, in the bar."

"Busy." Roberto gestured vaguely. "The usual, maybe more so. Some of the people from the salvage tugs were in." He grimaced appreciatively. "They spend a lot."

Laird nodded. "How about Señor Cuvier's people?"

"*Sí.*" Roberto understood and nodded. "The same two as before."

"Did you talk to them?"

He shook his head. "We were too busy, Señor Laird—and *Mamá* was behind the bar."

He brought Laird's breakfast, then left him alone. The other couple departed, and Mamá Isabel began restocking the bottles behind the bar. Laird ate slowly, hardly conscious of taste. With the Mercado busy, anyone could have sneaked upstairs from the bar to his room, and the Mercado didn't rise to luxuries like locks on the doors.

"*Buenos días,*" said Mamá Isabel loudly from behind the bar.

He glanced up, then tried to keep a look of surprise from his face. Janos Cuvier had just walked in, followed by Captain Van Holst. Giving a fractional nod in Mamá Isabel's direction, Cuvier gestured to the *Sea Robin*'s captain to wait where he was and came over alone, an anxious expression on his thin, pinched face.

"You feeling all right?" he asked, taking a chair and sitting opposite Laird without waiting for an invitation. "Laura told me about last night—and that you were knifed."

"I was lucky," answered Laird with deliberate mildness.

"That's not how she tells it." Cuvier ran a bony hand over his bald, sun-reddened skull and pursed his lips. "I felt sick when I heard. I sent you there. If anything had happened to that girl—anything worse—"

"It didn't." Laird allowed himself a slight grin. "She packs a fairly lethal handbag."

Cuvier looked at him blankly, then shrugged. Over at the bar, Van Holst had lit a small cheroot and was waiting patiently.

"I came to thank you," said Cuvier. He pursed his lips again. "Laura feels the same, of course—even more so. Unfortunately, she won't have a chance of seeing you before we leave this evening." He shook his head in apology. "There's too much to do before we go. However, she did ask me to tell you that any time you're in Switzerland, near our head office—"

"Tell her I'll look in," nodded Laird. "I'll probably head back to London tomorrow."

"No loose ends?" The parchment-thin face opposite eyed him closely.

"Not till we get Harry Novak's final report on the *Sea Robin*. Then—well, it's a London decision."

"Of course." Janos Cuvier gave a satisfied nod and got to his feet. "I'll let you finish your breakfast."

"One thing," said Laird casually. "We may need another statement from the ship's chief engineer. Any idea how we can contact him?"

"No." Cuvier seemed to tense, his eyes suddenly hard and watchful. Then he was smiling again. "Paul Raynal may have an address. I'll ask him. Goodbye, Mr. Laird."

He turned on his heel and left, Van Holst coming to life again and following him out.

Laird finished his last cup of coffee and smoked a cigarette. Something had happened, he was sure now. Maybe the message from Laura was genuine, but after last night—no, he doubted it. Or at least, that she'd wanted it that way. He could find out later, by appearing at the front door of the Casa Turo. And Cuvier's reaction when he'd asked about the *Sea Robin*'s engineer—he gave a humourless grin at the memory, then shoved back his chair.

It was time he checked on what was going on at the harbour and out where the salvage tugs were working.

*

Outside, the wind seemed to have died. But the grey clouds were moving lazily overhead and an edge of angrier black was beginning to come in from the sea. The very air felt oppressive. Although he had the Seat's keys in his pocket, Laird decided he'd prefer to walk.

Despite the short distance, his shirt was damp with perspiration and sticking to his back by the time he reached the harbour gates. The usual scatter of fishing boats were tied along the quay and a small coaster was unloading bottled gas. But the area of quay reserved for the salvage boats was deserted and empty. Laird hesitated, surprised, then saw a small launch coming in.

He was waiting when it tied up beside some stone steps and Harry Novak came ashore. The salvage tug master, scarred face unshaven, grunted a greeting, then took off his cap and wiped his brow.

"There's a storm on the way. Sooner it breaks, the better." His harsh voice didn't have its usual rasping edge. "I was going to come lookin' for you."

"It's that kind of a morning," said Laird neutrally. He stuck his hands in his pockets. "Why?"

"Your pal Jingles Reilly." Novak gestured out towards the sea. "He's sick, pretty bad—we've just ferried a doctor out to the *Beroe*, to have a look at him."

Laird frowned, remembering the last time he'd seen the *Beroe*'s mate and chief diver. "He didn't feel too good yesterday—"

"And he's a damned sight worse today." Novak shrugged. He fidgeted, eyeing Laird with caution. "You can borrow the launch for a trip out. I'm on my way to see Cuvier."

"You know he's leaving today?"

"He said that might happen." Novak hesitated, then gave a shrug. "It'll make life easier. What about you—are you staying on?"

"It depends." Laird was on his guard. Any time Harry Novak made moderately friendly noises, there had to be a reason. Turning, he thumbed towards the deserted stretch of quay. "Things seem quiet."

"For the moment." Novak gave a quick, defensive scowl. "We worked damned late last night getting that load of wine ashore, all of it. Then Raynal said there might be a problem with trucks today, so—well, we're taking a break, spending the time havin' another look at the ship as a whole."

"Worried?" asked Laird in a casual voice.

"About what?" Novak stiffened at the suggestion, and his voice took on a blustering note. "I'm not singing or dancing about this one, mister. But I know what I'm doin'—"

"I hope so," said Laird. "You're the expert. It's your reputation on the line, not mine."

"Right." Novak moistened his lips and breathed out noisily. "Look, it's agreed, isn't it? I do some additional survey work and then—well, your damned bosses decide." He swallowed as Laird didn't answer, and tried again. "Maybe there are a couple of problems, but that's how it goes on a salvage job. You should know that."

"I hadn't forgotten," said Laird. "I learned a lot when I sailed with you, Novak. Most of it easy to remember."

They parted on that, Harry Novak stalking off towards the village without a backward glance, Laird going down the stone steps to the waiting launch. As soon as Laird was aboard, the seaman who had been lounging at the controls cast off her mooring line and set the little boat moving.

They cleared the harbour, pitching in the moderate swell, an occasional curtain of spray hissing aboard. The seaman, young, red-haired and chewing gum, grinned each time it happened but said little. Keeping a grip of the cockpit rail, watching the steady, almost sullen pattern of the water and the way it had changed in colour to a shade like steel-grey, Laird knew Harry Novak was right about one thing. That storm was on the way.

When it came, the reef of rock farther out might protect the *Sea*

Robin as it probably protected most of the wide sweep of bay around San Ferdinand. But anything might happen.

A brighter flash of silver caught his eye as the launch dipped in another swell. It was another dead fish, floating belly-up just under the surface. He saw a couple more a moment later.

"Plenty more like them," the young seaman remarked, noting his interest and raising his voice above the engine's noisy throb. "Wouldn't like to be a fish. Not much of a life, is it?"

Laird smiled dutifully. They'd sink down soon enough, food for the always waiting, always hungry bottom life.

Curious, he kept watching, but there were no others. Then the launch was nearing the two salvage tugs and the sunken cargo ship, the swell still creaming in across her almost submerged deck, and making a mock island of her superstructure. He grabbed at a companionway ladder as the launch drifted in against the *Beroe* and climbed aboard as the small boat swung away. One of the salvage tug's crew gave him a helping hand as he reached the deck.

"I'm out to see Jingles Reilly," said Laird. "How is he?"

"Not good." The man grimaced in a way that showed a mouthful of bad teeth. "You'd better talk to the skipper."

Laird followed him along the deck, noting that the only men who seemed to be working were lashing down gear and rigging storm lines. Things appeared to be the same over on the *Scomber*. Neither salvage tug was taking chances.

Captain Weller was in his cabin, located under the salvage tug's bridge. Laird knocked on the door and a shout invited him in. Weller raised a mildly surprised eyebrow, then nodded a greeting.

"Good to see you, Laird." He wasn't alone. A slim, small man in a dark suit and white open-necked shirt was standing near him. "Out to find out about Jingles?"

Laird nodded.

"This is Dr. Mendes, from San Ferdinand." Weller completed the introductions, then added sombrely, "He reckons we should get Jingles ashore."

"I would prefer it." Mendes paused and brightened at Captain Weller's offer of a drink. Then, as Weller produced a bottle of whisky and glasses, he turned to Laird and shrugged. "Your friend is a very ill man, Señor Laird."

"What's wrong with him?" asked Laird bluntly.

"That's what I'm still trying to establish." Mendes paused, made a grateful noise, and accepted his drink from Weller. He sipped it appreciatively while Weller brought over two more, for Laird and himself, then added wryly, "Señor Laird, your friend appears to be suffering from acute food poisoning. But there is the additional complication of an apparent cardiac condition."

"His heart?" Laird threw a surprised glance at Weller. "But he was diving—"

"I didn't know," said Weller indignantly. "I'm a sailor, not a nursemaid."

"He seems to have been unaware of it himself," murmured Mendes. He sipped his drink again and brightened. "At the moment, I have him under sedation. For a start, that reduces the physical strain on the heart—he was suffering the usual symptoms of poisoning, from pain and nausea to faintness and vomiting."

Laird nodded. Several things could be added to that list, from sweating and headaches to blurred vision, then frightening, uncontrollable shivering and twitching.

"What about treatment?"

Mendes pondered briefly, using a finger to scratch the tip of his nose.

"That depends. First, we have to identify the cause—the bacteria or toxin." For a moment, he looked worried. "Of course, that can take time."

"What about other cases, ashore?"

"No. Though I might have expected others." Mendes grimaced. "A few of the young people at the student camp are unwell. I was called there earlier. But their problem is much milder, probably just faulty hygiene." He finished his drink at a gulp and turned to Weller. "Captain, I should go ashore and make the necessary arrangements."

"I'll have a boat ready," agreed Weller. He looked at Laird. "Want to see him before you go? He's sleeping."

They went aft together. Jingles Reilly was in his cabin, lying in his bunk. His face was almost as pale as the sheets, his eyes were closed, and he hardly seemed to be breathing. Mendes checked his pulse, then signalled them out again.

"Slightly steadier, Captain," he said once they were in the companionway. "But *sí*, I will be happier when I get him ashore."

The *Beroe*'s launch was waiting alongside. Captain Weller came with them to the rail and stood there, watching. The moment

Laird and the doctor were aboard, he signalled the man at the helm and the launch snarled away, taking an arrow-straight course towards the harbour.

*

The few minutes in the launch didn't give much opportunity for conversation, and Mendes made it plain he didn't like boat travel. By the time they reached the shelter of the harbour wall, the little doctor looked positively ill.

First up on the quay, he hurried off. Laird followed at a more leisurely pace, and as he reached the top of the steps, a hand touched his arm.

"Señor Laird." Roberto beamed at him. "*Mamá* sent me to find you."

"What's wrong now?" Laird spoke wearily, his emotions still affected by the way he'd seen Jingles Reilly. "Whatever it is—"

"Nothing wrong, Señor Laird." The young Spaniard blinked, his smile fading a little. "There was another telephone call for you, from a Señor Edwards. He said it was *urgente* you called him."

"Nothing more?" Laird was surprised at the message.

"I don't know," admitted Roberto. "*Mamá* took the call."

"All right." Laird twisted a grin. "I didn't mean to bite your head off. Thanks for coming down."

Cheerful again, Roberto ambled off to talk to a group of fishermen while Laird continued on his way. There were two public telephone kiosks just outside the harbour gate. One was out of order, but he got a working tone from the other, fed it some coins, then dialled the consular number in Málaga.

He had to wait before he was put through to Francis Edwards. An occasional truck or car passed along the street, stirring some small life into the oppressive air. In an alleyway opposite, an old woman dressed in black had given up and dozed on a chair in the shade. He stopped watching her to slap at a mosquito that had invaded the kiosk, then heard Edwards come on the line.

"The message I got said this was urgent," Laird told him.

"Not exactly." The plump consular official sounded embarrassed. "But it's a good way of making sure a message is delivered. Uh—are you still interested in your missing engineer?"

"In finding him," agreed Laird. He pressed the receiver closer to his ear as a truck rumbled past. "Why?"

"Something that might be worth following up." Edwards lowered his voice, which didn't help. "But look, I've got to be careful about this. We've already had a moan about you from the Guardia Civil, asking why you're stirring things up again about that poor devil Henderson. There's a Captain Alvarez—"

"I got the same moan, direct from the local horse's mouth," said Laird drily. "What's the 'something'?"

"My contact at the hospital in Marbella came up with this. She—ah—well, she's one of the medical staff and she was asking around." Edwards hesitated again, then took the plunge. "When Constantinos, the first officer, left hospital, he was supposed to go to the airport with Grant, your chief engineer, right? Well, the car that collected Constantinos from hospital was an agency rental job, with a driver."

Laird shaped a silent whistle of interest.

"Which agency?"

"A small one, Garaje Amarilla—someone noticed the name on the doors. It's a filling station, not much more, about two kilometres west of Marbella—that's on your side of the place." Edwards paused hopefully. "Perhaps they could tell you something, eh?"

"It's worth trying," agreed Laird gratefully. "All right, now it's my turn. Have you heard anything about the Spanish government making peeved noises about the *Sea Robin*?"

"No, not yet." Edwards was surprised.

"Looks like you're going to, fairly soon," Laird told him. "Call it a friendly warning."

"Oh God," said Edwards unhappily. "I think I'll apply for leave."

Laird hung up, left the kiosk, and stood thinking about what Edwards had told him. The hire car was a slender lead, and doing anything about it meant another drive to Marbella. But at least it gave him something positive to do.

A first, low rumble of thunder muttered through the air, and he glanced up. There were more black clouds than grey overhead. The storm might still be distant, but when it arrived, San Ferdinand would certainly know about it.

He shrugged and started walking, heading towards the Mercado to collect the Seat. Then a vehicle horn hooted and he heard someone call his name. Adam Warner's ramshackle grey van was parked a short distance ahead, on the other side of the street, and Helen Warner stood in front of it, beckoning.

Crossing over, dodging between two plodding horse-drawn

carts, Laird reached her. Instead of her usual outfit of shirt and shorts, she was wearing a beach dress with a zip front. The zip had worked its way open enough to show most of the bikini top she was wearing beneath.

"Good morning, Andrew." Her smile was warm and friendly as she thumbed towards the van's driving cab. "Someone wants to say thank you. He's fine again."

Piet, the young fair-haired student who had tangled with the sea urchin's spikes, grinned at him through the windshield glass. Laird raised a hand in greeting, then switched his attention back to Helen.

"How about your other patients?" he asked.

"You've heard?"

Laird nodded and almost grinned at the disgust on her face.

"It's like trouble just naturally comes your way," he mused. "What happened this time?"

"They decided to have a party last night." Helen combed a hand through her short fair hair in something like despair. "Eat, drink and be-merry style—and this morning most of them think they're dying." She paused as another low rumble of thunder sounded overhead, and managed a chuckle. "With our kind of luck, next thing is we'll be flooded out by this lot. Who told you about it?"

"Dr. Mendes," explained Laird. He didn't expand on why. "Where is your brother?"

"Dying like the rest," she said. "Apart from two of the girls and Piet, they're all lying around. Dr. Mendes said food poisoning, lined them up for an injection, and they're on a diet with plenty of liquid—liquid meaning no alcohol."

Laird nodded. "How did you escape it?"

"Four of us did. Piet was still feeling miserable, and stayed in his tent. The girls had an invite to a dance at a hotel along the coast—I took them in the van, then hung around like Mother Hen." Her eyes twinkled. "Mind you, I got a couple of interesting propositions. Another time, I'll maybe go on my own."

"Any idea what laid them low?"

She shook her head. "Dr. Mendes asked, but gave up. They brought in their own food—and drink. They did their own cooking." Pausing, she glanced up at the menacing sky. "I'm in to pick up some bland-diet stuff. Look, say hello to Piet, will you? He'd like it."

Laird watched as she hurried into the nearest shop, then he opened the cab door and slid in beside Piet.

"Hi." The fair-haired student gave a shy grin. "Uh—thanks for yesterday. The others told me what you did. They—well, I'm glad you were around."

"Next time you're diving, remember the old saying: Look before you grab," advised Laird.

"I will." Piet nodded earnestly. He shook his head with something close to awe. "I got one hell of a fright when it happened, believe me."

Laird grinned. But he had Piet to himself and there was no sense in wasting the chance.

"Maybe you can help me," he said slowly. "And no comebacks afterwards—that's a promise."

"Is it about the *Sea Robin*?" Piet hesitated and looked worried. "That's finished. We promised Adam Warner—"

"You could be helping him," said Laird. He leaned back against the cab seat, watching the fair-haired student. "You want to do that, don't you?"

Piet bit his lip, then gave a reluctant nod.

"You've been out at the ship a few times. You collected what we'll call souvenirs." Laird made it a statement of fact. "But I think something else happened on one of your late-night pirate trips—something Warner doesn't know about, but could be the reason the *Sea Robin*'s owners have it in for him." He paused. "I want to hear about it."

"It wasn't much." Piet squirmed in his seat and looked away. Outside, another roll of nearing thunder rumbled through the air. "Nobody got hurt or—well, anything."

"Right," encouraged Laird. "Go on."

Piet shrugged. "Three of us sneaked out of camp about two in the morning. We—well, we had scuba gear and we took one of the rubber boats. We motored part of the way, paddled in the rest, went aboard the ship and—uh—"

"Prowled," said Laird deliberately. "Did you get much?"

"Some reasonable gear," admitted Piet. "We had it in a sack. Bits and pieces—"

Laird shook his head. "I don't need a catalogue. Then what?"

"We started back, paddling again." Piet chewed his lip. "It was dark that night, really dark. Eventually, we started up the outboard engine—and it was just after that we saw the other boat."

"What other boat?" demanded Laird, frowning.

"A launch," said Piet. "She hadn't any lights and she was almost on top of us." He rubbed a hand along the van's steering wheel and sighed. "We hadn't expected the shipping people to run any kind of patrol further out. But there she was, creeping along." He stopped and looked at Laird, earnestly. "Look, you meant it—no comebacks?"

"I meant it," agreed Laird, holding on to his patience.

"Okay." Piet began to enjoy telling his story. "They put a spotlight on us, just as we dumped the sack over the side to get rid of—well, the evidence. But—uh—we had a couple of emergency flares with us, I didn't feel like being caught, and they were close, really close." He grinned sheepishly. "So I pulled the igniter tab on one and heaved it into their boat."

Laird stared at him. "You know what could have happened?"

"When I thought about it, afterwards," admitted the youngster. "But it worked, scared the hell out of them when it ignited. And we got away."

Lips pursed, Laird nodded. "You get a good look at them?"

"Like they were floodlit. There were two of them—the Spaniard who drives the white Mercedes and one of Cuvier's staff. The young dark-haired one—I think he's called Hans."

"Hans Botha." Laird pictured the sudden, blinding glare of the flare at such close quarters and winced. "Anything else?"

"Only one thing." Piet gave a puzzled frown. "Either they didn't report it to the local Guardia or they just didn't know who we were in our scuba gear. We didn't hear anything afterwards." He looked sideways at Laird. "The flare went out quickly enough. They must have kicked it overboard and the boat couldn't have been more than singed. But we certainly scared them, almost as much as they scared us. The last I saw before that, Botha was starting to heave a life-raft over the side."

"A damned-fool stunt like that could have killed them," said Laird, and saw the grin fade from Piet's face. "When was this?"

"A few nights back," said Piet vaguely. "But—"

"When?" Not totally certain why, Laird took a wild stab. "The same night the first Clanmore man was in that accident?"

Piet nodded.

The same night, but some hours later, Andrew Laird wanted to make sense of it, quite apart from the brash way the students had refused to be scared off by the experience. He heard Piet clear his throat, but ignored the youngster, trying to think.

The cab door swung open.

"That's done." Helen Warner was back, two grocery bags in her arms. The smile on her lips faded a little as she saw Piet's expression, and she looked at Laird. "Something wrong, Andrew?"

"No." Laird got out of the cab and helped her aboard with her shopping. "Everything's fine. Right, Piet?"

He nodded uneasily and started the engine.

"Everything looks that way," said Helen sarcastically. She frowned up at the heavy black clouds. "And that lot is getting too near for comfort. Time we got back, Piet." She glanced at Laird. "Any chance you'll be out at the camp later?"

"To visit the sick?"

"They're not worth sympathy," she said firmly. "But you could rescue me for a change."

"I might do that," Laird agreed. Closing the cab door, he stood back as Piet slammed the van into gear.

The rusty vehicle jerked on its way with a tyre-spinning squeal of rubber, its driver obviously glad to get away.

*

A first drop of rain landed on Andrew Laird's cheek as he reached the Hostal Mercado and walked round the back to where the Seat was parked. Other drops began appearing on the windshield glass as he got aboard and set the little car moving.

By the time he was out of San Ferdinand and on the road for Marbella, the rain was coming down steadily and he switched on headlamps and wipers. The rain became worse. The roadside verges rapidly became so much liquid red mud, churned by wheels that went through it, then spattering over any vehicle within reach.

Laird drove carefully, letting other traffic on the road set the pace. Inland, some of the mountain peaks had vanished into the blackness of the moving clouds. Occasionally, they showed again in sharp relief as a fresh fork of lightning stabbed between them, to be followed by yet another drumroll of thunder. Here and there, rainwater from the hills poured across the road in angry, shallow torrents.

Part of his mind stayed occupied with what Piet had told him, some of his thoughts were on how to tackle his approach when he got to the filling station. The kilometres clicked past, the rain kept falling and then, suddenly, he saw a lonely little building on ahead.

A couple of minutes later, he drove into the Garaje Amarilla. Like its name, it was painted yellow and amounted to a shabby forecourt area with some fuel pumps, a small shop and office combined, and what looked like a repair bay. Two yellow hire cars with "Garaje Amarilla" on their doors were parked to one side, rain bouncing from their roofs.

Stopping the Seat near the shop door, Laird saw the only occupant was a girl who was sitting at a cash desk. She was reading a book. Switching off the engine, Laird made a dive through the downpour and into the shop. As he closed the door behind him, the girl looked up, smiled, then went back to her book as he turned to the merchandise shelves.

His shirt had been soaked in the brief dash from the car and the shop stock included a cheap line in waterproof jackets. The only one roughly his size was a sickly shade of green, but he took it over to the cash desk.

He paid for the jacket, waited until she had rung up the sale, then beckoned her back again. She had a chubby, pretty face, wore an oil-company sweater tucked into denim trousers, and looked still in her teens.

"Do you handle the hire-car bookings?" asked Laird.

"Sí." She reached for a ledger and pencil. "For when, señor?"

"No, it's not for me." He grinned at her. "A friend of mine had a booking with you a few days ago, to the airport at Málaga. Do you remember it?"

"I think so." She checked the ledger, then nodded. "Señor Constantinos—from the hospital to the airport. Is that the one?"

Laird nodded. "Was there another passenger with him?"

She looked at the ledger again. "No, señor; why?"

"You're sure?" Laird shaped a puzzled frown. "He telephoned me. There was some luggage mix-up at the airport. I thought—"

"No, señor." She shook her head firmly. "It would be listed." A trace of amusement entered her voice. "Anyway, I think I would remember. Things are quiet here."

"Maybe I should talk to the driver," said Laird. "Where can I find him?"

"Jaime took the hire." Going over to the cash desk, she pressed a call button. "He is our mechanic, señor."

Laird waited, then heard another door at the rear open and

turned. The man in mechanic's overalls who had come through from the repair bay froze a few steps inside the shop and stared at him, his mouth dropping open.

"Jaime—" began the girl, then stopped in surprise.

The mechanic, tall, thin, dark-haired and in his twenties, was already backing away. There was a deep, badly swollen cut on one side of his cheek, a cut the exact size and shape of Laird's belt buckle.

"Jaime—" tried the girl again, in a frightened voice.

Laird started towards him, ducked as the man grabbed a can of oil and threw it at his head, then made a pounce to close the gap. Swearing, the mechanic took another quick step back, seized a display stand, and toppled it between them. Tins of polish, packaged spares and a confusion of other items spilled loose as the stand crashed down.

Turning, the man ran back into the repair bay while Laird, caught up in the stand, struggled free and pushed it aside. The girl was screaming as he ran through the doorway and looked around the workshop. It was empty, but there was another open door at the far end. He heard a motor cycle start up, then the howl of its engine as it drove away.

Laird got to the other door in time to see the machine, rider crouching low in the saddle, making a bouncing turn as it reached the road. Then it was gone, disappearing into the rain, the sound of its engine drowned by another roll of thunder.

Sighing, he went back through the repair bay to find the connecting door to the shop was closed and locked. He was still clutching the waterproof jacket and, pulling it on, he went out into the rain and tried the forecourt door. It was locked. He could see the girl standing beside the cash desk, staring at him, and holding a heavy spanner in one hand.

Waving goodbye to her through the glass, Laird went back to his car and got aboard. The motor cycle had headed off in the direction of Marbella, but he knew heading in that direction would be a waste of time.

There was a pack of cigarettes in the car, left there from the previous night. Laird lit one, sat for a moment just listening to the rain beating on the thin metal roof, then keyed the ignition switch. The Seat's engine was damp and spluttered for a moment before it came to life. The wipers battling to keep the windshield clear, he turned the car and started on the road back towards San Ferdinand.

There was more traffic than before, in both directions—headlights that appeared out of the murk, shapes that caused miniature bow waves as they hit flooded sections of the highway. But, though lightning still scorched down and the thunder seemed to be banging exactly overhead, the rain did seem to be gradually easing.

Perhaps that was why it happened. Cruising along behind a car and caravan trailer outfit that had Dutch registration plates, Laird noticed a truck coming towards them, heading in the opposite direction. Suddenly, another set of headlights appeared, overtaking the truck. It was a car, accelerating hard.

Too hard. Moments later, the car was sliding, aquaplaning on the wet road surface, out of control, heading for the Dutch trailer outfit. Brake lights flared as the Dutchman saw the danger, then the trailer outfit was also skidding, beginning to jack-knife—and it was Laird's turn.

He heard the impact as the two cars ahead collided, saw the other spin away, and wrenched hard at the steering wheel as the rear of the trailer caravan swung like a wild pendulum.

The Seat almost made it clear—but not enough. There was a rasp of metal as it grazed the rear of the caravan, then the little car pitched and skidded to a shuddering halt.

The first car, the one which had caused it all, had overturned. Other traffic had halted, and Laird joined the drivers who ran through the rain to rescue the couple aboard. They were young, bruised, cut by broken glass, but otherwise unhurt. The Dutch driver had a wife with a badly cut forehead and two children who were howling in the back seat.

At that, they'd been lucky. The front of the Dutch car was badly stove in, the rear of the trailer caravan now boasted a gaping hole.

The road was blocked. As more traffic came to a halt, two gendarmes on motor cycles weaved through, stopped, dismounted, and came over.

Laird turned away and splashed back to look at the Seat. Some metal had crumpled, a tyre had blown, but with luck the car would still drive. Swearing, rain running down the back of his neck, he went round to fetch the spare wheel.

The trunk was unlocked but the handle was stiff. He gave it a wrench, the lid opened, and he stared at what was inside, almost retching, forgetting the rain, the crash, everything else.

Sergeant Ramón García lay dead in the tiny space, his tricorn hat laid neatly beside him, blank eyes staring out at Laird, a thin patch of dried blood staining the front of his uniform tunic.

Laird heard a gasp behind him, then a frantic shout. He turned, saw a lorry driver, saw the man's accusing face, then the two gendarmes running over. One was hauling out his pistol as he came.

Sighing, Laird raised his hands and waited for them.

CHAPTER 6

The police station cell at Marbella was small, with concrete walls and a smell of stale human sweat. It had a steel door with a centre peep-hole and the weak glow of a single overhead light was protected by armoured glass. The sole item of furniture was a wire-frame bunk.

They had taken his shoes, his belt and anything in his pockets. They had let him keep his watch. He had fresh bruises in two or three places—police anywhere were liable to be that way when one of their own had been killed and they had a prisoner.

But once he was in the cell, he was left alone. Occasionally, he could hear a door bang outside in the corridor. A protesting drunk was brought in. Another prisoner shouted and roared until he was hauled away and apparently didn't come back. A few times, the spyhole in the door slid open, and an eye peered at him briefly.

Graffiti had been scrawled here and there on the concrete walls. Most of it was in Spanish, but not all—and one previous English-speaking occupant had pencilled a few choice Anglo-Saxon obscenities around a carefully drawn copy of the Union Jack. But once Andrew Laird had read them, there was nothing else to do. He sat on the wire-framed bunk, wondering what was happening outside, grimly aware there was nothing he could do to hurry whatever process was under way.

He had been brought in at noon. It was almost three hours later when the cell door was unlocked and swung open. A stolid-faced guard came in and dropped Laird's shoes at his feet, while another stayed filling the doorway.

"Mover." The first man thumbed at the doorway as Laird pulled on his shoes.

He went between them out of the cell block and along a corridor, then up a stairway to an upper floor. One of the men stopped at a door, knocked, then opened the door and signalled Laird to go in.

He found himself in a plainly furnished office. The storm had passed, bright sunshine was pouring in through an open window, and as the door closed behind him, leaving the guards outside, he realized that two men were already in the room. Laird peered against the glare of the sun, trying to make out faces, then the plumper of the two figures came towards him.

"Good to see you, Laird," said Francis Edwards with awkward geniality. The consular official gave him a quick, moist handshake, then fiddled awkwardly with the edge of his regimental tie. "I trust you've—ah—been reasonably treated?"

"Reasonably," said Laird.

His eyes were on the other man, a stocky, dark-haired individual who wore a civilian suit but who looked as though he would have been much more at home in a uniform. Standing with his back to the window, the stranger gave him a slight nod.

"Ah—of course—" Edwards made a sideways shuffle with his feet and indicated the stranger. "Laird, this is Captain Juan Alvarez of the Guardia Civil. Captain Alvarez is the officer investigating this whole—ah—regrettable matter."

"Very regrettable," said Alvarez drily. He moved from the window, a man with craggy features and skin the colour of teak. He was about forty, with green, animal-like eyes under dark, bushy eyebrows. "Particularly for Sergeant García." He nodded towards two chairs placed in front of his desk. "Sit down, Señor Laird. You too, of course, Señor Edwards."

As they did, the Guardia captain went round and settled behind the desk. Looking at Laird again, he said nothing for a moment, then sighed, opened a drawer, took out an envelope, and slid it across the desk towards Laird.

"Yours," he said curtly.

Laird opened the envelope. Inside lay his belt, his cigarettes and lighter, all the other things that had been taken from him. He glanced quickly at Edwards, then at Alvarez. Alvarez shrugged.

"You are a fortunate man," said Alvarez. "We start with Sergeant García's body found in the trunk of a car you are driving. We learn the cause of death was a stab through the heart with a knife. There are slight traces of blood in your room at the Hostal Mercado—leaving aside a blood-stained shirt and jacket, which are another matter. Then Señora Vegas tells us that a spring-blade knife she noticed in your room this morning is missing." He pursed his lips. "Not good, would you agree?"

"Not good at all," admitted Laird.

"Initial reactions." Edwards quickly cleared his throat. "Totally understandable—"

"Señor Laird, I said you were fortunate." Alvarez hardly seemed to hear them. "First, what kind of a *zonzo* would have behaved the way you did? Then—" For the first time, a twist of humour touched his lips. "—yes, you have a surprising number of friends. A procession of them give you an alibi for the whole morning. I have also been plagued by a priest, then, even, eventually, by Señora Vegas—and that Mamá Isabel is a formidable lady. When even the relatives of the dead are on your side, you are in a position of some strength."

"And?" Laird felt some of the tension inside him begin to fade, but waited.

"After you left the Mercado this morning, there was a time when Señora Vegas was there alone, in the kitchen. The Mercado has a rear fire-escape door, seldom used—or locked." Alvarez shrugged. "The *médicos* cannot give an exact time of death, but the possibilities fit. I believe Sergeant García, for his own reasons, made what he hoped would be a secret visit to your room. But he discovered someone else doing the same and was killed—perhaps with the knife which you left there."

"Then his body was sneaked out that back way," suggested Edwards helpfully.

"And your car was there. Perhaps the idea appealed to his killer. It was certainly convenient." Alvarez tapped a finger on his desk top, frowning. "It leaves gaps, but it provides a starting point." He paused. "So you are free to go, Señor Laird. But I would prefer if you stayed and we talked about some of your other activities here. I've already discussed them with Señor Edwards."

"I've explained that—ah—my involvement has been limited."

Edwards shifted uncomfortably in his chair. "Naturally, any consular assistance wasn't intended to cause difficulties for the Spanish authorities."

"Naturally." Alvarez made a mock bow in his direction, but his eyes were hard. "But I wonder about Señor Laird."

"Maybe I didn't have enough to make anyone listen," said Laird quietly, still getting used to a sense of relief.

"I think you have now." Alvarez glanced deliberately at Edwards. "Thank you for your help in this."

"A pleasure." Edwards took his cue and rose eagerly. "You know how to contact me, of course—at any time."

He left. As the door of the office closed again, Alvarez sighed with undisguised relief. Opening another of the desk drawers, he produced a bottle of brandy and two chipped glasses, poured a stiff measure into each glass, and pushed one across to Laird.

"Suppose I begin." He nursed his glass, watching Laird over the rim, not touching it with his lips. "First, something that may interest you. The Cuvier Corporation people have left San Ferdinand."

"All of them?" Laird didn't try to hide his surprise. "But—"

"All of them. A little earlier than expected." Alvarez shrugged. "They left before noon. The staff at the Casa Turo were told that a flight schedule had been rearranged." He tasted the brandy, his eyes still watching Laird. "I have heard from Mamá Isabel about some photographs. Father Sebastian has told me about a journey you made together, and what you saw. In between there were other things—including a telephone conversation with your London office."

"And you want my version of it all." Laird nodded.

The time he'd spent waiting in the police station cell had given him a chance to assemble what he knew in some kind of order. Moistening his lips with the brandy, taking another occasional sip as he talked, he went through it from the beginning, sticking to basics except where an aspect seemed to need more detail.

Even listening to his own words, he knew some of it sounded flimsy. But other parts were different, did matter—and he saw that Captain Juan Alvarez seemed to feel the same. Occasionally the Guardia Civil officer interrupted with a question. Mostly he stayed quiet, scribbling an occasional note on a pad beside him. At the finish, Alvarez sucked his lips, then silently topped up both glasses from the brandy bottle.

"*Gracias,* Señor Laird." He looked briefly at his notes, then shook his head in almost bewildered fashion. "All right, I could say what still matters most to me is that one of my men has been murdered. But there is something wrong here—something very wrong. Yet if you had come to me earlier—"

"I'd have been wasting my time?"

Alvarez winced, then nodded reluctantly. He turned to his notepad again, flicking through the pages, then looked up.

"I spoke to a man called Morris at your London office. He was very anxious to contact you about Grant, the chief engineer on the *Sea Robin*. You sent them photographs?"

"Yes."

"It seems he has other names. Two at least, apart from his own—which is not Grant," said Alvarez wryly. "He also has an unfortunate history of being aboard ships that happen to sink. In fact, he might be called an expert in the matter—he served a five-year sentence on the last occasion." His manner sobered. "Your friend Henderson was involved in the claim investigation after one of the earlier sinkings, when nothing could be proved. It was a number of years ago, but—" He left it there.

It was Laird's turn to sit silent. If Charlie Henderson had thought he recognized Grant, if Grant had also recognized Henderson, then it could certainly have been a motive for murder.

Provided the background stakes were high enough, and that was where any neat style of package collapsed. The Cuvier Corporation might have money problems of some kind, but Janos Cuvier had pressed consistently for the *Sea Robin* to be salvaged.

Or was it the *Sea Robin* that mattered? Could it be something aboard the ship that was important, part of her cargo? He bit his lip, thinking of the convoys of trucks arriving and departing from San Ferdinand harbour.

"Señor Laird?" Alvarez was waiting, puzzled.

"A notion. Something I'll need to think about." Laird forced his mind back to more immediate realities. "Did Osgood Morris say anything about the Cuvier companies?"

"No." Alvarez showed faint amusement. "He was more immediately concerned with your situation. By then, I was able to reassure him."

"How long ago?" asked Laird suspiciously.

"About an hour or so," said Alvarez. He gestured the matter aside. "*Sí*, and now I have a number of things to do, to think about.

This driver Vicente, for instance—I have an idea we know him. What will you do? Go back to San Ferdinand?"

Laird nodded.

"Then I will stay in touch. We are going to need your help."

Rising, Laird picked up the envelope with his possessions and Alvarez went with him to the office door. One of the guards was still waiting in the corridor.

"He will show you the way out," said Alvarez softly. "Otherwise it might be difficult."

*

When he had arrived, Andrew Laird had been bundled in through a rear courtyard. He left by the main street door, his escort giving a formal salute as they parted.

He stood in the warm, bright sunlight, letting it soak into him, enjoying the sheer luxury of being free again. Ignoring the stares of passers-by, he buckled his belt round his waist, put the rest of the envelope's contents back in his pockets, and tossed the envelope into a wastebasket.

A car horn hooted impatiently from across the street. He looked, then stared in disbelief before he crossed over. The car was an old Ford. The man behind the wheel was Harry Novak, who leaned over to open the passenger door.

"Get in," said Novak, his scarred face scowling. "I was gettin' to think they'd changed their minds about turning you loose."

"What the hell are you doing here?" asked Laird, climbing aboard and closing the door again.

"Protecting my interests," said the tug master. "Clanmore is footing my bill, right? I reckoned the cops would hold on to your car and someone would have to collect you. Where are we heading? San Ferdinand?"

Laird nodded and settled back, watching Novak start the car and set it moving.

"Getting worried, Novak?" he asked softly.

"Till I get paid, I always worry." Novak concentrated on driving for a moment or two, then gave him a sideways glance. "What are you hinting at this time?"

"The way Cuvier has pulled out," said Laird. "It might make a difference to the way you should see things."

"Should it?" Novak gave an evasive shrug and horn-blasted a

weaving motor-cyclist from their path. "I've got some bad news for you about Jingles Reilly."

Laird froze, with a cigarette halfway to his mouth.

"Is he worse?"

"Worse as you can get," said Novak brutally. "He's dead—he snuffed out in the ambulance soon after they got him ashore. That local quack Mendes says it was heart failure." He shrugged. "Bad luck. Jingles was like you—a soft touch. But he knew the salvage game."

"Yes." Laird had a sudden mental picture of Jingles Reilly, not the man he'd seen lying ill, but the lively individual he'd sailed with. Yet he knew very little about him. "What about family?"

"He had a wife once, somewhere." Novak grunted his disinterest. "But he was just a *Beroe* man when he died—Captain Weller will arrange things. You know Weller, he'll make a meal of it."

They drove on in silence for a spell, clear of Marbella, out past the yellow filling station. The road was still steaming dry after the storm, streaked here and there with deposits of mud or pools of water.

"What's goin' on?" asked Novak suddenly. He moistened his lips. "You know what I mean, Laird—what's it all about?"

"So far, two killings—Charlie Henderson and Sergeant García," Laird told him. He saw Novak's eyes widen, noticed the way the man's grip tightened on the steering wheel. "Maybe you know as much about the rest of it as I do."

"Me?" Novak quickly shook his head. "I've been doin' my job, that's all."

"What about the way you've been doing it?" suggested Laird.

"Now look—" Novak jerked round, sending the car into a swerve, and swore as he corrected it again. "—you show my reports to anybody, right? You get anyone you want to check that hull, and you know what you'll get?"

"Yes." Laird had no illusions. Harry Novak's survey reports would be found accurate, as far as they went. "I could bet they'd go along with you—as far as that takes them."

"Well then?" Novak was triumphant.

"Listen to me," said Laird wearily. "The *Sea Robin* is trouble—real trouble. If you did any kind of private deal with Cuvier, it still might be the kind that could get lost in the paperwork. Might—if it helped us."

Novak swallowed, then his mouth closed like a trap, his scarred face became a hard, expressionless mask.

Laird settled back and closed his eyes, listening to the car travel on. He knew Harry Novak was worried. But whatever Novak decided, it would be in his own time.

*

They reached San Ferdinand a little after five and Novak dropped him outside the Hostal Mercado, then drove off again without a word of goodbye.

Laird had been uncertain about what kind of welcome, if any, he would get. When he walked in, he still wasn't sure. The bar was empty, a handwritten sign on the counter said it was closed for the day, and every table had been cleared.

He heard a slow shuffle of feet, and Mamá Isabel came towards him. She still wore her hat, but otherwise she was dressed in black. Her broad face showed no hostility, but her sharp little eyes were slightly puffy round the lids.

"Señor Laird." She gave a fractional nod. "Captain Alvarez telephoned. I—I have had to give you another room. The Guardia have sealed the one you were in. They—" She stopped and shrugged.

"I'm sorry. About all that happened," said Laird.

"*Gracias.*" Her mouth tightened for a moment. "Ramón García was my cousin. In some ways he was a fool, but there were times when he meant well." She straightened her shoulders. "Father Sebastian is here. He wants to see you."

Laird followed her behind the bar and into a small sitting room. The priest rose from a chair. In the background, Roberto's chubby face gave a wary greeting.

"They listened to you?" Father Sebastian gripped Laird's hand in his own.

"They did." Laird nodded.

"Good." The priest showed his relief. "I told them what I could. *Sí* . . . and I have tried to explain a little of it to Mamá Isabel, to help her understand."

She had gone past them, over to Roberto, and mother and son exchanged a glance but said nothing. Father Sebastian smiled at them.

"I have told Roberto that nothing he did with his camera caused any of this," added Father Sebastian. "You would agree?"

"Totally," said Laird, knowing it mattered. "But those photographs are going to help find the men who killed his uncle."

Roberto looked happier. He glanced at Mamá Isabel, and squeezed her arm. Satisfied, Father Sebastian glanced at his old-fashioned wrist-watch.

"I must go," he apologized. "I have an appointment—a christening to arrange." Picking up his crash helmet from a table, he started for the door.

"Could you give me a lift?" asked Laird. "It's local."

The priest nodded and they went out together.

Father Sebastian's motor cycle was parked at the side of the Mercado. An idea stirred in Laird's mind as they reached it.

"How much do you know about the local two-wheeled world?" he asked.

The priest blinked. "A reasonable amount, I suppose. Enthusiasts cling together. But—"

"I'm interested in a little biker team probably based around Marbella. About all I know is that one of them is named Jaime." Laird described the rider, and the rest of what had happened.

"Some of the wild ones." Father Sebastian grimaced. "I can ask. The wound on this Jaime's face should help, though if the Guardia Civil are also looking for him it will not be easy." He paused. "Have you heard the other thing that happened here? One of the men on the salvage tugs has died."

"Yes, I knew him," said Laird.

"Dr. Mendes said it was not unexpected. A great pity." Father Sebastian got aboard the Suzuki. "Where am I taking you?"

"To Adam Warner's student camp."

"Ah." A smile touched the priest's lips.

"Meaning?" asked Laird.

"His sister has been at the Mercado several times today, ever since she heard you were arrested," murmured Father Sebastian. "When she heard you had been released—sí, she was very happy. Or have you another reason?"

"Yes," said Laird shortly, "I have."

It was easy to think of Helen Warner, but when he did, then suddenly, Laura's face was there too. What had happened to her? How much did she really know about Janos Cuvier's plotting? How much, if at all, was she part of it?

But he did have another reason. He got on the pillion seat as the Suzuki started up.

*

Father Sebastian dropped him at the roadside within sight of the student camp. Then, as the priest's motor cycle buzzed away, Laird walked the rest of the distance. The rough ground was still muddy in patches, some of the sparse grass had been flattened by the thunderstorm's downpour, but the camp seemed intact.

He'd been seen. A girl, hanging out bedding beside one of the tents, waved, then called. Helen Warner emerged from another tent, saw him, and almost ran to meet him.

"So they did see sense—" A relief on her tanned face, she hugged him, then stood back, smiling. "You had a lot of people worried."

"Including me," admitted Laird. She looked tired behind her smile. Her beach dress was grubby and crumpled and her legs showed traces of dried mud. Whatever it had been like here during the storm, Helen Warner hadn't had it easy. Instinctively, he reached out and brushed a stray lock of hair back from her forehead. "How are things with your invalids?"

"Not much change." She shook her head, a trace of worry in her eyes. "But I suppose it's still their own damned fault." She hesitated. "About Sergeant García—Andrew, what did happen? Do they know yet?"

"No. Not for sure."

She bit her lip. "Does it go back to the *Sea Robin*? Things you've said, things I heard this afternoon—"

He nodded. "It looks that way. That's why I'm here. I want to talk to Piet."

"Piet?" Helen showed her surprise. "Why?"

"Something he told me didn't make much sense before." Laird shrugged. "It might now—I'm not sure. Where is he?"

"Down at the beach. I gave him a load of dishes to wash." She glanced back at the tents. "I'd come with you, but—"

"No need," Laird assured her. "How's Adam?"

"As sick as the rest, but twice as sorry for himself," she said. "He may be my brother, but I'm running out of sympathy for him."

Laird grinned and left her.

Following one of the narrow, well-worn tracks through the scrub, he reached the beach. The storm had flooded most of the trenches Warner's students had dug in the coarse mixture of sand and shingle, some had collapsed, a lot of work had obviously gone to waste. Piet was crouching ankle-deep at the water's edge, a hamper of dishes on the sand behind him. He gave the plate in his hand a final rinse in an incoming wave, then turned, saw Laird, and came over.

"How was jail?" he asked cheekily.

"I don't recommend it." Hands in his trouser pockets, Laird considered the fair-haired student for a moment. "I need your help, Piet. For real."

"All right." Piet eyed him with a trace of doubt. "But doing what?"

"That story you told me, about the launch you met on your way back from the *Sea Robin*." Laird paused. "Could you take a boat back again—to exactly where it happened?"

"Now? In daylight?" Piet stared at him. "Why?"

"Could you? Yes or no?"

Fingering the plate he was holding, Piet turned and frowned out at the sea. He looked first to where the *Sea Robin* lay off-shore, only one of the salvage tugs beside her for the moment. Then, lips moving silently, his frown deepening, he looked along the coast in both directions.

"I think so," he said slowly. "It was at night, but we did line up a couple of marks on shore." He shrugged. "We had an idea about going back out to get the stuff we dumped. Then it didn't seem so clever." He tried again. "But—"

"You said the men in the launch were heaving a life-raft over the side." Laird let the words sink home. "Maybe it wasn't a life-raft. Maybe they had something of their own to hide."

"And you want to find out?" Piet's eyes widened in understanding. Suddenly, he sent the plate in his hand spinning out into the water, and chuckled as it sank. "You're on."

*

They set off from the shore aboard one of the camp's rubber dinghies. The outboard motor at her stern rasping busily, the little boat pushed steadily through the light swell, with Piet steering. Squatting on the damp rubber floor in front of him, Laird examined the set of scuba breathing gear he'd borrowed from the camp's equipment. The single air tank was almost full, the gear was similar enough to equipment he'd used.

Laird eyed it wryly. Piet had offered to go down. But it still wasn't much more than twenty-four hours since the young Dutchman had been dragged ashore unconscious from his last adventure. If he had thought it out more carefully, he might have asked for divers from the tugs. But that would have meant explaining too much about very little.

Several minutes later, Piet eased the outboard's throttle almost all the way back and the dinghy slowed to little more than a crawl. He looked around yet again, checking his position, and gave a satisfied grunt.

"About here—I think," he said. Then he asked doubtfully, "You're sure you'll be okay?"

Stripped to his underpants, the scuba harness clipped over his shoulders, the cold metal of the air cylinder rubbing his back, Laird nodded. The adhesive dressing over the cut on his arm was coming loose, but there was nothing he could do about that. He flexed his arm muscles experimentally, and the long tattoo marks rippled with movement.

"Ready?" asked Piet.

"Ready."

The dinghy was almost drifting, swaying with the swell. Pulling down the face mask, Laird slipped over the side. Then he duck-dived and went swimming down, regulator valve clicking steadily, a plume of bubbles marking his progress.

The water was pleasantly warm, Mediterranean-clear. As it began to lose its brightness and filter to a pale blue, he saw a squadron of slow-moving, almost transparent jellyfish pulsing ahead of him, long, thin, whip-like tentacles trailing behind them. Small, brightly coloured fish darted everywhere.

A warning pain began building up behind his eyes. He thought, then remembered, and forced air up from his mouth into the face-piece area. Pressure equalized, the pain faded, and he resumed the basic discipline of regular breathing and an unhurried, kicking crawl-beat.

Piet had reckoned they were in about sixty feet of water, and his estimate could hardly have been more accurate. The depth gauge strapped to Laird's wrist was quivering just past that mark when he touched the bottom ooze.

Pausing, letting the fine mist of disturbed sand settle, he looked around. The bottom was a flat underwater plain, littered with boulders, an occasional patch of dark-green weed swaying as it was teased by some undersea current. A whole school of the same tiny, multi-coloured fish flickered past, and farther out, at the limit of his visibility, something much bigger, grey and powerful, moved lazily.

Watching until it disappeared, Laird felt suddenly glad of the diving knife Piet had insisted he strap to one leg. Sixty feet of depth was pretty well shallow-water diving. But it was deep enough for there to be no guarantee that the natives were friendly.

He set to work, taking a specially thick patch of weed as his centre point, swimming out from there just a few feet above the bottom ooze. Gradually, he let the circle widen.

He saw boulders and fish, more wavering banks of weed, and knew a heart-stopping moment when he passed over a giant black snake that turned out to be an old, abandoned trawl warp. There were traces of other man-made litter, including an old car tyre and a metal bed-end.

But nothing more.

Trying to curb his disappointment, he kicked for the surface, broke water a short distance from the boat, and spat out his mouthpiece.

"No luck?" asked Piet.

"Nothing." Laird rested his arms on the rubber hull and shook his head. "Are you sure you've got it right?"

Piet nodded. "Except—well, maybe we should be a shade east of here."

"Thanks," said Laird sarcastically.

He let the boat tow him over, then went down again, to the same underwater desert with its patches of weed and occasional rocks.

This time, he tried something different. It amounted to his own grid pattern, a methodical progression, with each leg lasting for as long as it took him to count from one to a hundred.

Even at that, he almost missed it. The bag was a pale canvas, almost invisible against the sand until he was swimming over it. Laird sank down beside it, opened the mouth of the bag, let a couple of tiny fish swim a frantic escape, then grinned to himself as he saw the collection of ship's fittings packed inside.

Piet's part of the story was true.

It was the encouragement he had needed. Laird began swimming again over the flat underwater landscape, the clicking of his demand valve no longer a monotony, his senses sharpened by a feeling he had to be right.

The sail-like shape of a giant ray exploded up from the ooze and made a quick, flapping escape as he approached. He saw more fish, glimpsed what could have been the weed-encrusted remains of a wreck, then swore under his breath and tensed, his crawl-beat kick slowing.

The same grey shape he had seen earlier was back, but nearer. The shark was swimming in slow deliberate circles round what looked like a clump of dark weed.

But it had sensed it had company. The circling ended, the grey body came barrelling round and swam towards Laird. Then it veered away and circled.

Somewhere, sometime, it had been injured. He saw the great scar that began close to its head and ran along its side. But it was still big, formidable and—erratic. Laird watched as it circled again. He had the diving knife ready, but this shark moved almost awkwardly, as if physical injury had left it not just crippled, but nervous.

There was only one way to find out. Twisting round, Laird kicked towards the grey killer shape and began venting extra air from his mask in a frothing gout of bubbles.

The shark reacted in panic to the strange attack. The scarred, lean body almost corkscrewed in a new direction and it fled, leaving Laird a shaken victor.

He gave himself a moment to steady his nerves, then swam over to see what had interested the prowling killer. What had seemed a thin clump of bottom weed was a canvas-wrapped bundle, roughly oblong in shape, the canvas lashed around it by turns of thin rope. It floated upright, tugging gently with the current on a thicker rope which anchored it to what looked like part of an old engine block.

Laird reached for the bundle. The mere touch of his fingers was enough to send it away, to drift back like a slow pendulum. He grabbed again, felt what was under the canvas, and felt a sudden nausea.

But he had to be sure. Steadying the bundle, gripping it with his legs, he used the diving knife to cut away the top binding of thin rope. An edge of canvas came loose and he peeled it back.

The dead man stared out at him. He had been middle-aged, almost plump, balding on top, his sparse hair rippling in the current.

How he had died came down to a bullet-hole between those staring eyes.

But the real horror was something else, something that left Laird feeling he was in the grip of an obscene nightmare.

The dead man was Charlie Henderson. Charlie Henderson who had been burned to death in a car crash. Who had been shipped home in a coffin. Who had been cremated in England the day before.

*

When he surfaced, the rubber boat was some distance away. But Piet saw him, waved, and the little craft turned towards him.

Floating, Laird spat out his mouthpiece and vomited.

Then he waited, let the dinghy come bumping against him, and Piet helped him aboard.

"Any luck?" asked Piet, then saw his face. "What's wrong? I thought I saw a shark—".

Laird shook his head. Tight-lipped, he took the small marker float they'd brought out, checked the line and the claw-shaped weight secured to it, then tossed it over. He watched the float bob in the waves for a moment, then stop drifting.

"What's down there?" persisted Piet.

"Let's get back." Laird moistened his lips, then drew a deep breath. "Just do it, Piet."

The fair-haired student, bewildered, shrugged and obeyed. Throttle wide open, the outboard engine's popping note became a busy rasp and they headed back towards the shore.

They got there, cut the engine, and hauled the light-weight hull up clear of the water. Piet left Laird alone while he got out of the scuba gear and changed back into his clothes. But by then his curiosity became too much.

"Are you going to tell me now?" he pleaded. "I mean—well, I took you out there, didn't I?"

The sea was blue and tranquil, the white crests of wavetops sparkled in the sun. The marker float was out there, though he couldn't see it, and down under that float the nightmare bundle would be swaying to the steady rhythm of the currents. Laird looked at his hands and was surprised to see they were steady again.

"I found a dead man," he said.

Mouth falling open, Piet stared at him.

"That's right," said Laird softly. "Shut your mouth, son." He gave a small, tight smile as Piet obeyed. "Now keep it that way, understand?"

He went up to the camp and over to where Adam Warner's van was parked. The ignition key was in the switch. As he got aboard, he saw one of the girls coming over to investigate.

"Tell Helen I've borrowed your transport," shouted Laird. "I'll be back."

She waved. Starting the vehicle, Laird sent it rattling off towards the road. The nearest telephone he knew about was at the Casa Turo. Captain Alvarez had said all of Janos Cuvier's people had gone, and he was prepared to take a chance on the rest.

It was a short drive. He parked the van outside the villa's front door, rang the doorbell, and the door was opened by the grey-haired major-domo. The man's eyes widened in recognition.

"Where's your telephone?" demanded Laird. *"Prisa . . .* it's important."

"Sí, Señor Laird." Hurriedly, the major-domo led him through to the same large room with the leather armchairs and goatskin rugs where he'd first met Janos Cuvier. But now it had a bare, empty air. Some of the furniture had already been covered in dust-sheets.

The telephone was on a corner table. As the major-domo left him, closing the door, Laird lifted the receiver, dialled the operator, and a few moments later was speaking to the Guardia Civil office in Marbella. Then he had to wait until Alvarez came on the line.

"Hola." Alvarez was friendly but impatient. "Señor Laird, we are pretty busy here. But—"

Laird cut him short. "I've found a body." He paused long enough to let Alvarez splutter. "It's in about sixty feet of water off Adam Warner's student camp. You'll need a boat and divers to bring it up."

"All right." Alvarez recovered fast. "Does this body have a name?"

"Charlie Henderson," said Laird wearily.

Alvarez groaned. "Your Henderson?"

"Yes."

"But—no, not now." Alvarez sounded shaken. "How did he die?"

"It looks like someone shot him," said Laird.

"Gracias." Alvarez paused, and Laird could hear him giving orders to someone beside him. Then he was back on the line. "I'll come straight over. Meet me at the camp."

The call ended and Laird hung up.

He glanced at his watch. The other person he wanted to speak to, urgently now, was Osgood Morris. But the Clanmore marine claims manager, a creature of habit, would have finished work for the day and be on his way home. Home was a house in the Home Counties commuter belt, and Morris was there three minutes after his train pulled in at the local station.

That wouldn't be for another fifteen minutes.

Leaving the room, Laird wandered around the abandoned villa and finally found the major-domo alone in the kitchen, drinking coffee. He accepted the offer of a cup and talked to the man. Between Laird's scanty Spanish and the major-domo's equally minimal English, the conversation stayed basic.

But he did get a picture of Janos Cuvier's unexpectedly early departure. There had been hurried packing, several telephone calls, a kind of urgency which the major-domo treated with disapproval. Then, before they left, Cuvier himself had made a room-to-room check through the villa to see that nothing had been left.

"And Señorita Laura—how was she?" asked Laird.

"She looked *muy triste* . . . sad." The man shrugged. "There was some shouting between her and Señor Cuvier. But that was not my business."

He knew nothing more. The Guardia Civil had come later, had asked him questions, looked around, then had gone. His main interest now was to be left alone to close down the villa until it was needed again.

Laird left him, went outside into the sunlight, and smoked a cigarette in the shadow of the purple bougainvillaea. He walked round the villa, poking into the outhouses, giving Osgood Morris a few extra minutes to get home. Then he went back in to the telephone, dialled Morris's number, and waited while the international trunks electronics cheeped and chattered.

Morris answered on the fourth ring. When he heard Laird's voice, he reacted with an indignant ferocity.

"You. They should have kept you locked up," he said bitterly over the line. "Things were in enough of a mess already. Have you any idea how much chaos this *Sea Robin* business is causing, how the chairman is reacting?"

"Osgood, just listen." Laird caught him as he paused to draw breath. "I've found Charlie Henderson."

"What do you mean, 'found'?" Morris's voice became a high-pitched snarl. "Now, look—"

"Charlie Henderson," repeated Laird. "You cremated the wrong body."

There was horrified silence for a moment, then Morris finally managed to speak.

"You mean a—some kind of a mix-up?"

"No. He was murdered. Or it looks that way," said Laird.

"And—and our body?" Morris's voice was a quaver of its former self.

"It's going to be hard to prove—now." But the answer had been firming in Laird's mind, building to a point where there seemed no alternative. "We're still looking for the *Sea Robin*'s engineer. They were about the same height and build, the same age. That car was a burn-out."

"Dear God," said Morris, making it a prayer. "I—who's paying for this call?"

"Probably the Cuvier Corporation—we're not," Laird assured him.

"Then hold on. I—I'm hardly in the house. I need a drink," declared Morris.

More than a minute passed. Faintly, Laird heard a woman's voice in the background and Morris answering her. Then Morris was back on the line.

"Let's get this straight," said Morris, partly recovered. "You're sure about—well, Henderson?"

"Yes."

"But what about his widow? What about—damn it, half the board of directors were at the service!" Morris groaned. "Why would anyone rig that kind of charade?"

"Charlie was shot," said Laird. "An autopsy could have found the bullet. But if they had another body, killed some other way—"

"A murder to hide a murder?" Osgood Morris was thinking again. "Someone is going to have to tell his wife. Someone is going to have to—" He pushed that aspect aside, with an obvious effort. "What about who killed him and why? I suppose it's all part of the same damned *Sea Robin* package?"

"It has to be."

"Well, their whole claim situation has already been frozen," said

Morris bitterly. "The board's unanimous authorization—and we're beginning to dig up a few unpleasant things about Cuvier's finances. Your information was right. He's in a shaky situation. If that damned ship had gone down somewhere else, in deep water, if he'd slapped in a total loss claim—"

"Maybe that was the way it was meant to be," said Laird quietly. He paused and turned as he heard the room door click open. The major-domo looked in, gave a quick, apologetic bob of his head, and closed the door again. "Osgood, what's Cuvier's main problem?"

"On the money side?" Morris made a derisory, throat-clearing noise. "He bought a chemical firm in Switzerland, pumped in a lot of money for some big new production plant, and it all went wrong."

"The plant?"

"The plant or the product, I'm not sure." Morris was vague, slightly puzzled. "Does it matter?"

"It could." The day was still warm, but suddenly Andrew Laird felt chilled. "How long would it take to find out?"

"Well, I can get on it tomorrow morning—" began Morris.

"I mean starting now," Laird suggested.

"Now?" Morris made a gurgling noise. "I'm just home, I haven't eaten, I—" He suddenly understood. "But if there was some kind of a link, the ship and her cargo—that's what you've got in mind?"

"Yes." Laird waited. Despite his weaknesses, Morris was no fool. A fool wouldn't have lasted five minutes in the Clanmore management team, and though Morris might not be a genius, he was certainly a survivor.

"Cargo." Morris said it softly, as if thinking aloud. "All right. The other thing we'll have to do is go through the list of companies who put goods aboard the *Sea Robin*, check them out, their background. Cargo—chemicals—hold on. Drums—barrels—wine, man. How about that load of wine she was carrying? Could that make any kind of sense?"

Laird didn't answer, but that was good enough for Morris. "I'll be in touch," he promised. "God knows when, but you'll have to wait. But try and stay out of more trouble—we've got enough."

He hung up, and Laird replaced his own receiver, his fingers suddenly clumsy, so many things which had been there for him to see now beginning to fall into place. Fall in a way that pointed to a new possibility, one that was frightening.

The major-domo was loitering in the hallway outside. Laird went straight past him, almost ran across to the parked van, and set it moving in a way that spat gravel over the nearest flower-beds.

He had to find out, but when he did, could enough be done in time?

*

Helen Warner and Piet made up a reception committee of two when he drove back into the student camp. She was gripping Piet's arm, and from the look on his face there was no other reason he was there.

"He told me," said Helen quietly as Laird reached her. "I won't say he wanted to, but he did. Is it true about—about what you found?"

"Yes." Laird stopped her saying more. "I want to ask Piet a question. I think you'd better hear it."

She was puzzled, but nodded and let go the student's arm. Piet shuffled his feet and looked equally bewildered.

"Piet, I need the truth on this," said Laird grimly. "What did you bring back from the *Sea Robin* that last time you were out?"

The young face opposite him went pale. Piet moistened his lips.

"You mean—"

"Two nights ago, when you came back and found me here," Laird told him curtly.

"Just—well, a collection of stuff." Piet managed a wavering grin. "Ordinary stuff, no bars of gold or—"

"Tell me." Laird saw Helen wanted to say something but gave her a quick, warning headshake. "Now, Piet."

Piet stood in silence, avoiding their gaze. Insects buzzed noisily among the scrub, a truck passed on the road, and the young student still said nothing.

"I've got to know, Piet," said Laird. "Nobody will blame anyone —here."

Piet hesitated and looked at Helen. She nodded, and he gave a resigned shrug.

"We—I went out with Tom, for another look around." He gestured vaguely. "We picked up one or two things, then we had this idea. We'd explored inside the ship a little below water, we knew where the galley was, and—"

"You decided to try there?" suggested Laird, helping him on.

Piet nodded.

"What did you get?"

"Some tins—fruit mostly, though some of the labels had gone. Then some cans of beer, a few bottles of wine." Piet eyed him warily. "There was meat and other stuff floating around, but I reckoned they'd have gone bad. But—well, there were two damn great lobsters swimming around. How they'd got in there—" He shook his head. "Plenty of feeding for them, I suppose."

"So you caught them while you were at it?"

"Yes."

"And when you brought them back here?"

"Kept them in a box, in the water." Piet managed a feeble attempt at a smile. "We do that back home."

"Then you had the idea of a party?" persisted Laird.

"Piet." Helen broke her silence, frowning. "I thought the party food, everything else, was bought. You told Adam—"

Piet nodded. "We thought he'd go through the roof if we told him the truth. I mean—wouldn't he?"

"I suppose so," she admitted, her eyes worried.

"But you were still sick last night," said Laird relentlessly. "So you missed the party, just like Helen and two of the girls. But you know what happened?"

"I talked to Tom," said Piet miserably. "This morning—he said we should keep our mouths shut. I mean—they'll be better in a day or so, won't they?"

"What about the party?" asked Helen sharply. "I want to know, Piet."

"Everything was used that we'd brought back—except a couple of tins of meat that didn't look right." Piet glanced at Laird and nodded. "Including the lobsters. They seemed okay. But—well, they weren't, were they?"

"I don't know," Laird told him.

"But they'll be over it in a day or two. Tom said that doctor told him—" The fair-haired youngster's voice faded on the words. He stared at Laird and Helen. Then he turned and almost ran from them, towards the shore.

Helen took a first step to go after him, then stopped. Beneath her suntan, her face had lost its colour. She ran a hand through her tousled fair hair, her blue eyes wide and anxious.

"What's wrong with them?" She seized his arm. "Andrew

. . . ?" She became angry when he didn't answer. "Andrew, we've got nine of them sick—nine and Adam. Tell me!"

"I'm not a doctor," he said.

"But you know something," she persisted.

"Let me talk to Adam first." He held up a hand in a quick warning. "We make it I'm just looking in to say hello."

Adam Warner was alone in his tent, lying on a camp bed, his thin body covered by a single, crumpled sheet. There was a faint smell of vomit clinging to the air, his bearded face was the colour of parchment, and he looked strangely frail without his spectacles.

He lifted a hand in a weak greeting as they came in.

"How are you feeling?" asked Laird.

"Hellish." Warner managed a grimace. His voice was slightly slurred and there was fresh perspiration on his forehead. "Like— like I've been put through a mangle." He lay back and nodded thankfully as Helen used a rag soaked in water to wipe his forehead. "Damn that beach cook-out. How are the kids, Helen?"

"Like you." She smiled at him. "No worse and—and feeling sorry for themselves."

"Why not?" grumbled Warner, then bit his lip and winced. "My head is sore, my guts are aching, sometimes it's like the tent is going round in circles and I'm going to pass out." He forced a grin towards Laird. "Maybe I should make a list."

"Why not?" Laird bent over him briefly. Adam Warner's eyes were watery, the pupils had contracted to less than half their normal size. "Vision blurred?"

"Hard to say. I've lost my damned glasses." Warner lay back again, shaking his head.

Laird went out of the tent. He walked a few paces, then waited until Helen emerged and joined him.

"Well?" she demanded.

"I think you'd better get that doctor back," he told her quietly. "Send Piet for him."

"Why?" She faced him determinedly. "Because it's not just food poisoning?"

"I told you," he said tiredly. "I'm not a doctor. Juan Alvarez is on his way here, if we need to raise more help."

"Andrew—" She made it a plea.

"There was someone else, a friend of mine," he said. "He was working around the *Sea Robin.* It looked like he had food poison-ing. He died, Helen."

She closed her eyes for a moment, shaking her head as if stunned.

"Why?" she asked in a near whisper.

"Something out there." Laird bit his lip. There had been the dead fish, there had been Jingles Reilly. Now there was this. "I don't know, Helen. But we've got to find out."

With ten lives at risk. Ten he knew about.

"I'll send Piet," said Helen, dry-lipped.

She turned and ran towards the shore.

CHAPTER 7

It was a close-run thing, but Captain Alvarez arrived with two carloads of men shortly before Dr. Mendes reached the camp. That meant Laird had time enough to speak briefly with Alvarez, time enough to persuade the already shaken Guardia Civil captain that he meant every word.

In turn, Juan Alvarez dealt with Dr. Mendes. The physician, a suddenly anxious man, departed with Helen to see his patients. Alvarez told his men to see what help they could give around the camp, then turned to Laird again.

"Where can we talk properly about this?" he demanded.

Laird led him to the office tent. Alvarez took a quick glance around, eyes flickering with interest as he saw the salvaged can-non. Then, taking a camp stool, he sat down beside one of the trestle tables.

"From the beginning again, *por favor,*" he ordered, his face looking more than ever as if carved from a block of hard mahog-any. "Slowly—this time, I want to try to understand."

Laird nodded, cleared a space on the table, and perched on the edge with his legs dangling. Then he went over the story in more detail. At the finish, Alvarez swore wearily under his breath and looked down at his clenched fists.

"Who else in San Ferdinand knows all this?"

"Helen." He had owed her that much. "Some of it, anyway."

"But when we come to the matter of the ship, this is all mostly guesswork? Even if that turns out to be true, even if she was carrying some chemical product, we don't know what it was?"

"Correct," admitted Laird. "But we've got to find out."

"Sí . . . and we also have a body to recover." Alvarez sucked his lips. "But suppose the ship was carrying this—this substance, why is it so important?"

"Because any discovery that it had been aboard could cost the Cuvier Corporation several million dollars. Janos Cuvier would be wiped out financially." Laird's eyes strayed to the old cannon as he answered. "As far as Cuvier is concerned, that's an adequate motive for murder."

"But—" Alvarez shook his head, bewildered.

"Clanmore Alliance covered the *Sea Robin* under standard marine insurance terms. If a ship is carrying hazardous cargo, then that cargo has to be specifically declared and a separate risk premium agreed. If that doesn't happen, if the ship is lost—" Laird shrugged. "It's in the small print, Captain. We could cancel all cover, no compensation. He loses his ship. He could be sued by the people who owned the rest of the cargo aboard. He's left with a wreck that the Spanish authorities already say they want moved— and he'd have to foot that bill."

"I understand—I think." Alvarez shifted on his camp stool and scowled at the ground. "But some of it makes no sense. The *Sea Robin* was meant to sink?"

"But not here. Somewhere out in the Atlantic, safe and deep," agreed Laird. "The way it happened off San Ferdinand was a foulup."

"Yet the ship was underinsured—why?"

Laird shrugged. That moved them into an area where he was a lot less confident.

"Probably deliberate. If an insurance company thinks something is overvalued, they worry. If they think it's undervalued, it's not their problem. Janos Cuvier needs money—a total loss claim paid out on the *Sea Robin*, and his worries were over."

Alvarez nodded uncertainly. "Fine. But that leaves the chemical—presuming it exists. Why have it aboard?"

"To get rid of it, maybe—Janos Cuvier doesn't do anything without a damned good reason," said Laird bitterly. "But I don't know."

"*Sí*, there's a lot we don't know," murmured Alvarez wryly. He grimaced. "I can't tell you anything good. For a start, Cuvier's people have vanished—all except a middle-aged woman, his secretary. We know she left from Málaga airport this afternoon on a flight to Geneva."

Laird stared at him. "No trace of any of them?"

"None—and we found nothing at the villa that helps in any way." Alvarez built a steeple with his fingertips, frowning. "Our only step forward is his driver, Vicente. I was right, we do know something about him. He has a prison record, he used to operate around Barcelona—and now he owns the Garaje Amarilla, has a number of interesting friends."

"Including motor-cyclists?"

Alvarez nodded.

"Cuvier must have quite a contact book," said Laird.

"People with money often have," said the Guardia captain. He stopped as one of his men entered, came over, and murmured to him. Alvarez nodded and beckoned to Laird. "The *médico* is finished. We'd better see him."

They found Dr. Mendes standing in the open, away from the tents. He was smoking a cigarette, his face worried and thoughtful.

"How are they?" asked Laird.

Dr. Mendes shrugged, the cigarette dangling from his lips. He said nothing.

"Like to translate that?" suggested Laird.

"None show any improvement, one or two are a little worse," said Mendes sulkily. "But if I am being asked to accept this is not food poisoning—"

"You're not being asked, Doctor. You're being told," said Alvarez curtly.

"Then what am I supposed to do—stick a pin in a list?" demanded Mendes indignantly. "*Sí*, there are some indications. It could be some other kind of poisoning. But what kind? Do you want me to take a gamble, pretend I'm in some Saturday-night poker game?"

"You may have to do that," Laird said brutally. "You saw how Jingles Reilly died."

"*Gracias.*" Mendes flushed, took the cigarette from his lips, and tossed it away. "I happen to be doing my best, Señor Laird. If that is not good enough—"

"We understand," said Alvarez quickly, stepping between them. He nodded soothingly. "What help do you need?"

Dr. Mendes sniffed but cooled down.

"I need blood samples taken to a laboratory—"

"Done. What else?"

"An autopsy on Reilly's body. That means a pathologist, tissue samples—"

"I will arrange it," promised Alvarez.

"And—" Mendes hesitated, then gave in. "—and Warner and these young people should be moved to hospital, for observation, until we can commence treatment. I have spoken to Señorita Warner, and she agrees." He gestured unhappily. "Laboratory tests can take time. At the moment their condition is still reasonable, medically. But if you are right, I don't know how much time we have."

Alvarez nodded, looked around, and raised his voice to a shout. "Tomás—"

A young Guardia sergeant came hurrying over. Alvarez took Dr. Mendes to meet him halfway and the three men stood talking for a moment. Then Mendes and the sergeant strode towards the office tent and Alvarez returned.

"Next, our body," said Alvarez, and gave a faint, humourless smile. "The dead sometimes have a lower priority than the living. Will there be any difficulty in finding the location?"

"We dropped a marker," Laird told him.

Alvarez was satisfied. "Two of my men are trained divers, and brought equipment. If you took them out—"

Laird stopped him. "Piet could do that."

"And you?" Alvarez raised an eyebrow.

"There's a man called Novak—Harry Novak," said Laird.

"The salvage expert?" Alvarez eyed him oddly. "Yes, I've heard of him."

"Novak knows a little, he's scared a little. I want to try him again —and I want him to know you're equally interested."

"In my spare time, I frighten babies and small children," said Alvarez. He grinned. *"Á su disposición . . .* whenever you're ready."

"Give me a minute," said Laird. "I'll meet you at your car."

He went looking for Helen and found her at work inside one of the tents. Four boys, equally pale-faced, were lying miserably on their camp beds. One was moaning quietly. Another looked up as Laird lifted the tent flap, saw him, and tried to twist a smile.

"Outside," said Helen.

He nodded, and she followed him out into the open.

"Andrew, what are the chances of finding out what this thing is?" she asked steadily.

"Good, I think." He hoped it wasn't too big a lie. "But they'll still be more comfortable in hospital."

"Yes." She wasn't completely fooled, and showed it. "I've told Adam I'll go with them, see everybody settled."

"And then?"

She shrugged. "Come back here, I suppose—at least for tonight. Dr. Mendes seems to feel that—well, that would be safe enough. I've got to decide what to do about the camp, and there's Piet and the two girls to think about." She paused and frowned. "Where is Piet?"

"Going out with a couple of Captain Alvarez's men." Laird pursed his lips. "They're bringing up Charlie Henderson's body. Piet's going as boatman—nothing more."

"That's bad enough. Couldn't you—?"

He shook his head. "I've something else to do."

One of the boys inside the tent called softly. Helen sighed.

"I'll keep in touch," promised Laird.

She nodded, and went back into the tent.

*

Captain Alvarez drove the police car, Laird beside him in the front passenger seat, the dashboard radio between them coming to life with an occasional muttered message interspersed with rasps of static. The road was busy with the nearest San Ferdinand could offer to the evening rush-hour of homebound traffic, and Alvarez didn't have much to say until they were almost at the harbour gates.

"I was thinking," he said suddenly, unexpectedly. "Yesterday, things were peaceful—the way they should be. Today? I have murder, sudden death, all the rest of this upheaval. People have vanished, are running or hiding—yet as a policeman, do you know what I've got?" He grunted derisively. "Not enough real evidence to arrest anyone. *Eso duele* . . . believe me, that hurts."

Laird glanced at him, and Alvarez surprised him with a wink.

"But it will come together, Señor Laird. My wife says I have a good horoscope this month—so things can only get better, eh?"

Both salvage tugs had come in and were berthed at the quayside. They passed the *Beroe*, with her flag hanging limp at halfmast as a token reminder of Jingles Reilly's death, then parked beside the *Scomber*.

Laird led the way up the gangway and aboard, Alvarez at his heels. A lone crewman on deck, leaning against the rail, eyed them with disinterest as they went past and headed for Harry Novak's cabin below the bridge.

Not bothering to knock, Laird opened the cabin door. The tug captain was lounging back on a frayed couch, in his shirt-sleeves, reading a magazine. He looked up, startled.

"What the hell do you want?" Scowling, he tossed the magazine aside and lumbered to his feet. He glared at Alvarez. "Whoever this is, you can both get out."

"I wouldn't advise it, Harry," Laird told him softly. "He's Captain Alvarez, from the Guardia Civil." He saw Novak's eyes narrow perceptibly, and nodded. "He wants to talk with you. Only I suggested maybe you and I should have a discussion of our own first."

"About what?" Some of Novak's bluster had faded. A wary expression showed on his scarred face.

"Perhaps I should leave that to Señor Laird, Captain," murmured Alvarez, glancing around the cabin with some interest. "*Sí* . . . so I will look around your ship for a few minutes. Then we can discuss things properly."

Novak stared at him, saying nothing, and Alvarez turned and went out. The cabin door closed behind him, and as it did, Novak came to life again.

"What's going on?" he asked hoarsely. "What the hell are you tryin' to get me into, Laird?"

"Wrong way round, Harry," said Laird. "I'm giving you a chance to get out from under—if you've sense enough. If you haven't"— he shrugged—"well, that's your problem. But don't expect me to weep."

Novak growled. Anger in his eyes, fists clenched, he took a half-step forward.

"You snivellin' little—"

It stopped there as Laird deliberately pistoned the flat of his hand against Novak's chest, just under his throat. Staggering back, Novak met the couch, stumbled, and thudded down on it.

"Get up from there before I say, and I'll throw you straight to the Guardia mob!" Laird's warning cut through the cabin's hot, still air. "You wouldn't like it, Harry."

"Then what the hell do you want?" Novak licked his lips, angry but nervous. "You barge in here an'—"

Laird stopped him. "It starts with murder, Harry."

"That Guardia sergeant?" Novak blinked. "But—"

"I'm talking about Charlie Henderson." Standing over him, Laird saw total surprise and bewilderment in Novak's expression. "He didn't die in that car accident. He was shot, then dumped in sixty feet of water with a chunk of scrap iron as an anchor. They're bringing him up now, Harry."

The colour drained from Novak's face. He licked his lips again, then swallowed.

"I didn't know. I—what about the body in the car? They said—"

Laird shrugged. "Does it matter—to you?"

Novak looked away. The last remnant of his bullying manner had gone, he was badly frightened.

"You can't tie me into anything like that," he said weakly. "No way."

"Maybe Captain Alvarez doesn't see things that way," said Laird. "Who could blame him? More important, Cuvier's people have gone. But you're available."

"Now listen—" Novak started to rise.

"No, Harry." Laird shoved him down again. "You listen. There's only one way you can wriggle out of this, keep Alvarez off your back. I want your story about what was going on—the real story."

"Suppose I talk?" Novak's coarse, scarred face showed his uncertainty. "What kind of deal am I left with afterwards? Look, you say you can square it with the police, but how about Clanmore? If I end up on any kind of black list—"

"Unless you've really fouled things up, you'll come out smelling of roses," said Laird. "Is that good enough?" He took Novak's silence as an adequate answer. "When did Cuvier get to you?"

"As soon as I got here—or at least Raynal, his shipping manager did," said Novak reluctantly. "Then I met Cuvier, and I said I'd do it."

Laird nodded. "Do what?"

"Spin things out for them, go for a possible salvage situation in my survey report." Novak looked up at him and grimaced. "It wasn't too difficult. It was only a preliminary report—hell, it's even accurate on detail as far as it goes."

"But?"

"But the *Sea Robin* is old, an' I know her kind," said Novak with a faint derision. "She may look okay, but try to float her and she'll break her back. Even if she didn't, there could be other problems. The job would cost a fortune." He forced a hasty grin. "Look, no way was it going that far. I told Cuvier I had a reputation to think about—"

"Naturally," murmured Laird. "So why did they say they were so anxious to push the idea?"

Novak shrugged. "All Cuvier told me was they had a problem with the hull insurance, that Clanmore might be awkward. They needed to win some time, sell you the notion they really wanted to float her again."

"How did you sell it to Captain Weller on *Beroe*?"

"Weller?" Novak sneered at the thought. "All he wants is a quiet life. He does what he's told."

Laird sighed and turned away. Novak's desk was on the other side of the cabin. Going over, he picked up a short, thin-bladed gutting knife Novak always used as a letter-opener and felt the tip with care.

"What about the cargo, Harry?"

Novak didn't answer.

"Harry?" He stabbed the knife down, leaving the blade quivering in the wood of the desk. "What about the cargo you brought ashore? Did Cuvier push for that?"

"Yes." Novak was nervous again. "It was—well, part of the deal."

"To get the wine ashore?"

Novak nodded.

"Why?"

"He said it could be awkward if it was found later," answered Novak unhappily. "Maybe it was hijacked, stolen—I don't know. But he said we had to get it off whatever happened, that I wasn't being paid to—" He stopped short.

"How much, Harry?" said Laird grimly. "How much was it all worth?"

"Two hundred thousand Swiss francs." Novak chewed his lip and glanced anxiously at Laird. "Look, we'd probably have brought the stuff ashore anyway. You know that." He paused hopefully. "That's the story—all I can tell you, so help me."

"Wrong," said Laird. "You saw the wine brought up. Were any of the drums damaged, leaking?"

"Only one of them." Novak was puzzled. "A chunk of steel had fallen on it, gashed it open like a tin-opener. But they wanted it up, took it away with the rest."

"Just one." Laird took a deep breath, trying to keep his voice steady and unemotional. "Who did the initial diving work inside the hull? Jingles Reilly?"

"Yes."

"Did anything happen to him?"

"He came up once, complaining he'd been hung up on some junk. Damaged his breathing gear, swallowed a few mouthfuls of water, that's all." Novak shifted uncomfortably on the couch, and shrugged. "There wasn't any real danger. He knew his job."

"He did." Laird pursed his lips. "What about your other divers? Any health complaints from them?"

"Eh?" Novak looked surprised. "Hell, show me a diver that doesn't moan. A couple have been bitching about headaches—sick headaches, for God's sake." Then he stopped, a cunning, suspicious glint in his eyes. "Wait a minute—what goes on?"

"Nothing, as far as you're concerned," said Laird. "Be glad, stay with what you know. Where is Cuvier now?"

"Meaning he didn't head for Switzerland?" Novak sucked his lips gloomily. "Hell, he didn't tell me anything much, except what to do and when to do it." He shrugged. "The rest of his team weren't the friendly type either—I wouldn't trust Raynal if I had him on the end of a fishing pole, and those two hard-case office boys they had along were like high-class Mafia graduates."

"You're the expert," Laird told him, and turned away. "What about the others—Captain Van Holst and Grant, his chief engineer?"

"Van Holst is garbage," said Novak. "Grant I don't know about— I only saw him a couple of times before he left."

"And the girl, Laura Cero?" Laird still kept his back to him.

"Miss Nose-in-the-Air?" Novak managed a chuckle. "She's smart, all right. Janos Cuvier made me the offer, but she spelled out exactly how it was all inside the law—or could be." He flinched as Laird swung round and he saw his face. "Look, that's how it was then. I—I didn't know there would be any kind of killing."

"No." Laird still felt as if he'd been hit in the stomach. But he knew Novak wasn't lying. He drew a deep breath. "Where did they take the cargo from here?"

"A warehouse down the coast. I've got the address." Novak rose cautiously and went over to his desk. He brought back a bundle of papers clipped together. "That's it—and the full list of what we landed."

Laird glanced at the top page, saw the printed letterhead, then folded the sheets and put them in his hip pocket.

"If that's it then—uh—we've still got a deal, right?" asked Novak hopefully.

"We've got a deal," agreed Laird. He heard a noise outside the cabin door, knew Alvarez was back, and said softly, "You're covered. But a few people are going to know. If any of us catch Captain Novak of the *Scomber* trying anything from now on, you'll find your hide nailed to your bridge deck. Remember that."

There was a knock at the door. It opened, and Alvarez looked in. He glanced at Laird, then nodded cheerfully to Novak.

"I enjoyed my little inspection tour, Captain," he said brightly. "You have a fine ship. Now, have we anything left to discuss?"

"Captain Novak's been co-operative," said Laird drily. "If you need it, I'm sure he'd give some kind of suitable statement later."

"*Gracias*, Captain," murmured Alvarez. "Then I won't take up any more of your valuable time."

"Go to hell," said Novak bitterly. "Both of you."

*

They went back ashore, got into the police car, and Alvarez settled in behind the wheel with a chuckle.

"I'm impressed," he mused. "He told you what you wanted?"

"All he knew," corrected Laird, handing over the bundle of papers. "That's his documentation for the cargo brought ashore, and where it was taken."

"You have a positive gift of gentle persuasion," murmured Alvarez, frowning at the printed letterhead. "This place is a few kilometres on the far side of Marbella, near Elviria." Returning the papers, he started the car. "*Bueno*. I think we should go there. But tell me the rest of the good captain's confessions."

The sun had been swallowed up over the horizon, the light was beginning to fade. As they left San Ferdinand in the gathering dusk, Alvarez kept the car at a fast cruising pace and listened while Laird described what he'd been told.

"So," he agreed soberly as Laird finished. "We have what Captain Novak chose to believe. But it still confirms that Cuvier's ship sank in the wrong place." He frowned, keeping his eyes on the road, fingers resting lightly on the steering wheel. "He was positive only one of those drums of so-called wine was damaged enough to leak?"

"Yes," said Laird flatly.

"Just one." Alvarez gave a soft whistle of alarm. "Yet if the effect could linger, be so dangerous—" He broke off as the car radio murmured to life, giving his call-sign. Scooping the microphone from its clip, he answered, listened to the murmuring voice while he drove one-handed, then acknowledged the message and gave some clipped orders in Spanish.

"Señor Henderson's body has been recovered and brought ashore," he said unemotionally, returning the microphone to its clip. He glanced at Laird. "They were a little worried by the failing light. It seems they also had some trouble with a somewhat angry shark."

"I should have mentioned that," admitted Laird.

"Perhaps." Alvarez's broad face showed a twitch of amusement. He drove on for a moment in silence, took the car round a sharp bend, then said innocently, "Were you surprised when Novak mentioned Señorita Cero's part in all this? I—ah—presume you were going to tell me about that."

"Meaning you were listening outside?" challenged Laird.

Alvarez nodded. "Part of the time."

"She's a lawyer," said Laird. "She does her job."

"And the rest depends on how much or how little she knows," said Alvarez. He gave Laird a thoughtful, sideways glance, then shrugged. "Do you trust Novak?"

"Now and again. Not too often."

"When you have him in a corner—I understand. Still, maybe I should tell you what happened when we—ah—accommodated you in that cell today. Several people protested, as you know, but one of the first was the same Captain Novak. The language he used to one of my sergeants was most educational. Does that alter your feelings?"

"No," said Laird.

But there were times when Harry Novak could be one of nature's oddities.

*

It was dark by the time they reached Marbella, where the neon signs were just coming to life for the start of another night's business. Once on the far side of the resort town, Alvarez used his radio again. Then a little later he left the main highway and the car drove for a spell along a quieter road.

Three kilometres farther on, they reached the start of a small, run-down industrial estate. Alvarez slowed, checking the few street signs, then suddenly grunted and took a right turn. A minute later there was a brief flash of headlights ahead, then they drew in and stopped beside another police car. It was parked outside a featureless two-storey warehouse building, and a second police car was stopped farther along.

"This is it," confirmed Alvarez, but he sounded puzzled. "There must be something wrong. They were supposed to wait."

He got out first. Laird followed but stayed in the background while Alvarez spoke to two uniformed Guardia Civil who appeared from the shadows. After a few minutes Alvarez nodded to the men, then beckoned Laird over.

"There's only the regular caretaker," he said. "My men met him in the street. All he knows is the place was empty, then the Cuvier Corporation suddenly rented it."

"But they've been here?" frowned Laird.

"Sí . . . on and off, right up until this afternoon," said Alvarez. "That's about all he can tell. The Cuvier people told him they didn't want him around during the day but he was to keep an eye on the place at night. He's inside."

They walked along to the main door of the warehouse. It was unlocked, and another of Alvarez's men saluted as they entered. Light spilled from a small, glass-walled office to one side, and an elderly man peered out at them from behind a desk. The rest of the warehouse was in total darkness.

"*Maravilloso,*" said Alvarez. He snapped an order, a man hurried into the little office, and a moment later the whole warehouse area was suddenly lit by bright overhead tubes. Alvarez nudged Laird and pointed.

The salvaged cargo from the *Sea Robin* lay in neat lines down the middle of the warehouse floor. First the packing cases, still marked from their salt-water immersion but dried out, then the glint of rows of stainless-steel wine containers.

"Do you believe it?" Alvarez grinned with relief.

Footsteps echoing, they hurried over the concrete floor and reached the containers. Grabbing the nearest with both hands, Alvarez rocked it on its rim and they heard a low slurp as the liquid inside moved in response, then settled again.

"Well?" asked Alvarez.

"It doesn't make sense," said Laird.

Biting his lip, he walked slowly along the line. At a rough count, it looked as though they were all there except for the damaged container. But if they were so important, would Janos Cuvier have left them unguarded? Conscious that Alvarez was watching, he tried moving another of the containers and knew it was full like the first.

Standing back, he looked at the intact seal and the serial number stencilled below it. All the others were the same.

"Remember how I told you I had a good horoscope?" said Alvarez, coming over.

But there had to be something wrong. Then Laird knew what it was.

"They've worked a switch," he told Alvarez bitterly. "These didn't come from the *Sea Robin.*"

Alvarez goggled at him. "Are you sure? Can you prove it?"

"I saw some of the wine coming ashore," said Laird. "The containers were the same as these, but unmarked—no serial numbers."

"Maybe you are wrong." Alvarez stopped smiling. "Perhaps that list Novak gave you—"

They checked the list. Every crate brought ashore from the cargo ship had a shipping or serial number listed beside it. The wine containers were simply listed in batches, with no serial numbers, only the note that one container was damaged but included.

Cuvier's first mistake led them to discover another. They made their own count of the containers, walking up and down the lines. The number tallied exactly with the number brought ashore—but none was damaged.

"I'll talk to the damn caretaker," said Alvarez.

He strode off towards the little office. Through the glass, Laird could see him scowling as he questioned the caretaker, who seemed to do little in reply but shake his head. At last, Alvarez gave up and marched back.

"Useless," he said, exasperated. "*Sí,* he says there were trucks coming and going. But they could have been stealing the warehouse from under him for all he knows—or cares."

Laird didn't answer. He was thinking of the detail involved in organizing the switch, the planning it had taken. Two hundred containers had been loaded at Marseilles, two hundred containers had been brought ashore, and Janos Cuvier still had two hundred containers to display in the warehouse—two hundred containers which Laird would gamble were filled with innocent low-grade wine. But what kind of lethal secret did the originals hold, what kind of secret that made them worth even murder to protect?

*

A little later, a downcast Alvarez drove him back to Marbella and they went up to the Guardia captain's office at the police barracks. Scowling, Alvarez waved him into the same chair he'd occupied earlier and only grunted when an orderly brought in two mugs of black coffee.

Sitting behind his desk, sipping the coffee, Alvarez gradually regained some semblance of humour again, though his eyes stayed angry.

"Pity about your horoscope," said Laird mildly.

"My horoscope according to my wife," corrected Alvarez. "Maybe she read the wrong damn birth-sign again." He sighed, and leaned his elbows on the desk. "Well, every police patrol along the Málaga coast is watching for your Janos Cuvier—not that I expect it to do much good. This man thinks two, maybe three steps ahead of anyone."

"Not all of the time," Laird consoled him.

"But most of it," repeated Alvarez. He grunted three words under his breath which didn't appear in any high school Spanish textbook. "I was wrong tonight, I may be wrong again, but when I get him, then *cuidado . . .* he can look out for real trouble."

Laird grinned and took a gulp of the coffee. It was the kind only a police station could produce and manage to pronounce drinkable.

"He has a few headaches already," he reminded Alvarez.

"Good." Alvarez drew some comfort from the thought. "*Sí,* and my idea at the moment is to keep it that way. As few people as possible will know what is happening. I can persuade my head-quarters that any hint to any newspaper is *prohibito*. We stay silent about your friend Henderson's body—"

"And Sergeant García's murder?" Laird raised an eyebrow. "How do you cope with that?"

"We already have. For the moment, our story there is that García was apparently murdered when he attempted to arrest a wanted criminal. There are always a few of those about, and San Ferdinand is a place the average reporter wouldn't find exciting. Put all that together, and Cuvier and his people may feel confused."

"But happier." Laird nodded.

It could help. Janos Cuvier had been working to a planned timetable. His timetable had been upset. But if he was left hoping that the whole operation might still succeed, succeed and leave the Cuvier Corporation completely clear of anything more than vague suspicion, that could be his weakness.

"These containers—the real ones." Alvarez put into words the other thought in Laird's mind. "What will he do with them now?"

Laird shook his head. But Janos Cuvier would certainly have that in hand.

They heard a nervous tap on the door. The same orderly crept in, warily laid a message slip in front of Alvarez, then beat a quick retreat.

Alvarez read the message, looked puzzled, studied it again, then slid it impatiently across the desk towards Laird.

"For you—whatever it means," he said. "Now I am a post office as well as everything else."

The telex was from Osgood Morris in London, addressed to Alvarez direct, but clearly sent that way because Morris was determined to establish Clanmore's position.

CLANMORE ANXIOUS OFFER FULLEST CO-OPERATION WITH SPANISH AUTHORITIES RE SEA ROBIN. OUR INTEREST HUMANITARIAN, NOT SUBJECT ANY LIABILITY CIVIL OR CRIMINAL RE SHIP OR CARGO WHATEVER CIRCUMSTANCES. ADVISE LAIRD THAT PROFESSOR DANIELS ARRIVES EXECUTIVE CHARTER, MÁLAGA AIRPORT, EARLIEST TOMORROW.

"Well?" demanded Alvarez as Laird finished reading and looked up. "I understand the first part. Your people are wiping their noses."

"Keeping them clean," said Laird.

"Same thing." Alvarez nursed his mug of coffee. "It means keep a good image but protect the shareholders. But who is this Daniels? Why do we need a professor—or is that some kind of code?"

"I don't know," said Laird.

But the name was a vague memory, the kind it seemed best to keep to himself.

"I'll have a car collect him," volunteered Alvarez. He grinned. "Maybe he knows about horoscopes."

*

A Guardia Civil car, one of the unmarked kind, took Laird back to San Ferdinand. He sat alone in the rear seat, nothing to do but watch the road and the back of his driver's neck.

He was glad. It gave him a chance to think again about Osgood Morris's telex message. He'd have to wait to find out if his notion about Daniels was correct. But Laird could read a lot more into the first half of the message than the bare words were intended to convey.

Clanmore Alliance had a major problem on its hands. It was one thing to deny legal liability, another altogether to deny any kind of responsibility if a situation could reach the stage when a foreign government might begin real pressures—and pressures of that kind could be damaging to the company's image as well as its pocket if they became public.

Osgood Morris wouldn't be happy until the *Sea Robin* situation and all it had come to mean was a neat package that belonged totally to the Cuvier Corporation. So far, it was a package that included three deaths—four if Jingles Reilly was added to the bill.

Laird closed his eyes for a moment against the glare of an oncoming truck's lights. The primary factor in it all were the two hundred steel containers and whatever secret they held. Alvarez was confident that the watch already slapped on the few roads out of the Málaga coastal strip meant they couldn't leave that way. Airfreight movements were even easier to check.

That left the sea, the scatter of little harbours and fishing ports where a vessel might slip in, load, and leave. But again the word was out, vigilant eyes were already watching, off-duty men being hauled in to keep the surveillance unbroken.

The Guardia Civil might wear funny hats and be disliked, sometimes feared, by many who had good reason to remember how things had been before Spain took the plunge back into democracy. They had earned that inherited reputation for harshness, even if officers like Juan Alvarez were beginning to establish a new kind of tough but reasoned professionalism.

What was certain was that they were efficient. Janos Cuvier wasn't going to find any easy way round them.

The car purred on. Laird smoked a cigarette, listened to the driver hum a tune under his breath, then the lights of San Ferdinand appeared as a glow ahead. He glanced at his watch, saw it was close to midnight, but decided it still wasn't too late.

"Por favor . . ." He leaned forward, tapped the man on the shoulder, and gestured towards the shore. "I want to stop at the Warner campsite."

"Las tiendas?" The man nodded dutifully, yawned, and took up the tune where he had left off.

They drove off the road and stopped. Getting out, Laird walked through the darkness towards the silhouettes of the tents. The night wind had a chill edge and the sea was coming in at a steady muttering surge. But nothing moved around the tents, there were no lights, no sounds. The tent flaps had been tied down, the few equipment boxes left out in the open were locked, the whole campsite had been deserted.

He went back to the car and they set off again for San Ferdinand. A few minutes later, he was dropped outside the Hostal Mercado and waited until the car had turned and was driving off before he went inside.

The bar area was dimly lit, the same notice on the counter said it was closed to outside trade, and the only customers were two resident guests who were drinking quietly at a corner table. Mamá Isabel, still in black, was sitting at the bar. She looked tired and old, but she managed to muster a welcome on her broad face and nodded towards the little sitting room behind her counter.

Laird went past her, then stopped in the doorway.

"Hello, Andrew," said Helen Warner quietly. "I told Mamá Isabel I'd wait till you got back."

She was in an ancient armchair, the room lit by the flickering glow from a wood fire which had burned down almost to the embers in the small stone hearth. A cup of coffee was on the floor beside her, she wore a patterned cotton dressing gown tied at the waist by a cord, and her feet were bare.

"I looked in at the camp," he told her.

"I meant us to stay there." She gave a slight smile. "But Mamá Isabel arrived, collected us, and brought us here. She said it made more sense."

"And she usually gets her way." Closing the door, Laird came over and sat on the arm of the chair, looking down at her. "How about Adam and the others?"

"I saw them settled at the hospital." Helen clasped her hands over her knees, the dying firelight playing tricks with her eyes. "They're more comfortable there. The staff say two of the boys seem to have improved. But otherwise, there's not much change."

Laird nodded his understanding. "As soon as the laboratory tests come up with some kind of result—"

"I know." She straightened her shoulders. "That's what I'm trying to convince myself will happen, at any rate. They said at the hospital to come back in the morning, that—well, things might look better by then." She looked up at him. "Has Captain Alvarez made any progress?"

"A little, not much." Laird touched her arm encouragingly. "But it's pretty much the same. Maybe tomorrow—"

"Yes." Helen rose from the chair, the long skirt of the dressing gown brushing her ankles. She considered him seriously for a moment. "I'll be leaving early for the hospital. Good-night, Andrew."

"Good-night," he said quietly.

She went out, closing the door again. Laird went over to the hearth, used the metal poker to push the last fragments of burning wood closer together, and watched a few fresh flames crackle to life.

He heard the door open again and turned. Mamá Isabel came in. Behind her, the bar was now empty and almost in darkness.

"I'm glad you brought them in," he told her. "It was a good thing to do."

"*Gracias.*" Mamá Isabel moved bulkily around the room, tidying as she spoke. "It seemed sensible. The boy is with Roberto, the two young girls are sharing a room. There was no problem." She paused, the brim of her hat casting a shadow over her face. "You are now in Room Four. Not as good as where you were, but comfortable."

"It'll be fine," Laird assured her.

"The señorita is in Room Three." Mamá Isabel lifted an ornament, then put it down again. "The other señorita, the one who came here—is she still with Cuvier people?"

"I don't know," said Laird. He shrugged. "It looks that way."

"Yo comprendo." Mamá Isabel stayed silent for a moment. "The one who is here—sometimes, when a woman is deeply troubled, it is not good to be alone."

She went out and he heard her padding footsteps fading.

Leaving the room, Laird went upstairs. He found Room Four, went in, and went over to the window. A car that hadn't been there before was parked across the road. It was empty, but two figures stood nearby. The faint moonlight glinted on their tricorn hats. One was carrying a machine pistol.

Captain Alvarez believed in protecting his assets.

He turned away, stood for a moment, then went back out into the corridor and tapped lightly on the door of Helen's room.

It opened slowly. Helen still wore her dressing gown, but it hung loose. She looked at him uncertainly, her eyes moist with tears.

Laird went into the little room, closed the door, and she came into his arms.

CHAPTER 8

Sometime around dawn, Andrew Laird heard a vehicle rattle away from the Mercado's backyard. He knew it meant Helen had left for the hospital at Marbella, cursed sleepily because he had intended to go with her, then drifted back to sleep.

It was a bright, sunny day when he came properly awake. Showered and shaved, he dressed quickly and went down to breakfast. Dressed again in black, Mamá Isabel was alone in the bar and clearing a table which had already been occupied. She finished the task before she came over to where Laird had sat down.

"The señorita was on her way at six," said Mamá Isabel. She

looked at him, gave a soft chuckle, turned, and waddled off towards the kitchen. Returning with a fresh pot of coffee, she laid it down, then said, "Captain Alvarez telephoned. I have to tell you he is at the *aeropuerto,* but the flight from London has been delayed. He does not know why."

Laird frowned. "That's all?"

"Except that he will meet you at the police station in San Ferdinand at ten." Mamá Isabel paused hopefully. "Does it mean someone who can help is coming?"

"That's what I've still got to find out," said Laird. He looked around at the other tables. "Where's Roberto?"

She shrugged. "He took the boy and the two girls out to their camp. They want to make sure everything is all right there. It will be, but it gave them something to do."

Laird ate breakfast slowly. The delay meant he had unexpected time to kill and nothing particularly useful to do with it. If anything that mattered had happened overnight, then Alvarez would have hinted at it in his message. But apparently it hadn't, and for the moment he knew he was surplus to anyone's requirements.

Eventually he abandoned the last half-cup of cold coffee, went out, and walked down towards the harbour. There was not as much as a wisp of cloud above, the day was already warm, and he was glad he wasn't wearing a jacket or tie.

Near the harbour, Laird stopped and looked out across the water. A light swell was swirling white in the sun around all that was visible of the *Sea Robin*. There were no boats around her, only a few circling gulls.

Moving on, he found the two salvage tugs still at their berths at the quayside. The *Beroe* was taking on diesel fuel from a tanker truck, and he saw Captain Weller standing signing a receipt form for the driver.

"Hello, Laird." Weller handed the receipt back to the tanker driver and came over. "I wanted to see you. We're sailing in about an hour."

"Both of you?" Laird glanced at the *Scomber,* but saw no sign of activity on her deck.

"No, Harry Novak is staying for another day." Weller frowned at the thought. "I'm not sure why. All he'll tell me is you Clanmore people are suspending any other work on the *Sea Robin* for a spell."

Laird nodded. "That's all he said?"

"That's all." Weller stuck his hands in his pockets and looked puzzled. "I wanted to wait long enough to see Jingles Reilly got a decent burial, but now it seems that will be a few days—Dr. Mendes says the body can't be released yet." He shrugged. "There's a towing job lying in Gibraltar—short haul, just round to Lisbon. Novak doesn't want it, so I might as well earn some money."

"Why not?" agreed Laird. He looked around again. "Where is Novak anyway?"

"In his cabin with a bottle, threatening anyone who comes near him." The *Beroe*'s captain pursed his lips disapprovingly. "Damn the man, that almost included me. I'd leave him alone."

"I will," murmured Laird.

He stayed at the harbour long enough to see the *Beroe* ease away from the quay and head out past the breakwater, heading west. Then he turned, walked past the still deserted *Scomber,* and went up through the village to the police station.

He was expected. A young Guardia corporal he hadn't seen before showed him into the room that had been Sergeant García's office. But any reminder that García had used it had already been removed. Even the ashtray on the desk had been emptied and cleaned.

He only had to wait about ten minutes, then Alvarez walked in. The Guardia captain was tired-eyed and unshaven, but the stranger who was with him was pink-cheeked, brisk and almost aggressively cheerful.

"Andrew Laird?" He crossed over and shook Laird's hand enthusiastically. "John Daniels—my fault you've been kept hanging about. Osgood Morris sends his regards." He winked. "Something like that, anyway."

Alvarez grunted, pulling forward a couple of chairs and seating himself behind the desk.

"Professor Daniels—" Alvarez gestured towards the chairs. As Laird and Daniels settled, he said stonily, "We stopped at the hospital on the way from the airport. But Professor Daniels wished to leave any discussion until now."

Daniels nodded agreement. He was a large, sandy-haired individual in his early fifties. His jacket was draped over one arm and he was wearing black cord trousers with an open-necked shirt and a stringy red-and-white cravat.

"Saves time, makes life easier," he declared firmly. "One of my basic rules. Another is that I don't care about what I don't need to know."

"Professor Daniels is a farming expert." Alvarez looked at Laird in something like despair. "It seems he is well known in that—that field."

"Reasonably," said Daniels modestly. "But that's misleading. I'm a scientist; chemistry is my subject, agricultural aspects my speciality." He settled himself more comfortably. "Every now and again, I earn a little extra in consultancy fees with Clanmore."

"That's why I thought I knew your name," said Laird softly. He nodded to Alvarez. "It was last year. Some farmers in Norfolk were being sued for a small fortune—"

"Alleged environmental pollution when some crop-spraying went wrong." Daniels chuckled. "Yes, I think I saved Clanmore quite a lot of money that time. But I've never been caught up in your marine department till now." He paused. "Before I forget, Osgood Morris drove me to the airport this morning—when I finally got away from the telephone. He says to tell you that this alleged shipment of wine was owned by a French company that doesn't seem to exist. The address they're using is in an apartment block."

"That helps," said Alvarez with minimal enthusiasm. He shrugged at Laird. "I can tell you easily enough how we have got on overnight. We seized one boatload of smuggled cigarettes, arrested three innocent tourists by mistake and embarrassed a politician who was sharing his yacht with a young—ah—lady who certainly wasn't his wife. Apart from that, nothing." He turned hopefully to Daniels. "Professor, why are you here—can you do better?"

"I think so," murmured Daniels. "I hope so."

"Well?" Alvarez was impatient.

"Don't rush me." Daniels smiled, showing a mouthful of strong, white teeth. "Captain, I spent most of the night tapping the scientific grapevine—and we're a garrulous bunch. Particularly some of you—ah—Europeans. God knows what my phone bill will be like, but Clanmore will be paying."

"One way or another," agreed Laird.

"Right." Daniels wasn't in any hurry. "First, a lot of thinking people today are in an environmental hang-up—protect the ecology, eat grass, live in caves. Then there's the opposition—aluminium breeding tubes and we should live on food pills." He shrugged. "I'm a midway man. But your modern farmer depends on chemicals for a decent profit. That means fertilizers; it also means pesticides and fungicides—"

"Poisons," suggested Alvarez, becoming more interested.

"Useful poisons," said Daniels cheerfully. "Nature is full of them. Your apple seed, apricots, peaches—they're stiff with cyanide compounds. There's a lovely story about old Leonardo da Vinci. He injected some extra cyanide into the bark of some fruit trees, waited until the fruit had grown, then sent a basketful round to a friend he didn't like. Goodbye friend."

Laird sighed. "Professor—"

"Sorry." Daniels gave an apologetic gesture. "What matters, gentlemen, is that today there's a multi-million-pound, -dollar, whatever, industry producing agricultural chemicals for crop protection. Highly toxic, totally safe as long as they're properly used. They've a vast market—and it's expanding. The profits can be enormous."

"*Gracias,*" said Alvarez politely. He frowned. "And the Cuvier Corporation . . . ?"

"Wanted a share," nodded Daniels. "They bought over a small Swiss chemicals firm with a modest order book and a reliable pesticides product. They invested in a fully automated production line in a brand-new factory. A lot of Third World countries were told that the Cuvier firm was going to produce a brand-new product, twice as effective as anything on the market."

For a moment there was a silence in the room except for a fly buzzing near the window. Laird moistened his lips. It was coming together, but he still wasn't sure.

"Could they do it?" he asked.

"Cuvier thought so," said Daniels drily. "Some of this is gossip— I'm on a couple of obscure United Nations committees, who live on rumour. Cuvier was some kind of refugee?"

Laird nodded. "Originally—from Romania."

"Well, he bought a cookbook recipe for his new pesticide from another exile—South American, needing money." Daniels frowned and became more serious. "It seems the small-scale laboratory tests were excellent. That can happen, does all the time— it's when you cut corners on the production work-up that things are liable to go to hell."

"And they did?"

Daniels nodded.

"What happened?" asked Alvarez.

"Something went wrong, the plant shut down almost immediately. Not a drop of Cuvier pesticide reached the market." Daniels grimaced. "You want more gossip, rumour?"

"We need it," said Laird deliberately.

"Cuvier came up with something horrific. Spray it on a field, and you'd have a desert for generations. A few particles on your skin, and you haven't time to sign your will." The pink-cheeked face was coldly sober. "A pesticide should have a rapid breakdown factor—two or three days, and your crop is pest-free but safe for consumption. This stuff stays actively toxic."

"Professor—" Alvarez leaned across his desk, openly worried. "—this chemical, how much was produced?"

"Nobody knows."

"But there must be a process, some way to render it harmless—"

"Is there?"

Alvarez swallowed. "Surely—"

"Captain, there's a world-wide howl every time nuclear waste is mentioned," said Daniels wearily. "I'm one of the people who believe toxic waste is a bigger problem—there's a damned sight more of it around. Industries have nightmares about what to do with their toxic waste, spend fortunes trying to render it harmless." He shrugged. "Every now and then there's a small disaster somewhere, people die. Why? Because fifty or a hundred years ago industrial junk was dumped on the nearest garbage tip. Our grandfathers left us a legacy of time bombs."

Laird frowned. "But that doesn't happen now."

"No—or not so often," grunted Daniels. "When it does, the law wields a big stick, and no boss likes to go to jail. But remember, both of you, Cuvier has produced something particularly vile and useless."

Alvarez looked bewildered. "But would that worry a man like Cuvier? He could store this poison, hide it—"

"He could also pour it into the nearest river," said Daniels sarcastically. "And kill the river—that used to happen. But now people worry about the environment, the ecology. According to a colleague of mine in Geneva, the environmentalists are sniffing around the Cuvier situation—and they know how to sniff."

Alvarez got up, went over to the window, and scowled out at the street below.

"So you say Cuvier has an expensive, useless factory and some devil's potion which he daren't keep?"

"Exactly." Daniels showed the same satisfaction he might have felt towards a backward student. "Don't let me mislead you. I don't rule out a reprocessing that would make it harmless—I'm simply saying that might cost another fortune."

Laird stirred. "But if he could get rid of the stuff totally, could claim that things did go wrong, but harmlessly?"

"Then he'd be in the clear," agreed Daniels. He smiled. "I gather it nearly happened, he nearly got away with it?"

"Yes."

Very nearly. If the *Sea Robin* had gone down in the Atlantic deep, then Janos Cuvier would have solved two problems. His failed pesticide would have vanished from sight. Laird thought of how an insurance pay-out on the ship as a total loss would have given Cuvier the hard cash he needed to keep the Cuvier Corporation financially intact.

But something else mattered.

"You were at the hospital. You saw Warner and his students?"

Professor Daniels nodded. "With all the symptoms of possible organophosphorous compound poisoning."

"Treatment?"

"Difficult, except that Cuvier's recipe was meant to be in what's called the anticholinesterase sector." The big man scratched his sandy hair and chose his words carefully. "Medically—well, Dr. Mendes is contacting a specialist in Madrid. Standard treatment begins with getting the patient to drink activated charcoal mixes. Then my bet would be injections of atropine sulphate." He cleared his throat encouragingly. "There are other back-ups."

"And their chances?" persisted Laird.

"Good, even better when the laboratory results give pointers. If the story about those lobsters is true, then what happened to Warner and those kids was minimal." Daniels looked at Laird, remembered what he'd heard, and made an apologetic noise. "I know, your diver friend wasn't so lucky. But that was when there would be a higher toxic concentration in the water."

"But this was the sea, just one container was damaged—days before," protested Alvarez. *"Lo siento* . . . it is still hard to believe."

"You'd better get used to it," Daniels told him coldly, then relented. "I'll try and explain. Take an ordinary pesticide and say you want to kill bugs in a field. The safe mix is probably half a cupful to two thousand litres of water. With Cuvier's brew, that would be devastation."

Alvarez sighed and looked at Laird, as if seeking some kind of support. He found none, gave up, and glanced at his wrist-watch. "Are you ready to go, Professor?" he asked.

"Yes." Daniels got to his feet and explained for Laird's benefit. "I want to collect sea-water samples from around the wreck—research material." He turned to Alvarez. "I'll need some of my kit from your car, and those lobsters eaten at the camp interest me. If there were any kitchen scraps left—"

"I could check that," volunteered Laird.

He saw Alvarez raise an eyebrow, as if the idea of anyone volunteering to paw through garbage bins struck him as odd. But Daniels accepted the offer happily.

Leaving the office, they followed Alvarez down to the police yard and over to his car. Two Guardia Civil were waiting beside it and watched with detached interest as Alvarez opened the trunk lid. There was a large wooden box inside, fastened by a padlock.

"Give me a minute." Daniels unlocked the box, swung back the lid, and brought out a small leather case. "This is what I need." He noticed Alvarez staring at the rest of the contents of the box and smiled. "Just a few things I thought I'd bring along."

Like Alvarez, Laird stepped closer. The box held respirator masks, face helmets, rubber boots and two bulky rubberized one-piece suits that might have been borrowed from a space programme.

"Standard safety equipment," said Daniels. "Any operator handling raw pesticide chemicals is supposed to be kitted out that way —I won't say they always are, but you can't legislate for fools."

"One of my men will walk down to the harbour with you." Alvarez drew a deep breath as Daniels closed the box again. "I—I have arranged a boat."

"Thanks. It won't take long." Daniels tucked the leather case under one arm. "One word of advice, Captain Alvarez. When you do find those containers, don't handle them too much. Let me have a look at them first—or get hold of someone else who knows what he's doing."

"Sí." Alvarez nodded soberly. "I won't forget."

Escorted by one of the waiting men, Daniels walked away. Once he was out of sight, Alvarez grimaced.

"Do you believe all he said?" he asked Laird.

Laird nodded. "He's the expert."

Alvarez sighed. "Another expert—one of ours—says your friend Henderson was killed by a single shot from a .32 automatic pistol, fired at close range. The weapon was probably an American Colt." He paused, slammed the trunk lid shut, then thumbed towards the police building. "I have some phone calls to make. But my car can take you out to Warner's camp, then come back for me. I thought we might go together to the Garaje Amarilla and have a talk with that girl at the cash desk."

"Any reason?" asked Laird.

"She should have calmed down," said Alvarez. "All we got from her yesterday was hysterics." He rubbed one foot along the ground, scowling at the result. "I've still got every available man looking for Cuvier and his people—inland, as well as along the coast. But—*sí*, we may have missed them."

"Do you believe that?" asked Laird.

"No, not yet." Alvarez gave him a crooked grin. "My wife says it is *imposible*. That damn horoscope of mine is still good."

*

The promised police car took Andrew Laird on the short journey from San Ferdinand out to the campsite, dropped him at the road verge, then disappeared back towards the village.

Walking towards the tents, Laird quickened his step as he saw Warner's van parked in its usual space. It meant, as he'd hoped, that Helen had returned from her hospital visit. He saw her a moment later, and she waved. But she wasn't alone. Standing beside her, clad in his motor-cycle leathers, Father Sebastian greeted Laird with a nod as he reached them.

"Good morning," said Helen with innocent formality. Her eyes met Laird's for a moment, with their own message, but there was relief in her smile. "I saw Professor Daniels—and Dr. Mendes says he's starting treatment."

Laird nodded. "Things look better—a lot better."

"I'm glad," said Father Sebastian simply. He gestured towards one of the tents. His Suzuki motor cycle was propped beside it, his crash helmet hanging from the handlebars. "I'm also glad you came, Señor Laird. I came over to find out if these young people needed help. But I also hoped to see you."

"Father Sebastian thinks he may know where Cuvier is hiding," said Helen uneasily. "But—"

"But I can't be sure," admitted the grey-haired priest ruefully. "Still . . ."

"Tell me," invited Laird. He looked around as he spoke, then swore under his breath. A thin column of smoke was rising from beyond the line of scrub that marked the start of the beach. "Helen, who's down there?"

"Piet and Roberto. They're burning rubbish—" She stopped, wide-eyed with surprise, as Laird left them and ran towards the spot.

He found Piet and Roberto standing frowning at a mound of rubbish. It was smoking feebly but on the brink of going out, and they stared at him as he made sure of that with a few handfuls of sand.

"Any kitchen rubbish in that lot?" asked Laird.

Piet nodded. "That's why the damn stuff won't burn. Maybe if we get some dry driftwood—"

"Leave it," Laird told them. He saw Helen and Father Sebastian approaching, their faces puzzled. "Better still, do me a favour. Piet, try and find any trimmings left over from those lobsters." He grinned at Piet's grimace. "Call it a penance for sins past—okay?"

Gloomily, Piet set to work.

"Can we ask what that was about?" asked Father Sebastian.

"Research," said Laird. "It'll keep, Father. What about Cuvier?"

"*Sí.* You asked me to find out what I could about this motor-cyclist named Jaime—the one with the injured face."

"I remember," said Laird. "But—"

"*Momento.*" Father Sebastian was politely firm. "One of the young people in my unfortunate flock is an enthusiastic biker. More important, before he—ah—had to marry in some haste and decided to reform, he was a member of the same two-wheeled gang as this Jaime."

"You're sure they're the same?" asked Helen.

"He saw Jaime yesterday morning—and saw his face," said the priest. "Does that satisfy you, my child?"

Helen glanced at Laird. He nodded.

"It seems there is a hideout they sometimes use," said Father Sebastian. "Do you know of the Marina Diane?" He saw their blank expressions and chuckled. "Plenty of people would like to forget about it. A development company planned to build a yachting marina, complete with hotel and restaurant. But they ran out of money before the building was half completed. That was a few years ago, but nothing has been done since then."

Laird frowned, his interest roused. "Any kind of a harbour there?"

"Some work was done on the marina basin." Father Sebastian shook his head. "How much, I don't know."

"Then how about road access?"

The priest shrugged. "There was a track, for construction trucks —but it has been overgrown with weeds for years." He eyed Laird. "The whole thing is some distance from the main road, out of sight."

Laird had to admit it was a possibility, maybe more than that. Except that Cuvier would need some kind of facility that would allow a boat to come in and load—if that was his plan. A lot depended on how much had been done to the marina basin.

"How far away is it?" he asked.

"A few kilometres." Father Sebastian glanced thoughtfully towards his motor cycle. "I could take you there in a matter of minutes."

"No," said Helen sharply. "Suppose—"

"My child, I am no hero. We would creep quietly away—but quickly." He turned hopefully to Laird. "It's a probability, nothing more. But if we could rule out probability, even that would be useful. Don't you agree?"

Laird hesitated, seeing the warning glitter in Helen's eyes. But he could sense Father Sebastian's enthusiasm—and his likely disappointment if he refused.

"Suppose we compromise," he suggested slowly. "Captain Alvarez is coming over here soon. So we go and take a look, Father. But nothing more—and when Alvarez arrives, Helen tells him where we've gone."

"You're mad," said Helen. "Both of you."

Father Sebastian looked at her for a moment, a twinkle in his blue eyes.

"But we will be carefully mad," he promised. "Do you think I would take my motor cycle anywhere it might get damaged?"

*

They left the campsite, Laird riding pillion again. The little Suzuki snarled its way along, heading east on the dusty road, the sun glinting brightly on its polished chrome.

"I forgot to tell you one thing, Señor Laird," shouted the priest over his shoulder.

"What's that?" Laird huddled closer to hear the answer.

"Jaime told my reformed sheep they'd been hired by a foreigner to do a job—one that finishes tonight," shouted Father Sebastian. "Does that make sense to you?"

"Yes." Laird huddled down against the wind and swore under his breath.

He'd been right. Janos Cuvier was working to a carefully organized timetable. He let himself sway with the Suzuki as it took a corner, then straightened, most of his view the rear of Father Sebastian's crash helmet. All that Daniels had said about the toxic chemical in those drums was still in his mind. But for Laird, it had become even more personal.

There was a score to even. People he'd known, people he'd liked were among the deaths that could already be laid at Cuvier's door. Yet, when they died, none of them had really known why it was happening.

The motor cycle buzzed on for a few more minutes. Then it slowed and Father Sebastian steered in and let the machine coast to a halt.

"There," he said, pointing.

It wasn't so much a track as a rough ribbon of flattened, stony ground that plunged away from the road, then twisted and disappeared behind scrub and weeds. A large grey lizard darted across it, stopped halfway, stared at them, then flickered the rest of the distance and vanished.

Laird nodded. "Let's try it."

They set off again, bumping over the track, the Suzuki travelling at a slow crawl, the noise of its exhaust reduced to a murmur.

Only a few seconds later, Father Sebastian gave a sudden grunt and nodded to his right. Scrub and weeds at the edge of the track had been flattened by what had to have been a large vehicle. In another moment, they dipped down into a hollow where weeds had almost obliterated the track—but now they were totally flattened and churned.

The trail of damaged weeds and undergrowth continued while the track wound its way through ground that was a mixture of scrub and low hillocks. At last, Father Sebastian stopped again, switched off his machine, and removed his crash helmet.

"We're near?" asked Laird.

The priest nodded. "*Sí.* To go closer, we walk." He propped the Suzuki carefully on its stand, left his crash helmet on the handle-bars again, then scratched his chin. "But not along this track, I think."

"There's another way?" Laird raised a surprised eyebrow.

Father Sebastian grinned and beckoned. Laird followed him a few paces into the scrub, then stared at a deep, broad storm drain immediately in front of them. It was old, man-made, at least twelve feet across and more than half that in depth.

"Our better way," said Father Sebastian proudly. "It runs straight down to the marina beach—which is one of the reasons the developers went bankrupt." He made to scramble down.

"Wait." Laird caught him by the arm. "We look, we leave—"

"Agreed."

"Or maybe I tell you to stop or ease back. Also agreed?"

The grey-haired priest looked ready to protest, then sighed and nodded.

"You remind me of my bishop," he said bitterly.

"Right now, I sympathize with him." Laird grinned. "Let's go."

They got down into the old storm drain, its cracked bottom strewn with boulders and patchy with vegetation. Laird took the lead, moving unhurriedly, watchful for any sign of movement ahead. Behind him, Father Sebastian tripped on a loose stone, muttered in an unpriestly way as it clattered, then grimaced and padded on again.

The storm drain began to take on a downward slope. The slope increased, and Father Sebastian called a soft warning. Laird stopped and let him catch up.

"What now?" asked Laird.

"We're there," said Father Sebastian, gasping a little. "*Sí,* unless you want to march in through the front door." He pointed to the left side of the drain. "If we go up there—"

He needed Laird's help to climb the steep banking, then they lay side by side in the long grass at the top and looked down on all there was of the Marina Diane. From where they were, the line of the storm drain ran towards a small cove. Beside it, almost filling the rest of the cove, the concrete of a half-completed breakwater had the sea swirling white around its edges.

A patch of scrub blocked Laird's view. He eased forward a fraction to clear it, brushed a hovering insect away, then froze, as, for the first time, he saw the rest of the Marina Diane.

It was a cluster of mostly roofless, skeletal buildings, located about the length of a football pitch away from where they lay. Bare brick and timber beams were fronted by a half-completed concrete walkway bounding the inner edge of the marine lagoon. Yachts would have moored there, crews should have been able to stroll directly into the marina restaurant or its bars.

Instead, a strange, shoe-box-like shape, almost shrouded in camouflage netting, floated in the water beside the walkway. It took a moment, then Laird recognized the squat outline of an old military landing craft. Big enough to carry tanks to an invasion beach, yet able to manoeuvre in and out of shallow water, no other craft its size could have used the marina as a hiding place.

"I was right!" Father Sebastian hissed the words excitedly, nudging him hard. "Look—"

A figure had emerged from under the netting and walked into the nearest of the derelict buildings. Laird waited, but nothing else moved, he could hear no sounds. He took another long look at the landing craft, noting a launch moored in the shadow of her blunt bow.

He signalled. They moved back a little, still crouching.

"I've got to make sure," said Laird quietly.

"*Sí.*" Father Sebastian nodded excitedly. "If we—"

"Not you," Laird told him. "We agreed, remember?"

"But—" Father Sebastian saw his expression, sighed, and nodded. "What if something happens?"

"Then don't linger," Laird said. "Get back to your two wheels and find Captain Alvarez."

The priest sniffed. "*Gracias.* While I wait, do you object if I pray?" He paused and a slight smile touched his lips. "Even if it didn't do you much good, it would help me."

Laird grinned, and began to wriggle down the slope.

*

The cover available, mostly scrub or an occasional outcrop of rock, had looked scanty when he started off. But he made the most of it.

Crouching, crawling, pausing every now and again, Andrew Laird made the edge of the tumbledown marina development in a final short sprint that brought him into the shelter of an unfinished brick boundary wall. He stayed there long enough to let his breathing steady, then worked along the wall to where it petered out. That brought him to a flat concrete foundation, intended for some kind of structure. A brick wall had been started to one side. Loose bricks and mounds of building sand were piled against it, planks of wood and steel rods were scattered around. The marina work force might just have been taking a lunch break—except that a spiny cactus stood proud from the middle of the largest mound of sand and the steel rods were flaked with rust.

Something moved. Laird tensed, then moistened his lips and relaxed as a lizard darted from one sun-baked heap of bricks and vanished under the shade of an abandoned barrow. Briefly, from somewhere among the buildings, there was a sound like hammering.

Then it stopped. Only the sea and the low murmur of the wind broke the almost brooding silence.

Cautiously, Laird crossed the gap to the other wall. From there, he had a clear view of the lowered bow ramp of the landing craft. But the angle was wrong to see into her flat load deck.

A half-formed doorway formed a gap to his left. Laird went through it into a maze of cinder-block partition walls with only beams and open sky overhead, then found an unglazed window.

It gave him the view he needed. As much as he could see of the load deck of the landing craft was lined down one side with glinting steel containers.

He had seen enough. Laird turned away, began to work his way back through the maze, stepped through a doorway, then came to a total, involuntary halt.

He had taken a wrong turning. He was in an open courtyard and Laura Cero stood only ten paces away, staring at him, her dark eyes wide with disbelief.

"Laura—" Laird swallowed and took a single step forward.

Her expression changed from disbelief to alarm and she looked past him. Laird heard a sharp metallic click, the sound of an automatic pistol's slide. Raising his arms, he turned slowly, resignedly.

One of Janos Cuvier's "utility twins," the fair-haired John Vasco, was leaning against another of the courtyard walls. The Luger pistol in his right hand was trained unwaveringly at Laird's middle.

"Why?" asked Laura Cero wearily. She ran a hand through her

jet-black hair in a despairing way. "You damned fool, Andrew—couldn't you have stayed away?"

Vasco came forward, his manner totally calm, and the muzzle of the pistol jammed into Laird's side.

"I think Mr. Cuvier will want to see you," he said, then glanced at Laura and nodded. "Lead the way, Miss Cero—please."

They left the courtyard and went along the concrete walkway at the edge of the marina. Laird managed a sideways glance at the lapping water. It was little more than six feet deep. His guess had been right. Only something as unexpected as a landing craft could have come in and loaded cargo. There was little likelihood of the Marina Diane being on Alvarez's surveillance list.

"We're going to the restaurant," said Vasco conversationally. The man grinned, prodding again with the gun. "But don't look for any kind of service, Mr. Laird."

They'd been seen. Laird heard a shout, saw a figure scurrying ahead, then Captain Van Holst appeared at the landing craft's bow ramp. The former master of the Sea Robin gaped, then turned to talk nervously to the fat figure of Vicente. Cuvier's driver wore overalls and was wiping his hands on an oily rag.

Ignoring them, Laura walked past with her low-heeled shoes tapping on the concrete and went into the two-storey building that immediately faced the vessel. Another long row of container drums lay in the shade at its open front, waiting to be loaded.

Laird slowed. The restaurant had a gaping, open front but was roofed. Inside was a dusty, skeletal shell with no rear wall. Two trucks had been backed in that way. Men were standing around them, and a glint of sunlight fell on a row of parked motor cycles.

"Move." The gun jabbed impatiently.

Laird followed Laura inside, then stopped again, mouth tightening.

Feet wide apart, an expression of controlled anger on his face, Janos Cuvier stood glaring at him beside a trestle table. Paul Raynal sat on a box behind the table, his sharp features perturbed.

"Where did you find him?" asked Cuvier harshly. His bald head was covered by a blue peaked cap, and like the others, he was wearing overalls. "Well?"

"Back there, Mr. Cuvier." Vasco pointed towards the way they'd come. "He popped up in the courtyard while I was keeping an eye on the girl, like you asked."

"I see." Cuvier chewed his lip. "Who's up on the roof, watching the track?"

"Hans Botha," lisped Raynal anxiously. "But—"

"Then he didn't come that way," snapped Cuvier. He took a step nearer Laird. "Any more of you out there?"

Laird shrugged. Van Holst and Vicente had joined them from outside, the group of bikers were drifting closer from the trucks. That left Laura, and she was standing well away from the others, as if deliberately isolating herself.

"Find out," he suggested.

"We will," said Cuvier. He glanced at Vicente. "That storm ditch?"

"*Sí.*" Vicente nodded. "Señor Cuvier, I warned you—"

"I know." Cuvier scowled at the table. "All right, get two of your rat pack out on their machines, tell them to check the track. Have another two do the same along the bottom of that storm ditch. Any trouble, straight back. Otherwise, one of each pair stays out." He turned to Raynal. "Get up and take over from Botha. I want him here."

Rising, Raynal hurried outside. Vicente crossed over to the group of young Spaniards, talked and gestured rapidly, and four of them ran towards the motor cycles. In a matter of seconds, four machines rasped out of the building, filling it briefly with the fumes of their exhausts.

"Next." Cuvier sat himself on the edge of the trestle table, one bony hand tapping the wood. "Laura, did he say anything?"

"No," she said, her face turned away.

Vasco gave a slight headshake in agreement.

"You." Cuvier beckoned Van Holst. "Don't just stand there with your mouth hanging open."

The Dutch captain moistened his lips and nodded anxiously.

"What you wan' me to do, Mr. Cuvier?" he asked, eyeing Laird warily.

"Here." Cuvier went behind the table, took a sawed-off shotgun which was lying on a box, and tossed it to the man. He swore under his breath as Van Holst caught it awkwardly. "Get outside and keep your eyes open."

Van Holst seemed glad to leave.

"Useless idiot. But we still need him." Cuvier prowled a few paces, then came back. "Laird, do we waste time with preliminaries, or do I just ask how much you know?"

"Most things," said Laird. "I'd say probably the lot." He glanced at the gun still pressed against his side. "I'm getting uncomfortable."

"All right." Cuvier glanced at Vasco, and the pressure eased. But the "utility twin" stayed close beside him. Cuvier pursed his lips. "What do you mean by most things?"

Laird shrugged. "The *Sea Robin*, what's in those containers, what really happened to Charlie Henderson." He looked deliberately towards Laura. "And the rest—it's quite a list."

She nodded, her face strained and white.

"I didn't know," she said in little more than a whisper. "I thought—"

"She thought all she was meant to think," said Cuvier almost sadly. "That I'd been somewhat foolish with some smuggled cargo and that I needed her help to get round some insurance difficulties." His thin lips tightened. "I didn't want to get her involved in the rest—and I needed a good lawyer."

"But things got out of control?" suggested Laird.

"Only when your man Henderson recognized our engineer," countered Cuvier. "All right, we had to kill Henderson—"

"Then you needed a body that didn't have a bullet between the eyes, and that took care of Grant," said Laird. He nodded towards Vasco. "Which of your educated killers did that one? Him, or his little friend?"

Vasco's expression didn't alter as he took a half-step forward. He cuffed Laird hard across the face, then glanced apologetically at Cuvier.

"Gently," said Cuvier, frowning, some of his confidence fading. "So—maybe I underestimated a little. And whatever you say, I presume the Spanish police share most of this knowledge?"

Laird nodded bleakly. He still wasn't certain of Laura Cero's role, but he knew only too well his own life was on a knife-edge.

"They do. And the Guardia Civil don't take kindly to one of their men being murdered."

Cuvier didn't answer for a moment. His hand tapped the trestle table again in a slow, monotonous tattoo.

"But how much can they prove?" he asked. He glanced out towards the containers. "Without evidence, there is only suspicion —and suspicion means nothing in law. Don't you agree, Laura?" She said nothing, and he shrugged. "Three deaths—"

"Four," corrected Laird. "There was a salvage diver—or maybe you didn't know. There's a bunch of kids in hospital—but I suppose you didn't know about that either."

He heard Laura gasp. Cuvier stared at him. Then footsteps hurried from the rear of the building and Hans Botha appeared. He looked flustered, his overalls were grimy, and the gun in his hand was a .32 Colt.

"Well?" asked Cuvier sharply.

"A couple of the bikers are heading back," reported the dark-haired gunman, glancing at his companion.

"Together?" demanded Cuvier.

"No. One on the track, Mr. Cuvier. The other just came out of the storm ditch—"

"Good." Cuvier allowed himself a grunt of relief. "Then maybe —yes, maybe he did come nosing alone."

He waited, ignoring Laird. In another minute, the two returning riders roared into the building, stopped beside the trucks, and talked to Vicente. The plump driver hurried over to Cuvier. Grinning, he slapped Father Sebastian's crash helmet on the table.

"They found this, Señor Cuvier—an' a motor cycle."

"That's all?"

"*Sí.* They are positive. But like you ordered, two of them are keeping watch."

"*Gracias,*" said Cuvier absently. He poked the crash helmet with a finger and glanced at Laird. "Borrowed?"

"Hired," said Laird, making a desperate try to appear indifferent. "It goes on expenses."

Cuvier shrugged, then frowned towards the trucks.

"How many to go?"

"Another sixty, maybe, Señor Cuvier," Vicente told him.

"I'll take a look." Cuvier turned at Vasco. "Keep Laird here." He glanced at Laura. "And—ah—keep an eye on Miss Cero. An eye, nothing more—you understand?"

He went off, Vicente at his side.

A moment passed. Vasco took out his cigarettes, lit one, moved impatiently, then glanced at Botha. Botha nodded.

"Back over there," he ordered Laird. "Against that wall, then sit down." He pointed at Laura. "I mean both of you. I'm not your uncle Cuvier."

They did as they'd been told, sitting side by side on the cold concrete. Laird caught a glimpse of one of the side rooms and saw sleeping bags and a bottled gas stove.

"When did you get here?" he asked quietly.

"Yesterday," said Laura in a low, empty voice. "Andrew, I—"

"You knew a little, not a lot. I know." Laird glanced towards the "utility twins." They had begun their own low-voiced, earnest conversation, glancing every now and again towards their captives. "What about the landing craft?"

"It came in last night." She wore a sweater and dark-blue slacks. They were creased and grubby and she had a smear of dirt on one cheek. "The crew that brought it in were picked up by another boat. We—they say Captain Van Holst and Vicente can handle it."

"Then what?"

"Janos planned to finish loading and leave tonight." Laura hesitated for a moment as Botha looked over. "Then he'll scuttle it in the nearest deep water. We'll have the launch and there'll be another boat waiting. He says we'll be ashore in North Africa before dawn."

"Is that what you want?"

"Now?" Her shoulders slumped. "Andrew, you said those students—"

He nodded.

"It was the pesticide?"

"Yes."

She shuddered, then gripped his arm hard. "But how—"

"Cut that out," rasped Vasco, coming over. The Luger in his hand jerked threateningly. "Shift—move apart. And stay quiet."

He waited until they had separated, then, satisfied, went back to where Botha, grinning, was watching.

The minutes crawled past. Laird watched as, directed by Cuvier, the leather-clad bikers unloaded more of the steel containers from the trucks and rolled them out to join the line outside waiting to be loaded aboard the landing craft. Once or twice Captain Van Holst appeared outside, clutching his shotgun uncertainly, looking anything but happy.

About half the containers left on the trucks had been rolled into position when there was an interruption. The young Spaniards stopped as one, and stood listening. A moment later, Laird heard the sound of motor-cycle engines and seconds after that the two riders who had been on guard duty raced their machines into the building and came to a skidding halt.

Surrounded by their companions, they were the centre of a

babble of conversation until first Vicente, then Cuvier shouldered their way through.

Suddenly, the bikers scattered. The two riders who had returned sat blipping their engines while the others started their machines. Then, in a pack, ignoring Cuvier's shouts and Vicente's attempt to stop them, they roared away through the gap at the rear. Laird had a brief, final glimpse of them, bouncing over the rough ground, already scattering, the noise of their exhausts fading.

Cuvier came hurrying back, his face a livid mask of fury. He vanished into the side room and reappeared, a rifle in his hands, just as Paul Raynal made an agitated arrival from his post on the roof.

"I know," snarled Cuvier before Raynal could draw breath. "Police. Those damned bikers saw them—now they've bailed out."

"Your rat pack leaving the sinking ship," suggested Laird.

Botha glared at him. The others didn't seem to hear.

"I saw two carloads," declared Raynal in an agitated lisp. "They've stopped up on the slope. What do we do?"

"Think." Cuvier glanced at the faces around him. "Get Laird—and Laura." He waited until they were brought over, then grabbed Laird by the shirt. "You knew, didn't you?"

"I hoped," Laird told him. "What do you want to do now? Stage Janos Cuvier's last stand?"

"No." Cuvier let him go, his voice hoarse with emotion, but still controlled. "Laird, you can't understand. I started from nothing, I built up to someone that matters. Then one mistake, just one—that damned pesticide idea." He moistened his lips. "All right, it caused all this, maybe it can still get me out—get all of us out."

"How?" asked Raynal, bewildered.

"Outside." Cuvier led them into the bright sunlight, over to the stacked container drums beside the waiting landing craft, then pointed. "That's what's holding them up there. They're frightened as long as we're sitting on it." He swung round at Laird again. "You tell them—there's enough toxic in that lot to turn half the Málaga coast into a disaster area."

"Or a killing ground," said Laird, shaken. "Look, Cuvier, you couldn't—"

"So we do a deal," grated Cuvier. "A business deal. We take the—" He broke off. "Van Holst—where is that damned Dutchman?"

Paul Raynal gave a startled yelp and pointed towards the water. Van Holst's bulky figure was scrambling across the deck of the launch tied alongside the landing craft. He had already freed the stern line, now he was fumbling with the remaining line at the bow.

"What the hell—" Cuvier ran to the edge of the concrete walk-way, his voice a bellow. "Van Holst, what are you playing at, you fool?"

"Getting out." The *Sea Robin*'s captain gestured warningly with the sawed-off shotgun in his right hand, his other hand fumbling with the bow line. "They—you paid me to sink a ship, Mr. Cuvier. None of the rest of this."

The bow line came free. Quickly, Van Holst began to back to-wards the cockpit of the launch as a slim gap of water began to separate it from the landing craft.

"Stop him," rasped Cuvier urgently. "Take him, Botha."

The .32 Colt in Botha's hand swung up, barked twice, and Van Holst jerked, but stayed upright.

Botha triggered again, and the Dutchman slumped. But as he fell, both barrels of the shotgun blasted wildly. The deadly double load of buckshot slammed along the line of containers. Thin steel punctured and ripped, Raynal screamed as a stray pellet gouged away half of one ear.

Van Holst lay dead on the deck of the drifting launch, Raynal was sobbing.

Then there was another sound, a gurgling, gushing hiss. Like the others, Laird turned and felt a wave of icy fear. Light green, sparkling innocently in the glare of the sun, liquid was spouting from half a dozen of the punctured containers, spreading in fast pools across the sun-baked concrete.

He heard Cuvier make a choked, horrified sound, saw one jet spraying over Vicente's trouser legs, then his nostrils caught a first faint whiff of rising fumes as Botha and Vasco began to lurch back, terror on their faces.

"Laura, the water—now." He seized her by the arm, shoving past an unseeing Cuvier. "Swim for it. Stay under."

He jumped, hauling her with him, and they hit the water to-gether. She rose instinctively and he pulled her under again, drag-ging her along, the landing craft a dark shadow beside them.

He made her stay down until her face contorted in a need for air. Then they surfaced briefly, gasping. Glancing back, Laird could still see the containers spurting their toxic death. Someone was screaming. A figure was crawling on hands and knees along the concrete. Someone else was in the water behind them, swimming frantically.

They went down again, came up for air, and a large white seabird spiralled down, one wing still flapping feebly as it splashed into the low waves. Vaporizing in the heat, the pesticide's poison was reaching up and out for victims.

The next time they came up, they were clear of the Marina Diane breakwater. Floating together in the swell, they rested for a moment. Another seabird flapped drunkenly from the shore, then plummeted down and died.

The wind was still light, off-shore, and blowing east. Laird pointed west and they went down again.

Ten minutes later they finally staggered ashore, safe but exhausted. A burly Guardia Civil grabbed Laura before she fell, another supported Laird and helped him onto dry land.

Then time, for the next half hour, became a confused jumble of impressions. Somehow, they were on the slope above the Marina Diane. He saw Alvarez and Professor Daniels, grotesque figures in respirators, face masks and protective clothing, stride down towards the buildings.

They came back alone.

But, unbelievably, Janos Cuvier was alive, dragged ashore in much the same way they had been. Vomiting, twitching, he lay on the grass beside one of the Guardia cars, too ill to be handcuffed.

"Señor Laird." Father Sebastian appeared from somewhere and smiled thankfully. "Andrew—for once, maybe, my prayers were worthwhile."

Propped on his elbows, Laird grinned up at him.

"Your prayers and Alvarez's horoscope, Father. Even a lapsed Presbyterian couldn't lose," he said thankfully. "How did you manage it?"

Father Sebastian pretended to wince.

"I didn't," he admitted. "I hid like a rabbit when those riders appeared."

Laird sat upright.

"Then how the—"

"Helen Warner," said the priest sadly. "She decided we were a pair of fools. She went to the Casa Turo and telephoned Captain Alvarez—who thought the same." He paused and shook his head in something close to awe. "Alvarez says that down there, at the Marina Diane, is like a foretaste of hell. Nothing lives—not an insect, not a blade of grass. It is the same in the water. Fish of every kind, even the seaweed—dead."

Laird nodded. A military helicopter was circling overhead, keeping at a respectful altitude. Another had landed nearby. A steady procession of vehicles seemed to be arriving, army uniforms were beginning to appear. The Marina Diane had become a full-scale emergency.

Yet only six of the drums had been punctured.

If there had been more, if the wind had been from the sea, heading inland—he drew a deep breath.

"It could have been worse," he said.

"*Sí.*" Father Sebastian nodded. "Professor Daniels says the same." He gave a small, wry smile. "He almost sounds disappointed. But I—ah—have a message for you, from Helen Warner. She is waiting in her van at the road. Alvarez won't allow her to come nearer."

Laura was a few feet away. Getting to his feet, Laird walked towards her. She looked at him, saying nothing.

"What are you going to do?" he asked quietly.

"Now?" She passed a hand over her damp, raven-black hair and gave an odd smile. She looked past him, towards Cuvier. Someone had wrapped a blanket round him. "If—when he recovers, what will happen?"

"Charges, a trial." Laird shrugged. "Probably the rest of his life in jail. Why?"

"I still owe him. For a little while, anyway." She gave a shrug that was empty of emotion. "Maybe that's not easy to understand."

"It isn't," said Laird. "But good luck with it."

He turned, and glanced at Father Sebastian.

The priest nodded, pointed towards the track, and Laird started walking.

Ten days later, it was raining hard at London's Heathrow Airport when the Iberia jet from Málaga touched down.

Wearing his best suit but with the belt with the seaman's buckle round his waist, Andrew Laird waited in the international arrivals hall.

A lot had happened since he'd got back. There had been endless reports to dictate for Clanmore Alliance. With Osgood Morris, he'd gone to the second funeral service for Charlie Henderson, where a widow in black had kissed him on the cheek in a special way.

They had told her that the company pension fund was paying a bonus. Osgood Morris had managed to cash Cuvier's cheque before the Cuvier Corporation's accounts were frozen.

There had been a meeting with Professor Daniels, who had brought his bill and a message from Alvarez.

Apart from Laura, only Cuvier had survived at the Marina Diane. The others had died, horribly but quickly. A section of beach would be closed for a long time. The sea around was barren of life, but the sea would heal—just as Janos Cuvier, wrecked physically, would live to stand trial on a catalogue of charges.

But the rest was brighter. Adam Warner's students had recovered completely and were already scattering across Europe, on their way home. The Cuvier Corporation's remaining assets would meet the cost of an elaborate reprocessing treatment devised by Daniels, a treatment he was certain would neutralize the remaining containers of toxic.

A door opened. The first of the Iberia passengers began to emerge from the immigration channel.

He saw Helen first. She wore a cream linen suit with a flared skirt. Her sun-bleached fair hair defied the grey English light and her blue eyes shone as he hugged her.

Then Adam Warner was pumping his hand. He was still pale, he wore a tweed jacket which looked several sizes too big for him, but he was beaming.

"You've heard?" asked Warner.

"About the *Sea Robin*?" Laird nodded.

The details had been worked out the previous day. The old cargo ship wasn't wanted off San Ferdinand, for more than one reason. Clearing the wreck meant a brutal demolition job, with explosives. Clanmore and the Spanish government would split the cost, then see what could be recovered later.

"I know about that, yes."

Warner nodded impatiently. "No, I mean the real news—about the *Emeraude*, my French three-decker." He ignored his sister's amused grin. "We've found her, Laird. At least, those divers who— well, recovered that body, spotted her."

A vague memory touched Laird's mind. He nodded.

"Good," he said politely.

"It's arranged," said Warner, eyes glinting behind his spectacles, his little beard quivering with enthusiasm. "I can get some university sponsorship, the Spanish say they'll help, and I'll take another camp back there next spring." He paused and smiled awkwardly. "That's when you're blowing up the *Sea Robin*, isn't it?"

"Probably." There was no rush, no particular timetable had been fixed.

"And—uh—Captain Novak of the *Scomber* has the job?" queried Warner.

"He's available," agreed Laird.

Warner cleared his throat. "I thought—well, maybe you could persuade Captain Novak to give us some assistance. Though I don't think we could pay him much. But a three-decker, Laird—"

"I'll talk to him," said Laird drily. "I think he'll listen."

Warner had a train to catch. He kissed his sister goodbye, picked up his case, and hurried towards the coach exit. Laird turned to Helen.

"How about you?" he asked quietly.

"I'm in no hurry," she said.

"I wondered," said Laird. "No hurry till when?"

"Till long enough." Her eyes were suddenly serious. "Except for one thing. Last time—it was for a reason, wasn't it?"

"That's over," said Laird.

She gave a slow smile, nodded, and took his arm.

Laird lifted her suitcase and they headed through the crowded terminal towards his car.